West 4th and Bank Street

A Novel

By Liz Molloy

West 4th and Bank Street

SC ISBN: 9781645385868
West 4th and Bank Street
By Liz Molloy
Cover design by Maggie Carroll

Published by Ten16 Press, an imprint of Orange Hat Publishing

www.orangehatpublishing.com
Wauwatosa, WI

For Mom, Dad, Kris, Dan & Chloe
Thank you for all your love and support. It means the world to me.

To Cody, Cali & Champ
Thank you for being the best dog companions a girl could ask for.

Chapter One

Emma will always choose to walk to work.

Rain or shine, unless there is a hurricane or blizzard outside, she will walk the exact one-mile distance from her parents' rowhouse in the West Village, the place where she was born and raised, to her office in Astor Place. Despite the snap of the frigid morning December air hitting the skin on her cheeks, Emma still decides to walk to work.

There is only one reason why Emma would choose to walk to and from work every day (it's not for the exercise, although it does help). It's to see the block between West 12th Street and Bank Street on West 4th Street.

With a hot cup of coffee in her mitten-covered hands, Emma walks along West 4th Street, crossing the cobblestoned street of West 12th, heading her way down the block. The block she has come to know like a family member, although she has never met nor spoken more than three words to any of its inhabitants. In all the neighborhoods in this city, Emma has never seen a singular block that has all its buildings so uniquely distinct, as if they all have a personality of their own, such that any passerby would notice its charm and forever remember walking by such a place. Even her own block, which is up one block from this one, doesn't match the same quality of magnetism. Every rowhouse on her street looks the same. So identical that the street number on the front door is its only distinguishing feature.

As she crosses the crosswalk, reaching her favorite block, Emma counts down to seeing all the people she has come to know in her head and the beautiful rowhouses they live in.

Right on the dot, she sees the old man with the crazy, static-sticking white hair who lives in 364, standing outside his front door. She can feel his sharp, cold, dark brown eyes from where she is on the sidewalk, keeping an eye out for his property. The batty old man does this every morning, monitoring his property during the morning and afternoon rush to make sure that no one is letting their dog relieve themselves in front of his white-bricked rowhouse or littering on his sidewalk. His property must always be clean and orderly. God forbid someone rides their bike or stops walking on his part of the sidewalk; Emma has heard the batty old man yell at passersby too many times to count. Luckily for her, she has only ever received a scowl from the batty old man, but from witnessing what he could do, she always walks on the opposite side of the street and never looks in his direction for too long.

Daring to take a quick glance across the street, Emma can see that the batty old man has his gaze locked on something in front of her, agitation forming in the creases in his wrinkled face. Emma follows his line of sight to a man a few feet in front of her, leaning against a brick wall and chatting enthusiastically on the phone while smoking a cigarette. She wonders what this man is doing to piss off the batty old man so much. Maybe it is his loud voice? Or that he is smoking? Could this man be his longtime nemesis? The list could be endless. She'll never know, this time or any other time, what the answer really is.

Her thoughts of the batty old man are cut short as the young, hot-shot finance man in 366 makes his way down the almost marble-like stairs, heading towards the black Mercedes that drives him directly to his office, which Emma assumes is on Wall Street. Just by looking at him and his home, Emma knows all there is to know about him. His short, sleek-cut black hair and clean-shaven face show he is a perfectionist. His three-piece Tom Ford suit and the Rolex on his left wrist show off his vanity, while his toned physique shows off his need to feel powerful.

The only thing about 366 she likes, other than being on her favorite block, is its exterior.

Emma feels envious of the head-to-toe dark brick-covered rowhouse, with vines of ivy encompassing one-half of the front, giving it a taste of nature in a city of concrete. The black windowsills are the icing on the cake, making the whole unit the epitome of expensive modernism. Emma can only imagine what the inside must be like.

With a quick glance across the street to her left, Emma spots the sweet middle-aged lady in 363, watering her plants by the front window. 363 is by far her favorite rowhouse on this block. You can see the thoughtfulness and care put into every detail on the exterior alone, from the Tiffany blue front door with the gold-plated hardware bordered by a thick white trim to the small white lantern hanging from the transom. Soft sandstone-colored bricks cover the whole front wall, and the top of the house features a detailed white custom trim. You know that this is a house that has been meticulously designed and stands out all on its own.

Emma doesn't know the lady who lives in 363, nor has she ever spoken to her. She doesn't know if she truly is a sweet and nice lady. But from her observations of her cheery, almost walking-on-air demeanor, Emma senses that is how she is. To her, 363 just seems to have it all together. Yes, she is at least thirty years older and has more life experience than her, but seeing someone who seems to have found the secret equation of true happiness and fulfillment in life would make anyone envious. Deep down, Emma knows that it's odd to think this way about a stranger, but she can't ignore the kindred spirit connection she has with this woman.

If only I could live with the purpose and contentment she does.

Over the years, Emma has developed a sort of fixation on her and even has a slight crush on her handsome son, someone she sees visit 363 from time to time. Even from afar, Emma couldn't help but take notice of him. From bringing his mother flowers every Sunday morning to shoveling her front steps after every snowfall, it's no wonder Emma has developed feelings for the kind and good-natured guy.

Will Emma ever admit that she sometimes takes this route to her destination just in case he happens to be walking to 363 at the very same time as she passes by, creating the meet-cute of her dreams? Absolutely not. But that is only between us hopeless romantics.

There have been times Emma wanted to start a conversation with 363 when she was outside her stoop, watering her plants on a crisp spring morning or dusting snow on a winter afternoon. But the only thing Emma has ever mustered is a smile and nod, maybe even sometimes a 'Hello' if she felt bold.

Once she reaches the end of the block, Emma mentally checks off the items on the list of the little things she hopes to see to start her day. Being able to check off seeing everyone on her favorite block from her list, Emma knows that today will be a good day. If even one item on her list is not checked off by the time she reaches Bank Street, it will throw off her rhythm and start her day off on the wrong foot.

Satisfied with today's checked-off list, she happily makes her way over to Astor Place, unbothered by the cold cutting into her face. If only everything else in Emma's life could be as predictable and give her the same amount of happiness.

She makes it to Astor Place, heading into the all-glass building that is SpikeSearch, the leading marketing firm of the tri-state area. As if she is a robot, following the nine-to-five morning routine, Emma grabs her employee ID card and swipes it onto the metal gate. The arms of the gate swing open and the elevator chimes, preset to go to the employee's floor upon the swipe of their card. Emma makes her way to the open elevator and takes the last sip of her coffee. Once the door closes, a small screen in front of her displays a slideshow transitioning from the local weather (25° with snow predicted in the afternoon), to CNBC for the stock market (SpikeSearch's stock is doing remarkably well this quarter), and a schedule of events the company is holding (sushi will be delivered for lunch and a ping-pong tournament starts today).

Looking to her right, Emma sees her reflection and all she can see staring back at her is the despair and fatigue in her eyes. She should be happy. Working at SpikeSearch was everything she worked tirelessly for, yet she still feels like something is missing. It isn't specifically her job that she is unsatisfied with; she has a great boss and enjoys what she does. She isn't one of the millions of zillennials drowning in student debt. She is, however, one of the millions who still lives at home with her parents, since living in New York City on your own costs you your liver and a kidney. Besides, Emma couldn't move out without Sadie, their goldendoodle, who got her through college.

She's made peace with living at home for now, but there are other things in her life that aren't what she hoped they'd be, being twenty-four and having never fallen in love or had a serious boyfriend, for one. There's the loss of communication with friends from high school and college that slowly dissipated as life went on, leaving only her family and Sadie as her social life. Emma knows that having a boyfriend will not make you happy or fulfilled, but maybe having a girlfriend with whom you can share all your dumbest and silliest remarks can help. Her mom, Abigail, is the only constant friend she has had throughout her whole life.

Emma has had only one best friend in her life, or at least she thought they were best friends. The story is simple: Two high schoolers who didn't belong to a clique became close friends and did everything together. Then once graduation passed and college came into full swing, the communication they promised to keep started to drift as it does from attending different schools. Until it's been months since they last spoke to each other, leading to years. It broke Emma when their friendship fizzled, as it showed her what years of friendship meant after mere months of being at different schools.

Emma shakes off the memories and the sudden feeling of sadness that arose from them and puts a smile on her face once the elevator dings to indicate her arrival on her floor.

She passes her co-workers, who have their heads bent down in front of their laptops and ears covered with wireless headphones, sitting at tabletops or in comfy lounge chairs, sipping on their first or second morning coffee. None of them talk to one another. That's the way things are in a relatively new company created by millennials and staffed with zillennials. They only talk face-to-face during in-person meetings. If something needs to be discussed outside of those meetings, that's what instant messaging is for. Why bother getting up and walking to the other side of the floor when you can just ask Josh straight from your laptop what exactly he needs for the next stakeholder presentation? The less human interaction, the better.

Emma walks down the hallway and heads towards the open space in the far corner with several open-spaced desks sitting in a square facing each other. That's another thing about working for a new company: they fully embrace open workspaces, which means no personal offices for anyone, not even for the CEO. It's supposed to help with collaboration, which is quite pointless when no one wants to collaborate while working, but at least it makes the most of Spike-Search's square footage.

As Emma reaches her team's area, she takes a seat at one of the empty desks near the window, desperate to feel some sunlight during the dark winter days. As Emma takes her laptop out from her backpack, her well-worn copy of *Pride and Prejudice* flops out onto the floor. Emma picks it up, and her pulse quickens as she feels the sturdy, hardcover in her hands, excited to continue re-reading one of her favorite books and reach the part when Mr. Darcy declares his love to Lizzie. Impatience runs through her body, knowing she will need to wait at least eight hours to get back to reading, yet she also feels the excitement of knowing that there is something to look forward to later today.

She places the book securely back in her backpack, right behind her good luck copy of *The Port to Sea.* Other people have a bracelet, a ring, or a keychain as a good luck charm, but Emma's good luck charm is the overly highlighted and annotated hardback cover of her favorite novel. She has carried it with her since she first read it back in her freshman year of high school when it hit the shelves and blew up into a national phenomenon. Emma, just like millions of others, fell in love with Madeleine and Beck's love story, and ever since then, she has hoped to find the same kind of unconditional love that they have.

Emma has never found conclusive data to prove that this copy actually gives her good luck. But the slightly superstitious part of her is too afraid to ever find out what will happen if she does go without it one day. Until that day comes when she has been proved otherwise, it will remain by her side as her good luck charm.

Instinctually, Emma places her fingertips over the top edge of the book, hoping whatever good luck it may have will send her positive energy for the rest of the day. As she zips her backpack shut and places it underneath her desk, her co-worker Astrid strolls into their area and takes a seat at the desk next to her.

"Morning," she says cheerily to Emma, as she removes her AirPods from her ears and unravels the multi-colored wool scarf from around her neck.

"Morning," Emma responds, smoothing her curly light auburn hair after taking off her beanie, then deciding to put it up in a loose ponytail based on the glance of herself in the monitor's reflection. "I can't believe how cold it already is, and it's only the middle of December."

"You're telling me!" says Astrid, while unpacking her laptop, water bottle, and other items onto her desk. "I always overlayer, then end up sweating bullets while on the subway."

"That's why you should walk to work," Emma says singingly.

Astrid laughs and shakes her head. "I don't know how you do it, and all year round too."

Emma laughs. "It's only a mile, Astrid. I'm not walking all the way from Central Park."

"Still! Even in this freezing weather, I would rather take the sweat traps of the subway cars than freeze my toes off." A welcome silence emerges between the two as they start looking through their emails and Slack messages, checking to see if there is anything pressing for them to look at first. Emma is able to have thirty minutes of uninterrupted silence until she hears her name being called a few feet away.

Picking her head up, she sees her boss's stopped by her teams area, looking right at her. "Do you have the latest numbers ready for the stakeholder meeting?" asks Wyatt with a heavily caffeinated smile on his face.

Emma sees that he had taken off his suit jacket and rolled his shirt sleeves high on his forearms. This is how she knows Wyatt has been at the office for at least two hours this morning, while she has been here for a mere thirty minutes. She shouldn't feel bad as she arrives at work well before many others in their office. But there is just something about having a boss who is *too* into his job, highlighting how dedicated an employee could be. Should be, some would argue.

Emma feels slightly off whenever this difference between them comes up. She tries to match his level of enthusiasm, hoping that would bridge the gap a bit, and nods. "I finished writing the script yesterday. I can run it again to get updated numbers and send you the full report in twenty minutes."

Wyatt smiles once more. "Always on top of everything. Thank you, Emma." He turns around to leave, then suddenly peeks his head back in. "Oh! And good morning to you both," he says finally, then makes his way to the other side of the floor.

"You were finally able to get that script to work?" asks Astrid.

"It wasn't all me. I had to ask Ben for help on it." Emma looks at the empty desk next to her. "Speaking of, have you seen him? I owe him a coffee for saving my butt."

Astrid shakes her head. "Not yet, but you know how the 6 train runs." She looks around them, ensuring no one can hear, and scoots her rolling chair closer to Emma, leaning over the desk to get into her personal space. Emma knows she is about to tell her some office secret that Astrid always somehow manages to gather as soon as it spreads, being the go-to person to verify office gossip. "I thought you should know. Since we took on three major clients this year, I heard that Wyatt wants to create a program manager position for the data science division and hire two more data analysts to our team. He already has the approved funding for it. It's just a matter of when. Have you thought about applying for it? I couldn't think of a person who is more qualified than you to lead our division."

Emma's eyes widen. "Me? I'm not even the best coder on our team. Wouldn't Ben be the best candidate to be the program manager?"

Astrid rolls her eyes. "Ben is the best coder, but he is terrible at multitasking and cannot give a presentation to save his life. He could literally present to the company which type of cookie is the best, and he still will bore us to tears. Emma, you may not be the best coder, but you are the best choice to be a project leader. I'm pretty sure Wyatt already has you in mind for the role."

"I... really?" she says, caught off guard. Being a program manager would mean much more work and responsibilities. *But this is everything you work for, a promotion, right? But do I even want to do it? Do I want to be a manager of a team, leading others and being the fall guy when things go awry?*

Astrid nods her head. "Yeah. I'm just giving you the heads-up, so you don't get blindsided by it. All I'm saying is to think about it, as everyone is sure that it will be offered to you first."

Uneasiness settles in Emma's stomach as the uncertainty about her future creeps in. The last thing she wants to be is one of those people whose career becomes their whole life. That is probably the only thing Emma does know about her life: what she *doesn't* want it to be. This new potential promotion is one step closer to that.

Becoming a data analyst wasn't her dream job. She didn't wake up one day and decide that she wants to decipher and analyze data for a living. Who would? But just like everyone else in her generation, she chose a career path not for her passion for it, but for its longevity and security. Now all she can think about is not how this would be great for her career, but if she wants to work twice the hours for something that she doesn't even love doing.

For the rest of the day, Emma's thoughts spiral out of control, and she feels a midlife crisis coming on, something she usually inflicts upon herself at least once a year. Emma sits staring at her monitor, repeating the same questions in her head: *What am I doing with my life? What do I* want *to do with my life?*

There is something about the upcoming holidays and new year that leads Emma to question everything in her life. Thank goodness today is her last day of work for the year and she has the remaining two-and-a-half weeks to unwind and not think about work. The thought of snuggling with Sadie on the windowsill bench, with a fuzzy blanket and a hot cup of tea along with one of the many books she has piled on her desk to read, brings a smile of relief onto her face.

By the late afternoon, she has tied up any loose ends and handed off any remaining work. She has a deep itch to leave work a bit early and make a quick trip to the Strand to reward herself for getting through the day. Although she has at least a dozen books to read, there are always more she could add to her pile.

She checks the time and sees it's not quite five yet.

Screw it, what does forty-five minutes mean when I'm out for the rest of the year?

Emma manages to escape the office without Wyatt knowing. He was very pleased with the report she prepared for his meeting with the stakeholders, so she knows that he wouldn't bother her for anything else so close to her time off. She takes her navy wool beanie out from her coat pocket and puts it on once inside the elevator. She looks at her reflection, and this time she sees a slight sparkle in her blue eyes. There is something about sneaking out and getting away with it that brings her a slight adrenaline rush. Besides, she gets to go to her favorite place in the world and get lost in the endless rows of books, letting all her worries slip away.

Beyond providing sheer enjoyment and entertainment, books have filled a big hole throughout her life. They helped fill the void of her nonexistent social life.

Emma had friends throughout elementary and middle school; she even had a friend group of her own. But once high school came along, everyone's priorities changed. The other members of the group decided to focus more on boys and popularity over keeping meaningful friendships. Emma, being the sole person in the group who didn't get this memo, was pushed out, leaving her to float around the social sphere of their high school. She was acknowledged occasionally but mainly ignored and thought of as someone who was just there, not as someone who was an integral part of the school's social scene. Not as someone who could be viewed as a person with her own thoughts and feelings, but as someone who was just a background character to serve all the main characters.

No matter what she did, Emma never found her place at her high school. For four years, Emma did what she had to do to endure and go on until she could leave her small school behind and start anew in college. The only way for Emma to escape her world, to fill the silence from the lack of people around her, was to become lost in the immersive world of books and feel close to the characters she came to know as actual friends. For four years, that was enough. She knew she could never truly be lonely when you could find new friends, new people to feel connected to, in the palm of your hand.

Since then, books have always had a special place in Emma's life. Even when her social life got better in college, there was always that craving to slip away into another world.

When Emma steps into the Strand bookstore, a wave of ease and euphoria creeps in, as if she has traveled far away for several months and finally has come back home. With nothing particular in mind, she walks aimlessly down the aisles, looking first in the new fiction section, then browsing her favorite genre, historical fiction. Lastly, she checks up on the genre that helped her through her darkest times in high school: young adult. Naturally, there are a dozen books she wants to take home but has masterfully decided to purchase only two books. Giddiness sets into her bones. The thrill of getting lost in a story is what Emma imagines it feels like to fall in love. Once she places her new books in her backpack, she makes her way back to her parents' rowhouse, naturally going out of her way to stroll down her favorite block.

The darkness doesn't bother Emma too much this early in the evening, up until the end of January, of course. Then seasonal depression kicks in, and Emma craves feeling the sun on her face and wishes she wasn't so tired that she wanted to go to bed at seven. At least at this time of year, there are Christmas lights to substitute for the lack of sunlight.

Rowhouse 363 always has the best lights during the holidays. Every year, it is always something different, and this year's light display is one of Emma's favorites. Tiny lights dangle from the edge of the rooftop on the second floor and cascade down to the top of the first-level windows. The lights flicker lightly and slowly from the top to bottom, as if snow is actually falling. From all the way at 11th Street and West 4th, Emma can see the fake snow falling. As she gets closer and closer to the block, her eyes are glued solid to 363, mesmerized by the lights.

She doesn't notice that something is off until she passes Bank Street and is a mere dozen feet away from 363. She sees a dark shadow moving in her peripheral vision to her left. Knowing that 364 does not put up any lights or any holiday décor out, she thought she must have imagined something, but when she squints her eyes, she is able to make out the silhouette of a very tall and long-limbed person hastily making their way out of 364, leaving the front door wide open as they rush along West 4th Street. A gasp escapes her. A chill runs down her spine, and it is not from the frigid weather.

No one ever goes into batty old man's place, much less runs out of it.

Emma checks up and down the street, seeing if anyone else noticed it. Unfortunately, she is the only other person on the block. She looks back at rowhouse 364's gaping front door, the light inside illuminating the dark street, wondering what she should do, if anything at all.

Did someone just break into batty old man's house?

Emma doesn't realize until her feet hit the steps that she has gradually made her way to 364's entrance. Her heart is beating out of her chest, preventing any coherent thoughts from forming in her head. Slowly she makes her way up the three steps and peeks inside.

"Hello?" she calls out, her voice breaking in pitch.

She opens the door further when no one answers and looks around. Emma senses movement by her feet and jumps with a yell, only to see that a cat is walking in between her legs.

"Oh, you scared that crap out of me." With her heart racing out of her chest, Emma bends down and scratches the cat's head; it purrs in return. "Where is your owner?" she asks the cat.

The cat lifts its paw and pats it on Emma's bare hand. She feels its paw is wet. Looking at her hand, she sees that it is not snow, as she initially thought, but blood. Panicked that someone needs help urgently, she takes out her phone, unlocks it, and is ready to call 911.

Emma follows the cat further inside the house, looking to find who the source of the blood is, and soon finds the batty old man's body in the living room, lying face down on the rug with a knife lodged in his back. The whole floor is soaked with his blood. She doesn't realize she has called 911 until she hears the operator's voice.

She doesn't realize she is standing there, staring directly at the dead body, waiting for the police and ambulance to come, until she feels a pair of hands drag her outside.

This is not how Emma wanted to start her winter vacation.

Chapter Two

Emma doesn't know how long she's been wrapped in the shock blanket. Nor does she know how long she has been sitting in the open back of the ambulance, staring at rowhouse 364 right in front of her. She doesn't register the bright flashing lights of the police cars or the yellow tape that now blocks the entrance of 364 until she notices someone standing in front of her, talking directly to her, waking her up from her trance. Blinking, she looks up at the figure; it's the sweet middle-aged lady who lives in rowhouse 363.

"Huh?" is all Emma can say.

The woman puts a thermal mug in Emma's hands and clasps her hands to hold on to it. "It's freezing out here. It looked like you could use some tea to warm you up, and some company," says the woman, with an empathetic smile on her face.

Emma dumbfoundedly looks down at her hands, realizing that she is holding the mug. She can slowly feel the warmth of the mug hitting her fingers underneath her wool gloves that someone must have put on for her. "Oh, thank you," she mumbles. Tiny sparks of excitement start to form in the back of her head; Emma can just barely feel them tickle alive. Finally! She is talking to 363. But the excitement can only travel so far. The rest of her is still too numb to feel much of anything just yet.

The woman takes a seat next to Emma on the edge of the ambulance. "It's tragic what happened. Although George was a miserable old brute, and a terrible neighbor," she nudges Emma with her shoulder, "can't say I feel sad for what happened to him. I'm assuming you found his body?"

Emma nods and slowly takes a sip of the tea, surprised by the sweet flavors of cinnamon and ginger hitting her taste buds.

"I can't imagine how disturbing that must have been to find another person like that. How are you feeling?" she asks.

Suddenly, everything that happened in the past hour comes back into mind. "I don't know. In shock, I guess."

The woman nods and stares straight ahead, as if she understands what it's like to be in shock. "I'm Winnie, by the way. Winnie Reynard. I live across the street in 363."

"I know," is what Emma wanted to say but refrained from speaking out loud. "I'm Emma," she says instead, turning to look Winnie in the face with a slight smile of gratitude, amazed by her generosity and empathy toward her, a complete stranger. "Thank you for the tea and for sitting out here with me. It helps to not be all alone with my thoughts."

"No one should be alone in a time like this. How come they have you sitting here? You aren't hurt, are you?"

Emma shakes her head. "No, I'm waiting for the detectives to show up. They wanted to ask some questions about what I saw."

Graciously, Winnie didn't ask her what she saw, seeming to not be just any other nosy neighbor. "I know I just met you—and you can say no if you want to— but if it's okay, I'd like to wait with you until they show up. If I were in your shoes, I wouldn't want to be sitting here all alone in the dark and cold waiting for who knows how long for detectives to show up," says Winnie.

Emma doesn't even take a second to consider her offer. Now that Winnie mentioned it, sitting here on her own would surely make her feel much worse. "I'd really like that, if you don't mind at all."

Winnie gives her an empathetic smile as they settle into a silent understanding of just wanting to be with another human being and not needing to fill the silence with chatter.

When the calming effects of the tea start kicking in, Emma's nerves seem to settle down. Her head and vision finally clear enough to take a closer look at the stranger sitting next to her. Yes, she always referred to her as the sweet middle-aged lady, but maybe her assumption about Winnie isn't too far from the truth. Indeed, she does look middle-aged, but in the way of looking too young for her age, her grey, almost white, straight hair giving her age away. But her eyes are green, nearly almost blue, with no signs of crow's feet or creasing skin on her forehead. Her frame shows that she is athletic, ready to join a yoga or cycle class whenever asked. There is some sort of effortlessness in her, looking beautiful while wearing no makeup and sporting sweats underneath a puffer coat.

She looks like one of those actresses who age gracefully.

There is something in her eyes that tells Emma that she can trust her and knows that she is comforting her from the goodness in her heart.

"So, what brought you to our little neighborhood here in the West Village and unfortunately finding George?" asks Winnie after a few silent moments.

"I walk down this block every day, walking to and from work in Astor Place. I live with my parents one block over near Jane Street," Emma points upwards, barely making out her parents' black front door.

"Oh! You're practically a neighbor!" Winnie exclaims. "That's the thing I love about this city, you meet new people every day, some who belong to the same small world you do. How strange, we live so close to each other and yet we have never met before."

Little do you know; I feel like I've known you for years.

Emma shifts slightly in her seat, thinking about what Winnie just said about them never meeting despite their close proximity. There were so many times she could have gone up to her and said hello. So many times they could have had this initial conversation, but she never was able to get the courage to do it. Emma doesn't know what's sadder, the fact that she never did get the courage to do it on her own, or the fact that it was the death of a neighbor that resulted in their first meeting.

In her peripheral vision, Emma sees one of the officers walk towards her. Dread slowly forms in her, hoping that she isn't coming over to tell her of any developments. There is only so much shock a person can handle in one day. "Miss Callahan," says the officer once she's in front of her and Winnie. "The detectives should be arriving in a few minutes. Is there anything we can do before they arrive?"

For a moment Emma thinks about having them tell her parents about what happened. But not wanting her parents to panic, she thinks better than to frighten them. Besides, she will be home soon to tell them on her own.

Emma shakes her head. "Thank you, but I'm alright."

"Just let me know if you need anything," offers the officer one more time. A glimmer of empathy courses through her eyes for a moment, then she heads back inside the rowhouse with the other officers.

"I hope they do come soon," says Emma. "Standing out here and waiting is making me anxious."

"We are always on someone else's time, never our own," says Winnie as she watches the officers move around them.

A ragged sigh comes out of Emma as she tilts her head back. "I'm just afraid that they think I had something to do with this."

Emma can feel the warmth of a hand on her arm. "I can't say for certain what they'll do, but the only thing you can do is give them honest answers," says Winnie. "I know that isn't helpful. I've never been in this situation either."

Emma nods her head, understanding what Winnie is trying to do: easing her mind and preventing her from panicking. She takes another sip of the tea, fully tasting the strong flavors. Surprise shows on her face, "Wow. This is delicious, by the way."

"Oh, thank you," says Winnie. "That's one of my favorite tea combinations. I call that one *ensoleillement*. It means 'sunshine' in French."

After almost finishing the tea and taking a few deep breaths, Emma can feel her anxiety start to wane and the terror from seeing a dead body slowly start to slip away. She knows that these emotions won't go away quickly, but feeling closer to her normal self gives her some reassurance that they will eventually. It also helps having Winnie around. But when Emma thinks about it, having Winnie around shouldn't be helping her. One would think her sweet and contagious disposition would make Emma feel worse, not better. Sometimes a stranger's good intentions can create more harm than good. But Emma cannot imagine going through this without Winnie.

She takes one final sip of the tea, emptying the mug. "You make your own teas?" asks Emma, grateful to be distracted from the visions appearing in her mind of the man's body encircled by a pool of blood.

Winnie nods. "It was something my grandmother loved to do back in France. She passed the skill to my mother, and my mother passed it on to me. I grow some herbs in my small garden on my back patio and make my own tea bags. I know it seems a bit silly. Why go through all that hassle when you can go to the store and buy a bunch of tea bags ready to be used? But it was one of the things I loved to do with my mémé. It reminds me of her and of home."

"You're from France?" asks Emma, surprised that she didn't hear any trace of an accent. She already had this deep, yearning curiosity to know about Winnie, but now she is even more intrigued. With every detail Winnie reveals, the more amazed and pleasantly surprised Emma is.

She nods. "Martigues, South of France, near Marseille."

This woman is amazing. She's French, makes her own teas, and has a gorgeous rowhouse. I bet this woman has truly lived.

"Is that why your front door is a turquoise blue?" Emma asks, gesturing towards the door.

Winnie looks over and laughs. "I never made that connection. I guess I subconsciously picked it to remind me of the sandy beaches and blue waters of the Mediterranean." She looks lovingly at it, as if lost in a dreamy memory.

"What made you move here?" Emma asks.

Winnie shakes her head. "We never planned on leaving France. But one day when I was ten, my dad was offered the job of his dreams in Chicago. He accepted it in a heartbeat. I knew enough English to get by, but I still had a heavy accent that I was made fun of relentlessly for."

Emma shakes her head, knowing how kids in school can be. "Kids can be very cruel. Was it hard to leave everything behind in Martigues?"

"It was, but the hardest part was leaving my grandmother, my mémé… She helped me a lot while I transitioned to my new life here in the States. Back then I had to mail her letters to stay in touch with her. My poor mémé got so many letters from me during my first few years living here. But nowadays," she shakes her head slightly to herself, "you can see your family virtually from thousands of miles away in an instant. I wish I had had that option when she was still alive."

"Have you gone back to visit since you left?"

Winnie shakes her head. "I always had plans to go back and visit but never did."

Emma sits with this knowledge for a moment, wondering why someone who clearly loved their home country never went back.

"Do you still have family in the States?" asks Emma, hoping to get Winnie to mention her son.

Winnie nods. "Only one. My parents eventually moved back to France. I think they missed it more than they'd like to admit."

Before Emma could ask a follow-up question about who that one remaining family member is, a man and a woman approach them after they parked their black Ford Fusion by Winnie's house. Emma assumes they are the detectives she has been waiting for and curses in her head. Of course, the detectives show up the moment when the conversation is getting good. She is eager to know all there is about Winnie. Her life, her family, her son. But now the time with her is gone, and she may never get a chance to know.

"Are you Miss Callahan?" asks the female detective, disrupting Emma's thoughts. Emma takes her eyes off Winnie and takes in the detectives before her. The woman looks like one of those detectives you'd find on a BBC limited series, wearing a big dark trench coat with an intense, serious face. The 'take no bull shit' kind of detective. Her partner looks exactly like what you would see on *Law & Order*. A stereotypical Italian with gelled, combed-over hair who would make the occasional terrible bad joke thinking he was a stand-up comic.

"Yes," responds Emma wearily.

"I'm Detective Moreno," says the female detective. She motions to the man next to her. "This is my partner Detective Cedrone. We want to ask you some questions regarding Mr. Krueger's death." Detective Moreno looks over at Winnie and gives her a blank stare, signaling that she is not needed for this conversation.

Winnie, getting the hint, leans over to Emma and whispers, "I'll be sitting over there on my stoop. If they give you any trouble, call for me."

Emma nods appreciatively at her. "Thank you."

Winnie gets up from her seat, nods curtly to the detectives, and walks across the street to her place, keeping her eye on Emma.

"Miss Callahan," says Detective Moreno, "can you go through the timeline of the events that led to your discovery of Mr. Krueger's body?" Her partner pulls out a notepad from his coat pocket, waiting to jot down Emma's statement.

A chill runs down Emma's spine, suddenly feeling the night's frigid temperature. She pulls the shock blanket closer to her as if that will help warm her up. She shifts in her seat, wanting to recall everything correctly for them. Not wanting to show any sign that she could have possibly done something to contribute to this man's demise. She picks up her head and looks at them directly. "I was walking up West 4th Street, toward home."

"Can you confirm for us your address?" asks Detective Cedrone.

Emma nods. "382 West 4th Street."

"And where were you coming from?" asks Detective Moreno.

"I work in Astor Place, so I walk to work every day. I left early from work today since I'm on vacation for the rest of the year. I headed to the Strand, as a treat, spent some time there, and bought some books. Then I headed home a bit after six but took my normal route to pass through these blocks on West 4th."

"How come?" interjects Moreno. "Wouldn't it have been easier to cut through West 12th?"

Sweat slowly seeps in her armpits, something Emma didn't know was possible in this weather.

How do I tell them about my obsession with walking a specific route without sounding like a psycho? Do I even say anything about it at all? What if they think I killed him?

Quickly, she makes her decision on what to say. She nods back at them. "It would, but I guess out of habit, I took my normal route home, not really thinking too much about it."

They nod, seeming to accept that answer. "What happened

when you reached this block?" asks Moreno.

It took her some time to go through it all, detailing every aspect of what happened. But she was able to tell the detectives everything. The way she was walking home, when she noticed the figure fleeing out the front door, finishing off with noticing the blood.

"The blood?" asks Detective Cedrone.

"On the cat," clarifies Emma. "There was blood on its paws. The cat walked further into the house, and I followed it, then saw the—" Emma pauses, unable to say the thing she saw: a man's dead body.

Moreno nods with understanding, then faces her partner. "So, it seems like the time of death is somewhere between six and six-thirty. We will have to wait for the autopsy to confirm it." She looks back over at Emma. "Did you know the deceased?"

Emma shakes her head. "No. I saw him from time to time when I walked by, but I never spoke to him."

Cedrone's head perks up, a thought coming into mind. "You said you cross by here to and from work? Monday through Friday?"

"Yeah…" says Emma cautiously.

"Have you ever seen or heard anything about Mr. Krueger that seemed a bit unusual? Or know if he had any issues with anyone in the neighborhood?"

Emma takes a moment to respond. Over her years walking down this block, she noticed a lot of things about its inhabitants, especially the batty old man. That's why she calls him the batty old man in her head. The question isn't whether she wants to share what she has seen, but how long do the detectives have to listen to her. "I mean, from what I've seen, he seemed to cause a bit of trouble for the area."

"How so?" asks Moreno.

"He was very… protective of his property and would often go after people who would litter or let their dog relieve themselves on it. He seemed to monitor his side of the sidewalk like a hawk. Deterring, practically harassing people."

"Would he get into verbal arguments with neighbors?" Cedrone asks.

Emma nods. "With strangers too. He took his ownership of this piece of sidewalk very seriously."

Cedrone smirks into a closed fist, sensing the slight humor in her voice. "Do you remember if there were any arguments recently? Anything that got really heated?"

Emma takes a moment to think, then suddenly recalls how she saw the batty old man staring at a man this morning. While it's definitely not an argument, it may mean something to them. "I did see him staring down at someone while on my morning commute, a man."

"What did this man look like?" asks Moreno.

"He was tall and slender, maybe in his mid-thirties?" She turns to point to the other side of the street. "He was standing over there, talking loudly on the phone and smoking a cigarette."

"Does the person you saw Mr. Krueger staring at have the same build as the person you saw leaving his house?"

Emma thinks for a moment again, then slowly nods her head, "It's possible."

Moreno reaches inside her jacket and takes out her phone, showing Emma a picture of a disgruntled middle-aged man. "Does this man look like the one you saw fleeing the crime scene earlier?"

Emma takes a close look at the picture of a lean, tall man in his fishing gear, standing in front of a large lake, holding up the big catch he just scored. She takes a deeper look into the man's build and hair texture, then closes her eyes to see if that matches the person she saw earlier. Not a lot of men are that same height with unusually long limbs, looking like he never quite grew into his body. "That man does have the same height and build as who I saw earlier, so it could be him. But I can't say that I got a good look at his face, with, you know, him running away from me and all."

"That's enough confirmation for me," says Cedrone as he shuts his notepad shut. He reaches behind him to unclip the walkie-talkie snapped to his belt and presses the receiver, "We have confirmation on the suspect, proceed to bring him in for questioning."

"Wait, you already caught the man?" asks Emma, flabbergasted.

Moreno nods, "We believe we have found a suspect, but I'm not at liberty to disclose anything further." Looking into Emma's eyes,

Moreno sees the fear inside them. "DNA retrieved from the crime scene should confirm, but between you and me, I'm confident you won't have to worry about a killer running around this neighborhood for any longer," Moreno assures.

And just like that, as quickly as the suspect took away George's life, did the police potentially find him and take him off the streets. This will give Emma—and to the rest of the neighborhood— some peace of mind that the killer is no longer running loose.

"Thank you, Miss Callahan, for your cooperation and help. May we reach out to you if we have any further questions?" asks Moreno.

Emma nods and gives them her cell number. Now that the detectives are content with her statement, she is free from the NYPD's grasp. Glancing over across the street, she sees that Winnie is still outside on her front step, just like she promised she would be. Winnie heads over to her as the detectives make their way inside George's house.

"How'd it go?" Winnie asks once she reaches her.

"Fine, I guess. I've never given a witness statement before, so I don't know how it should go." Emma shrugs her shoulders. "I guess it doesn't really matter since it seems like they already know who broke in and killed George."

Winnie looks at Emma with surprise. "Really? Well, I'm glad that they were able to figure that out so quickly. I don't know if I could have gone to bed soundly, knowing the killer was still out there."

Emma nods her head in agreement. Looking down, she realizes that she is still holding Winnie's empty mug. "Oh," she hands it back to her, "I forgot I had this. Thank you again for the tea, and for everything."

"No problem at all, I'm glad that it helped." They both take a moment, unsure of where to go from here. "Do you want me to walk you home?" Winnie offers eventually.

"Oh, I don't want to bother you when you've already been so nice and went out of the way for me."

"Please, you're one block up from me. Come, let's get you home and you can take a nice, hot shower to thaw."

Suddenly feeling how cold and tired she is, Emma agrees, too drained to try to persuade her otherwise. Side by side, they start making their way up West 4th, leaving the flashing lights of the police cars behind them. Silence lingers between them. Emma wants to speak, say something to her, anything to keep her mind off that dead body. She wants to slip back into the conversation they had before the detectives showed up. Or more like, she *needs* to go back to it. For just the briefest moment, her normal conversation with Winnie distracted her from not focusing solely on the body.

And now all she wants is to go back to that moment.

Now that she's scratched the surface, Emma wants to know all there is about Winnie. She imagines all the possibilities, all the stories Winnie could share about her life. But how can she ask her all these questions without being too nosy or coming off as prying?

Instead, Emma thinks back to how her day started like any other and how it ended up like this.

And I thought the idea of me being the top person for that promotion was the worst thing to happen today.

A laugh of disbelief escapes out of her mouth without realizing it.

"What's so funny?" asks Winnie.

"Oh, sorry, I didn't know I laughed out loud. I was thinking about something that happened earlier and thought that was the worst thing to happen to me today," Emma laughs. "Boy was I wrong!"

"What happened?" asks Winnie, with a hint of concern in her voice.

Emma flicks her hand nonchalantly. "It was a work thing, nothing that important. Looking back at it now, it just seems so silly that I was so worked up over it. I mean, look at George. I don't think he woke up today thinking someone would break into his house and stab him in the back."

"Yeah, I don't think so either," says Winnie.

"I'm relieved that I'm off for the rest of the year. That way I can rewatch all of *New Girl* and eat all the ice cream I want, so I can try to forget this ever happened."

"You know..." starts Winnie, thinking out loud, "if you ever want to talk about it, or not talk about it but just want some company, you are always welcome to stop by my place."

Wait… did she actually invite me over?

While she appreciates the offer, Emma knows she won't accept it, not when Winnie has already done so much for her, a stranger. "Thank you, that is really generous of you to offer."

"I mean it, stop by whenever you want. None of my students will come by until after the New Year, so I don't have any commitments for the rest of the year."

"Students?"

Winnie chuckles at the perplexed look on Emma's face. "I'm a private tutor. My home also works as my classroom as well as my tea sanctuary."

"Oh, wow," says Emma, slightly caught off guard. She hadn't envisioned Winnie as an educator. She always thought she was an artist, a painter, someone creative. "What do you tutor?" she asks.

"Literature and French, of course," she says teasingly. They both giggle.

"Right, I should have guessed that," says Emma, in between giggles. "That's amazing. I always wanted to learn French but chose Spanish in middle school."

Winnie's eyes open wide with enthusiasm, an idea sparking into her head. "Oh, I can teach you!"

Uncertainty creeps into Emma, not used to knowing someone who is as kind and willing to go so far out of their way for someone. "That's really kind of you, but I don't want to make you teach me when you are on your winter break."

"Oh shush, it would be my pleasure! Besides, you would be my only student who is actually eager to learn the language. Most of my students are snobby rich kids whose parents want them to know French just to sound prestigious and be obnoxious about knowing it. I mean it, you are more than welcome to come over. We'll have some tea, and I'll teach you some French, and you can repay me with your lovely hospitality. What do you say?"

Emma thinks for a few moments. The zillennial in her doesn't want to be a burden on Winnie, but the other part of her can see this as an opportunity to spend time with her and learn more about her life. But with everything that just happened, how physically and emotionally tired she is, Emma can't, and doesn't want to, commit to a decision right now. All she can think about is going home, showering away the stench of tonight, and curling up into a ball in her bed. She can see her parents' front door. She needs to walk only a few more steps, and she will be protected within the walls of her home.

Emma looks back at Winnie, feeling pulled toward her front door. "After everything that happened today, I need to take tonight to think about it."

"Of course. I'm surprised you've been holding up this well. If you do decide to take up on my offer, feel free to stop by whenever you like. My door is always open. Well, not literally open, but you know what I mean."

Emma nods, wondering how to politely end this conversation without seeming like an ungrateful brat. "Well, this is me," she says while nodding at her parents' rowhouse. "I really do appreciate what you did for me tonight. Not many people would have done that, especially for a stranger."

"I just saw someone who needed some comfort in a time of need. It's the least I could have done." Winnie reaches out and lightly touches Emma's arm. "I'm sorry that you had to get sucked into all of this."

An anxious laugh comes out of Emma. "Yeah, me too."

"Well, goodnight, Emma. I hope to see you soon."

Once the pair gives their final farewells, Emma eagerly heads towards home. As she makes her final steps to the door, disbelief courses through her. Not only from what she just witnessed, but also the fact that she finally got to speak with the woman from 363, or as she found out tonight, Winnie. As she unlocks the front door, she feels like the universe is presenting her with an opportunity; for what, Emma doesn't know, but she's tempted to find out.

August 21, 1988

My Dearest Mémé,

I sincerely want to apologize to you. I know it's been too long since I last wrote to you, especially after Russel and I got back home from our honeymoon. You know how time seems to pass quickly once you've said 'yes' to that one question all women dream of being asked.

The day I am writing this is the first day in a long time when I can finally take a moment to reflect and breathe. Now that I have time to unwind, I must admit that there are things I have overlooked or been blind to, hitting me in a wave of sudden realization.

I'm scared to write down what I want to say, as it would no longer just be in my head but something real. But I must share it with you, as I'll unravel if I don't. We both know that ma mère's thoughts and feelings are about marriage and duty, which is why I can't share with her what I hope I can articulate to you. You are the only one who will understand and support me, no matter what.

Here it goes...

After being married for exactly one month, I should feel as happy and elated as I was before I said 'I do'. I should feel like we are in la lune de miel, but it wasn't until today when I realized that married life is proving to be very different than I thought it would be.

I don't know how to describe this to you, as I cannot even describe it to myself. It's almost like something is changing, or shifting, right underneath your nose and it unsettles me. It's like the real truth unveiled itself once the wedding and honeymoon passed. All I can say for certain is that this new life scares me. I feel nothing but emptiness and loneliness. I do not know what I could do to make it better.

I thought that maybe getting a job; feeling like I am a part of something other than my marriage, would help lift my spirit. But when I brought this subject up to Russel, he rejected the idea as soon as he said it aloud. He tells me that being his life partner is more than enough work and that he 'needs me' to be home to help him excel (and possibly make it to senior principal) at the new architecture company he started working at this summer as a first-level architect.

Mémé, I've worked very hard to graduate NYU with honors—and with a double major in Literature and French! Don't you think I should be using it in some capacity? I want to use my degree, in either teaching or doing some translating work. But no. Russel insists that he needs me and that his career is our family's number one priority. (I'm quite surprised children is not on the top of his list.) One of my NYU professors even highly recommended me as a candidate for a job at the U.N! It was so hard for me to say no when the job was offered to me, since I wanted to say yes terribly.

Can you imagine how humiliating and embarrassing it must have been for my professor to hear that I said no, after everything they did to help me get the job? It's the eighties for goodness' sake; women are allowed to work and make their own living! Why can't Russel see that this will make me happy? We really are never going to escape the patriarchal society we have been trapped and enslaved in for centuries, are we? If the women who fought so hard for our rights could see where things are for us now... Je ne veux même pas penser à ça ....

I desperately need your help and guidance, Mémé, as I have no idea what I should do.

I never felt such heavy hopelessness before...

Ton petit soleil,

Winnie

P.S. I found that mixing chamomile with lavender and rose helps to soothe the soul in difficult times. I'm naming this tea blend: jusque là

Chapter Three

Emma can start to feel her fingers and toes again once she steps inside her house. Her mom has the fireplace going, and every muscle in Emma's body wishes to fall asleep in front of it to forget today's events. As she takes off her beanie, coat, and shoes, Emma feels what this evening has done to her. She leans against the coat tree, her head resting on her wool coat, and takes a few deep breaths. Sadie comes running into the entry and jumps on the backside of Emma, practically knocking her down.

"Hi, Sades," says Emma, kneeling to give her dog head scratches and kisses.

"Emma? Is that you?" calls her mother, sounding far away from within the kitchen.

Emma stands back up and looks in the mirror on the opposite wall of the entryway. Her eyes have turned into a deep blue, like the chasm of the ocean. While her face is ghastly white, her freckles stand out like bright, burning stars on a clear night. Looking down, she sees that her hands are shaking. Now that she is safe and sound at home, she can lose her composure.

"Emma…?" calls Abigail again, this time closer as she heads towards her daughter in the entryway. She reaches up to her, places a hand on Emma's shoulder, and looks at her daughter through the mirror. "Are you alright?" she asks, full of concern for the state of her only child.

Tears start to well up into Emma's eyes, and she turns to face her mother and melts into an embrace. "No," she mumbles into Abigail's hair, with tears seeping into her sweater.

Her mother wraps her arms around Emma, instinctually swaying from side to side. She strokes her head, a method she used when Emma was a baby and crying her heart out. It goes like this for a few minutes, the two women holding on to each other as if their bodies have melded into one another. When Emma finally stops crying, her mother steps away and wipes away her tears with the sleeve of her sweater. "Come inside, and I'll make you a cup of hot chocolate. Are you hungry?"

Emma nods, while trying to calm herself down. Abigail puts an arm around Emma's shoulder and guides her to the back of their house where the kitchen resides. Emma takes a seat at the stool by the kitchen island, while her mother boils some milk and makes her a peanut butter and jelly sandwich. While Emma slowly eats the sandwich and sips on the creamy hot chocolate, Abigail watches her uncertainly, waiting for when she is ready to divulge what is troubling her.

Emma pushes the empty plate and mug further into the island, signaling she is done and ready to talk. "Thank you, that is exactly what I needed," she says with a satisfied sigh.

Abigail leans across the island and grabs Emma's hands. "What happened, Ems? The last time I saw you even remotely upset was when Zayn Malik left One Direction. What has you so rattled?"

Emma laughs at that memory, looking back at how insignificant all her problems seemed then when she was a handful of years younger. "You know how you always imagine what it would be like if you were to encounter certain situations?"

Her mother nods. "Of course, that's how we empathize with people."

Emma lets out a sigh. "Well, one of those situations actually happened to me today."

Abigail straightens up, worry slowly consuming her body, igniting her mother bear mode. "Emma, did something happen to you?"

Emma puts her hands up for reassurance. "It wasn't me, I'm fine. Well, physically I'm fine."

"Then what happened?"

"I...", Emma looks down at her lap, "found a dead body."

"What? A dead body!"

"Actually, I think I witnessed someone's murder."

Abigail's eyes bulge out of her head, frightened by the words her daughter said. She rushes back over to the entry hall near the staircase and yells up to the upper floor, "Oliver! Get down here!"

"What is it?" comes the voice of Emma's father from his office upstairs.

"It's urgent, just come down here!" Abigail comes back into the kitchen and takes a seat next to Emma.

Footsteps can be heard creaking overhead, trailing down the stairs to the kitchen where the two women sit. "Yes?" says Oliver to his wife and daughter. His glasses are sitting on the bridge of his nose, his greying hair sticking out in all directions. This is how the women know that he was deep into reviewing a legal case he is currently working on, one where he can't share too much information with either one of them.

Having both her parents in the room, Emma finally feels like she is in the safe place she needs. The mental wall she didn't know she built can finally crumble. She no longer feels that she needs to hold back or put up a façade. She has never had to do that with her parents, and never has she felt this grateful that she could, until now.

Abigail lightly nudges Emma, signaling her to speak.

"I, um, found a dead body," she says to her parents.

"Where?" asks Abigail.

"On our street, one block over. I saw a man run out of a house and left the door open, so I went in, and that's where I found the body."

"Jesus…" mutters Oliver under his breath.

"And it was murder? Not just an accident?" asks her mother.

"The man had a knife stuck in his back. I don't think there is any possible way that could have been an accident. Unless some Final Destination shit happened to him, which I don't think is very likely."

"And you called 9-1-1 right away?" asks her father.

"Of course I did, Dad," she says with annoyance, slightly hurt that her father thinks she would be so foolish not to do so.

He nods in approval. "Did you see anything? Touch anything? Did you share everything you know with the police? Is there anything that you *didn't* share?" These are the questions Oliver Callahan, the lawyer, asks all his clients, making sure he covers all bases to understand the legal ramifications. But this is the first time he ever had to ask this of his daughter.

Emma nods. "I told the police everything and told them how I came across the body. I didn't touch anything and I was as cooperative as I could be, like you always told me."

Relief spreads across Oliver's face, and quickly he goes from Oliver Callahan, the lawyer, to Oliver Callahan, Emma's father. He comes over to stand beside Emma and holds on to her, letting her rest her head on his chest as he comforts her. "I just can't believe it," says Oliver, "a murder, in our own neighborhood…"

"The detectives told me they already caught the suspect," says Emma. "So, we don't have to worry about a killer being on the loose tonight."

"Oh, thank God, I was starting to worry we would have to securely lock our doors with the furniture," says Abigail. She reaches out to stroke Emma's hair, sending comforting tingles down her daughter's spine. In this moment, Emma doesn't feel like a twenty-four-year-old, but a young kid, being consoled after having a nightmare, except this time, the nightmare is real. A rotten corpse that frightened her good. "But are you okay, Ems? That must have been traumatizing to see something like that."

"It's just…I can't get the image of that man's body out of my head." Emma looks up at her parents, her eyes pleading for help. "How can I ever get it out of my head?"

"I wish we knew how, baby," says Abigail. "Thankfully you are off work for a while, you can take all the time you need to process it. I may be jumping here, but you can always go see a counselor or a therapist too. The last thing we want you to feel is that you need to force yourself to get over this. You witnessed something that a human being should never have to see, don't ever invalidate yourself of that."

Emma reaches out for her mother's hand on her lap, giving it a tight squeeze, appreciating her psychologist mind and empath nature to understand the spiral of emotions she is feeling. "Thankfully, one of the neighbors on the street came over and kept me company while I was waiting for the detectives to show up. If it weren't for her, I don't know how I would have managed to get home, even though I was so close by."

"That was very gracious of her," says Abigail. "At least we know there is some humanity left out there."

Emma lets out a small laugh. "She actually offered to have me over at her place if I ever want to talk to someone about it." She shakes her head at herself. "Can you imagine meeting the nicest person in the world during the worst time of your life?"

"Strangely, that's how life is, dear," says Oliver.

Looking at her mom, Emma can see that she is deep in thought, her nose squinched with that look she has when an idea is brewing in her head. "We should really thank her somehow," says Abigail. Her eyes light up once the idea has finally come into place. "Oh! We should have her over for dinner. That way we can meet her and thank her in person."

"I haven't decided yet if I want to take her up on her offer…", trails Emma.

Not a second later does a realization hit her. A chill runs through her as she thinks about the block.

What if I can't ever walk down my favorite block ever again? What if I'm too scarred from tonight that I can never go near it again?

"Well, if you do decide to visit her, which you should," says Abigail, interrupting Emma from spiraling, "invite her over, please."

"Sure… yeah…" says Emma, lost in her own mind at the dreadful thought.

Suddenly, she feels the weight of exhaustion and fatigue that has settled into every bone and muscle in her body. All her thoughts go quiet. All except for one: a helpless desire to put this whole day behind her as soon as possible. "I think I'm going to head upstairs, shower, and lie down in bed for the rest of the night," she says, hoping some time to decompress will help.

"Do you want to watch a movie together later?" asks Abigail. "Try to take your mind off of it?"

Emma nods, knowing that the last thing she wants tonight is to be alone.

"Okay," consoles Abigail, "you can pick the movie, and I can make us some popcorn."

Once upstairs in her bedroom, Emma closes her door and flops onto her bed with Sadie lying down next to her. She stares straight up at the ceiling while petting Sadie for comfort. She can hear the clanking and clatter of the room's radiator, the sloshing of car tires going over wet snow on the street, even the rhythmic breathing coming from Sadie. All while still seeing the image of the batty old man's dead body with a knife handle sticking out its back, surrounded by a pool of fresh blood seeping into the rug.

There was just so much blood…

Suddenly feeling dirty, Emma rushes to her bathroom, takes off her clothes, and scrubs herself clean in the shower. Getting into every nook and cranny, deep in her cuticles and nail beds, as if she is trying to wash away the blood on her, although there is none. The hot water warms up her body. Slowly in increments, she raises the heat of the water, wanting to feel the burn on her skin. Hoping that the hot water burns the image of the batty old man out of her head. She stands there for several minutes, knowing that once she gets out, she will have to deal with the events of this evening. For a few minutes, she doesn't want to be Emma Callahan but just any other young woman in this boisterous city.

Once the water has gone cold, Emma is forced to leave her safe little bubble and go back out into the world. She wraps her body in a bathrobe and wipes the steam off the bathroom mirror, looking at her reflection. Her pale skin is now a pinky-red from the hot water and the forceful scrubbing, almost matching the color of her hair. She still feels dirty, as if there is no real way to wipe yourself clean after seeing a dead body.

Staring at herself, Emma wonders how so much bad luck could have happened to her in one day. How a seemingly normal day can go sour so quickly. She thinks back to the moment when she touched her good luck charm, thinking it would send her some good vibes.

Instead, all she got was bad luck. She starts to doubt if her copy of *The Port to Sea* was ever her good luck charm.

But today wasn't all that bad, right? I mean, if tonight never happened, I wouldn't have met Winnie. So maybe the book is my good luck charm? A good luck charm with a sick, twisted sense of humor.

The more she thinks of that positive spin, the more she starts to accept that truth behind it. If it weren't for the death of the batty old man, then she likely wouldn't have ever met Winnie nor have known that her name is Winnie and not "sweet middle-aged lady". If she focuses only on this positive spin, then maybe it will help her to process everything that happened and move on. Thinking only of the good things that are going on in her life, not on the negative.

As Emma brushes her wet hair and sets her curls, she thinks about the short glimpse into Winnie's life she showed her. Her hometown in France, the family tradition of making their own teas, being a tutor of her native language in a different country. She wonders how someone who came from a faraway place ended up right here in West Village, one block away from her, and wants to know much more about her.

Once she has finally completed her after-shower routine, Emma looks back at herself in the mirror, looking at all the features she sees in front of her. She knows there is no difference between the woman she sees now versus who she was earlier this morning, but Emma knows that the two do not look the same. As if tonight not only changed her mentally but physically.

She thinks back to Winnie's offer, how she could stop by if she ever needed someone to talk to. Closing her eyes, Emma can imagine herself sitting by Winnie's front window, a cup of tea in her hands, deep in a life-changing conversation with her. Then in another flash, she can see herself talking to Winnie's son, finally being able to meet the man she has had a secret crush on for months. Excitement flames inside her from all the possibilities.

Emma opens her eyes, looking at the stranger before her once more. The old Emma would shy away and go back to her normal life. But the Emma from before is already changing; she is no longer the person she used to be. So, what's stopping her from leaning into this new version?

She already discovered a dead body—the worst thing she will ever experience in her life— whatever she could possibly lose by getting out of her comfort zone is nothing in comparison.

Chapter Four

The hours from Friday night to Sunday morning passed by in a blur. There wasn't a moment Emma was by herself; every second she was with one or both of her parents. For once, she appreciated their company at all hours. Whether it was binge-watching *Jane the Virgin* with her mom or sitting in her dad's study reading while he silently goes through pages and pages of documents, every moment she was with someone. Besides using the bathroom, of course.

When she wakes up from the rising sun on Sunday morning, she still feels sluggish and fatigued. Her nights are still consumed with nightmares and restlessness. Flashing images of the batty old man's body and blood are still buried in the deep corners of her mind, always lingering, waiting to haunt her when she tries to forget.

Out of habit, she reaches for her phone on the nightstand, scrolling through her unopened emails and checking social media to wake up her brain. She glances at the time on the top left of the screen, realizing it's barely close to seven. Never in her life has Emma been a morning person, but for the past two mornings, her lack of sleep has forced her to become one.

She continues to scroll through her phone, not quite ready to get up from her warm and comfy bed. Besides, she knows how Sadie will be cranky if Emma gets out of bed before their usual time. Out of curiosity, Emma searches for information about Martigues, Winnie's hometown. Reading through a site called The Europe Tourist, Emma learns about the history of the canal-infused commune. She's mesmerized by the bright, warm colors of the buildings, the tantalizing blue of the Mediterranean Sea, the rows of docked fresh white row boats along the canals, the effervescent greenery that is on every patio and bridge. It looks like paradise. Suddenly, Emma wishes she could run to JFK and take a plane to this beautiful place, wanting to escape for just a little bit.

I may not be able to go to Martigues, but I can visit the second-best thing to it.

With her new plan in mind, Emma again feels energy buzzing in her body, feeling excited and optimistic that she can forget about Friday night for a few hours.

As she gets up and starts getting ready, Emma pauses at the bathroom sink, toothbrush in hand. She thinks for a few moments about how the zillennial in her doesn't want to be a burden on Winnie, showing up at her house unannounced on a Sunday morning. But the other part of her, the new Emma who is eager to know more about this woman and her life, is screaming deep down to say yes, wanting to do something adventurous and out of character for once. It doesn't take her much convincing; she caves easily, ready to start making decisions that her old self would never make. Wanting to escape from her boring, scheduled life of a corporate-working twenty-something.

Impatient to start living as this new version of her and head to Winnie's, she rushes through the rest of her morning routine in her bathroom. She takes out her hair from the messy bun she put in during last night's movie watch-in-bed and hopes her hair is in decent condition. Luckily, it's salvageable. She decides to braid her hair on the side with a head scarf woven in between the braids, bringing a contrast of blue against her light auburn hair. As she finishes her last braid, a thought makes her stop in mid-plait.

What if she's busy? Or worse, what if I run into her son?

Her head starts to run in several directions. What should she wear? How should she look? Settling for a natural, not over-the-top look, she applies only mascara and blush on her face. Embracing her half-Irish heritage, Emma gave up on covering her freckles ages ago. She has grown to love them for what they are: a part of her.

Rushing back into her room, she goes to her small closet and opens the door that has been forced shut. Bursting on the hooks are dresses, shirts, and skirts of all kinds. Just one of the many minor downsides of living in an old rowhouse, the storage space is irritably minimal.

Emma frantically searches for something to wear, wanting to look respectable but not too overdressed. Cute but not seeming to try too hard.

She decides on a pair of plaid corduroys that flare out on the bottom and pairs it with a black high-neck sweater, blending warmth with fashion. Sadie lays down on Emma's unmade bed while she gets dressed, giving her a look as if she's asking where she is going. Once dressed, Emma kneels on her bed and scratches Sadie behind her ear, one of her favorite spots. "I know, Sades. I'm just as shocked as you are that I'm going out on a weekend."

Sadie places a paw on Emma's arm, as if asking her not to go and to stay in bed with her instead. Emma giggles. "You silly girl. I'm home for the next few weeks. We can stay in all we want then." Sadie jumps up and gives Emma a kiss on the cheek, approving of the plan.

"You like the fit?" Emma stands back up and poses for Sadie, as if she is in a teen movie makeover montage. Sadie tilts her head to the side, confused, not giving her much feedback.

"I'm going to take that as a yes." Emma gives Sadie one last kiss on the head, grabs her bag hanging on the closet door, and makes her way downstairs, creaking floors and all.

"I'm going to go to Winnie's. I'll be back later," she yells out into the void of the house, knowing her parents will hear from wherever they are.

"Alright!" yells her dad, most likely in his office.

"Love you!" yells her mom, most likely in the family room watching the CBS Sunday Morning Show.

Emma bundles up in several layers: wool coat, scarf, mittens, and earmuffs. After tying up her Doc Martens, she heads out into the cold and walks the one block to Winnie's house.

At least I don't have to walk too far.

The excitement propelling her forward vanishes as she gets closer to the block. Fear immobilizes her as she reaches the street corner. She hasn't seen the block since that night and forgot she would have to walk through it to get to Winnie's. Closing her eyes, she takes a deep breath.

I can do this. I can walk across the street and down the block. There is no body; it's just a normal Sunday morning.

Before she can give herself a chance to chicken out, she walks across the street and heads right for rowhouse 363, not daring to sneak a glance at 364, despite seeing the yellow police tape in her peripheral vision. She feels a bit of relief once she reaches the turquoise blue front door, with her back facing 364, completely out of sight. Her heart beats out of her chest once she rings the doorbell, excited yet nervous. Despite the cold, she can feel sweat forming in her armpits. This feels like an interview, wanting to get the job as someone welcomed into Winnie's inner circle. For some reason, she is more determined to get this 'job' than when she had four rounds of interviews for SpikeSearch.

Emma doesn't know why she is so desperate for Winnie to accept and welcome her. Maybe it's the people-pleaser in her, wanting everyone to like her, or maybe it's wanting to become her friend, or maybe it's the knowledge she will have a higher chance of running into her son if she comes by often.

Before she knows it, the front door opens with a burst of warmth hitting her face. Winnie stands in front of her, exuding effortless grace once again. She's wearing a blue cashmere wrap with jeans and a long white sleeve. Her hair is somewhat wet, as if she did a morning workout.

There's a look of surprise on her face that turns into joy. "Emma!" says Winnie, grinning.

Emma looks down at her feet, pushing down the awkwardness rising inside her. Once she regains her composure, she looks back up at Winnie. "I don't usually show up at someone's house without notice, but I didn't know how to reach you. I hope it's okay I stopped by now? Unless this is a bad time for you, then I could always swing by another time," she says while silently hoping that this isn't.

"No, of course it's okay. I meant it when I said my door is always open." Winnie steps aside, giving Emma enough space to walk through. "Please come in."

Emma had envisioned many times what 363 would look like. She couldn't decide if Winnie would have a colorless, minimalistic home with a museum vibe, or a colorful house covered in every square inch, with every item having a specific purpose. Never in a million years did she think she would ever get to find out what it was truly like inside.

Before her, she sees charm, warmth, character—a place that has been lived in and cared for. The hardwood is worn down, but in a rustic way. Above her is a chandelier that looks like it came from a medieval Spanish castle. She can see a lively library on her left with shelves upon shelves of books, a desk with stacks of journals and loose-leaf paper resting on top. In the middle of the library is a soft brown leather couch that looks perfect for a nap. To finish it off, plants fill in every empty space. To Emma, it's her reading room dream come true. She longs to go through the rows of books, curious to know what kind of collection Winnie has.

"Can I take your coat?" Winnie asks, breaking Emma's gaze away from the library.

"Oh, yes, please." Emma takes off her coat and hands it over. "Would you like me to take my shoes off?" she asks while gesturing to her boots. She hopes Winnie says no, as it's as big of a pain to get Docs off as it is to get them on.

Winnie waves her off nonchalantly. "Only if you want to."

Once Winnie hangs her coat in the hall closet, she motions for Emma to come into the kitchen. As Emma makes her way deeper into the house, she looks at every corner, searching for any tidbits of Winnie she can find. She sees several framed photos on display. Emma believes photos can easily show a glimpse into the person. So much so, one can just look at a few to understand a bit about that person's life. Many of the pictures Winnie has on display are of her son throughout his life. From the few that Emma can see, it's clear that the two of them are very close.

What strikes Emma the most is not the number of pictures of mother and son, but the lack of other faces frequently appearing in the photos. She doesn't know what to make of that just yet, so she makes a mental footnote to keep that in mind throughout her visit.

As she makes her way closer to the kitchen, Emma experiences olfactory overload. Freshly ground coffee. Melted butter and cheese. Suddenly, her stomach makes a loud growl from gnawing hunger. She places her hand over her stomach, hoping to dampen the sound.

Walking into the kitchen, Emma is magically transported to another time and place. Cream-colored stone tiles cover the floor. Warm brown cabinetry with glass on the doors to show off the unique plates and cups Winnie has collected over the years. A small island with a farmhouse sink is placed in the middle of the room, a rack of pots and pans hanging above, and two rustic stools with beige cushions placed on the side closest to her. What delights Emma most is the brickwork on the walls above the stainless-steel range on the farther kitchen wall. If Emma were to ever see an upscale European countryside kitchen, she knows that this is what it would look like.

She follows Winnie to the island, where piles of clean bowls, pans, and utensils have been stacked, awaiting use. "I was just about to make some breakfast. Are you hungry?"

Emma nods. "Starving, actually."

"Do you like omelets and coffee?" asks Winnie as she opens the fridge to take out cartons of eggs and milk.

"Love them," replies Emma. "Would you like any help?"

"I'd love some help. I'm guessing you never learned how to make a French omelet?" Emma shakes her head, confirming Winnie's suspicion. "My mother taught me at a young age how to whip up a classic French omelet in no time. I will teach you her secret recipe," says Winnie with a wink and a hint of mischief in her smile.

Emma watches and listens attentively to Winnie's instructions, being conscious not to make a mess or fail miserably at the small tasks Winnie gives her. Since she intruded on her Sunday morning, the last thing she wants to do is give her more trouble.

Before she knows it, the table is set with two nicely plated Food Network-quality omelets, two cups of hot, freshly made coffee, and a bowl of freshly cut fruit.

"*Bon appétit*!" says Winnie as they sit down and start to eat their breakfast.

Before any awkward silences emerge, one of the things Emma hates most in the world, Winnie speaks as if she isn't hosting a total stranger at her house, but a friend. "How are you holding up, after the whole…", she waves her fork in the air, hesitant to finish the rest of her sentence.

Emma knows that her response to this question could change the trajectory of their friendship. She sees two roads forming in her head. The path on her left starts uncomfortably with honesty but ends up leading to a genuine, meaningful friendship, making the discomfort worth it. Then there is the path on the right, where she puts up a façade for niceties and their friendship never quite feels real but only shallow, superficial, leading it to be a short-lived one. Emma knows that if she wants to know Winnie, become friends with her, and learn from her life experiences, she will have to choose the former, despite how uncomfortable it will be at first. "Honestly, it has been tough," she admits. "I totally had a mental breakdown after we parted ways on Friday night, and since then I've been holding it together and trying to get George's dead body out of my head."

Winnie nods, listening intently to her while taking a sip of coffee. "One should never have to experience such a tragic event but feel reassured that you will heal from seeing such a thing. Has your family been supportive?"

Emma nods while taking a sip of the strongest coffee she has ever tasted. The kick of the strong grounds sends a buzz of energy down to her core. "Graciously, yes. My parents have always been understanding. My dad is an attorney, and my mom is a psychologist, so between them both, they understand all sides of the incident, from the emotional impact to the legal implications."

Winnie smiles. "They seem like quite a pair."

"They've been married for twenty-seven years and are still going strong," Emma takes another bite, this time getting a mouthful of

Gruyère cheese. "Oh my god!" she moans while covering her full mouth. "This is amazing."

"*Merci beaucoup*," says Winnie beamingly. "I'm assuming you know what that means?" she teases her.

Emma laughs and nods. "That and '*oui*' are the only words I do know."

Winnie sits up straight in her seat as an idea occurs to her. "We can use our breakfast for your first lesson." She lifts her fork and points at it. "*La fourchette*," she says with a clear French accent. Gone is the American accent Emma is used to, and now it sounds like a different woman is sitting before her. Winnie then points to her coffee mug, "*Le café*." Her gaze goes down to their now-empty plates, "Omelette is still *l'omelette*, just spelled and pronounced slightly differently." She then waves her hand around the table, signifying the meal as a whole. "*Le petit déjeuner. Ma nouvelle amie Emma et moi, nous prenons le petit déjeuner.*"

"What did you say?" Emma asks.

Winnie smiles at her. "My new friend Emma and I are having breakfast."

Emma's cheeks turn pink as Winnie mentions that she thinks of her as a friend already. "And *le café*!" exclaims Emma, lifting her cup to take its final sip.

"Someone's a quick learner."

Emma laughs, "Being the coffee addict I am, I would easily remember that first."

"So, Emma, besides being a coffee addict and having the recent misfortune of uncovering a dead body, tell me about yourself. Who is Emma? What's your story?"

Caught off guard by her bluntness, Emma does not know where to begin but then remembers that there isn't too much to her story. It's quite short and simple. "I wish I had a lot to say about myself." She plays with her napkin, suddenly self-conscious about how lonely and boring her life is. "My life is more like a short story than a novel."

"Short stories are masterpieces too," says Winnie as she looks at her sympathetically. She leans forward and whispers, "Besides, they are my favorite kind of prose."

Feeling seen and understood, Emma smiles. For the first time, she feels like her life story is one worth sharing. Winnie gives her an encouraging look, challenging her to tell her short story.

"Well," Emma starts, "I was born and raised here in the city. I even grew up in the same house we live in now. I'm an only child, although I don't think by choice. When I was eight, I'm pretty sure that my mom had a miscarriage as she was very ill for a while. After that, I noticed that they stopped talking about me having a younger sibling, and I stopped asking them to give me one, as I had a feeling that they couldn't have another. All my life, it's only been us three and our dog, Sadie."

"I cannot even imagine suffering a loss like what your parents have gone through," says Winnie. Empathetic eyes stare back at Emma with a hint of recognition lingering, leaving Emma to wonder if she too has gone through her own familial tragedy. "I'm an only child too," Winnie finally says, "and my son is as well. I never had any other kids besides him."

Images of Winnie's family pictures flash back into her mind, recalling how most of them are of only her and her son. Emma takes a quick glance at Winnie's left hand that is now resting on top of the table and notices that she isn't wearing a ring. Emma doesn't recall Winnie wearing one on Friday night either. With the evidence presented to her, a hypothesis forms in her head. One that makes her question where the father of her son is. If he is still in their lives, or if anything happened to him.

Emma, remembering she isn't supposed to know of her son, hopes the look on her face shows some sort of surprise. "You have a son?" she asks, selling her faux cluelessness.

Winnie's eyes light up, a smile of pride and love spreading across her lips. She nods. "His name is Noah, and he is the best thing to ever happen to me. He might be a few years older than you. He'll be turning twenty-eight next month." Her eyes widen. "My god, my little boy is almost thirty."

Emma does some calculations to figure out how old she could be. From her youthful appearance, she must have been very young when she had him. "Does he live here in the city?" Emma asks, keeping up with the charade.

"Yes, thankfully, he got a teaching job here. I don't know what I would have done if he ended up hundreds of miles away. What do you do for work? I can't recall if you told me earlier," Winnie asks before she takes another sip of coffee.

Emma shakes her head, "I don't think I did. I'm a data analyst at SpikeSearch."

Winnie squinches her face in thought. "I don't think I ever heard of that company."

"You wouldn't unless you were one of our clients. It's a marketing and PR firm. We have a wide range of clients from Bloomingdale's to Coachella. We even do some work for politicians and celebrities, though I've been there two years and have yet to meet any of them."

"Pardon my ignorance, but what exactly does a data analyst do?" Winnie says, confused.

Emma shrugs, signaling that it's less glamorous than it sounds, almost demeaning her work. "We collect data, honestly. Then my team and I go through the data and draft up reports for upper management to present to their clients. It's all numbers, code, and pretty charts."

Winnie hesitates, taking in what she said. "And you're not happy," she says curiously.

Emma's breath catches in her throat. Not only does she feel caught off guard by what Winnie said but feels like the air is being sucked out of her whole body. Winnie voiced out into the world what is always deep in Emma's mind but has never been spoken aloud, not even to her parents. Yet Winnie immediately figured it out.

Perplexed, Emma racks her brain to go through everything she told Winnie, wondering if she indicated at all her unhappiness. Coming up empty-handed, eventually she asks, "How could you tell?"

"It's easy to tell when someone else is unhappy when you've been unhappy yourself for a long time," says Winnie with a hint of sadness in her voice. "It's the way you phrased what you do for a living. Even when you said earlier that your life is more like a short story than a novel. That tells me you feel stuck, lost, and possibly that you feel behind." Winnie's eyes lock with Emma's, asking her silently if she guessed correctly.

Feeling cornered, Emma isn't sure what to say in response. She doesn't feel uncomfortable by Winnie's bluntness. If anything, she feels relieved to be able to open up to someone who seems to understand what concerns she has been burying for several months. She wants to unload about her unhappiness, how she doesn't feel fulfilled or have a purpose, how she is afraid she will never fall in love and will die alone. The gates are open, allowing her to run through and pour out everything to whomever is willing to listen on the other side. So, what's the harm in sprinting and unleashing her worries to a stranger?

Emma smiles meekly at Winnie. "You're not wrong. In fact, you're very far from being wrong. What caused you to feel the same way?"

A nervous laugh escapes from Winnie, then she looks off to the side for a moment, shaking her head slightly at herself. "Oh, a lot of things. Family… love… life…", she says with a sigh, then looks back at Emma with recognition. "There are beautiful, euphoric moments, but there are heartbreaking and painful ones too. I wish I could tell you that it all gets better as you get older, but the truth is that it gets much more complex and challenging." Winnie gets up from her seat, taking her empty mug with her and points to Emma's. "Would you like another?"

"Oh, no, thank you. I think this cup alone will keep me awake until I'm ready to go to bed. What kind of coffee is it? I never had such a vibrant coffee that wakes up all my senses in one sip."

Winnie walks over to the kitchen counter and pours herself another cup. "It's not the grounds that make it that way." She raises up the clear kettle-looking item in her hand. "Using a French press makes a world of difference."

She takes a sip of the freshly poured cup and looks out somewhere in the distance of the kitchen. "You know what I did when I was your age to help figure out my thoughts and feelings?" She turns to look back at Emma. "Poetry. There is something so freeing in being able to express your emotions while also being so concise."

Winnie sighs. "I still have my collection of journals in my study from when I was a young girl to a middle-aged woman." Her focus drifts again, then she realizes she got lost deep in her own thoughts. Winnie shakes her head at herself and looks at Emma, with a laugh escaping her lips. "I'm sorry about that. Here I am preaching about writing when you came here to learn French!"

"Has it helped you? Writing?" asks Emma, open to trying anything to ease her troubles.

"It has, and yet it also broke me," says Winnie under her breath. Emma isn't sure if Winnie got lost in her thoughts again and said that out loud without meaning to. She has noticed over their morning together that the answers Winnie provides skirt around the truth—never providing the full details but not coming off as disingenuous either. Which makes Emma even more intrigued about her.

"How so?" asks Emma, acting on her piqued curiosity.

"I wrote a book several years ago," explains Winnie, "and it was sold to a publisher without my permission." She pinches the bridge of her nose, shaking her head with closed eyes. "If that book hadn't been sold without using my name, I wouldn't be here worrying about paying the mortgage and on the cusp of losing my house." Realizing what she just said, she jolts back up, looking at Emma. "I'm so sorry, I didn't mean to bring that up. I've just been under a lot of financial stress; the tutoring business hasn't been going well for a while."

Winnie gives Emma a reassuring smile and a wave of nonchalance, but Emma senses that she may be covering up the severity of her situation. "But don't worry," says Winnie, "it will all be fine. I have until the summer to figure out some things before I have to put the house on the market."

But Emma can't help but worry. Never expecting that Winnie would ever leave West 4th Street, this news shocks her. She thinks about Winnie's house and how it has become part of her neighborhood, her home. The possibility of Winnie not being here, that the house could have a new owner, sends her into an uncomfortable, deep sadness.

"But as I was saying about writing," says Winnie, changing the conversation back to what she initially meant to talk about, "I always tell my students to at least try it. Who knows, it may help you to get clarity with what you want or need in life." A thought comes through Winnie's head, making her perk up. "That's an idea!"

She walks over to the banquette and sits across from Emma. "We can make this your first assignment. Try writing a poem to express how you are feeling."

"When is the due date?" asks Emma, like the model student she was all through school.

Winnie laughs. "There is none, hon. This isn't school. It doesn't need to be ready to turn in by a certain date. There are no rules with poetry, which makes it one of the hardest forms of writing. It will take time for it to feel right to you. But don't write it for me—you are writing this for you and you alone. Don't overthink it—let the words flow out of you."

Emma gives her a slightly skeptical look. Being unfamiliar with poetry, she's unsure how this could help her. "I know, I know," says Winnie, raising her hands up in defense. "It's easier said than done. Especially how they programmed you kids to feel like you must always get everything right in school. It's kind of a strange concept, writing what comes from your soul, with no rules or guidelines."

Emma considers her 'assignment', wondering if it could help provide her with any clarity or help her let out her emotions. "I'll give it a try," she says reluctantly, doubtful about how much it will help.

Winnie places her hand on top of Emma's. "Don't feel like you have to do this. If you try and it does nothing for you, then that's not the method for you." Before she can say another word, the front door suddenly opens, bringing in the sound of late morning traffic and a rush of cold air.

"Mom?" calls a voice from beyond the kitchen as the front door closes.

As she hears an unfamiliar male voice, the color drains from Emma's face, her skin becoming an ashy white. Her heart starts to beat rapidly, her palms start to get hot, and she perspires as she realizes who the visitor is. For months, she has dreamed of the day when their paths will finally cross. Now that it is finally happening, Emma tries to recall any of the scenarios she imagined, hoping to bring forth the calm, cool, and collected person she envisioned she would be in this moment. But her mind goes blank as pure panic prevents any of her brain cells from working.

Confused, Winnie gets up and walks toward the entryway. "Noah? What are you doing here?" she asks, filled with motherly concern.

"Didn't you read any of my texts? The Wi-Fi is out on my block, and I need to enter these grades before midnight, so I need to work here until it gets fixed." Emma can hear the stranger, who she now knows for certain is Winnie's son, take off his shoes and jacket and make himself at home in her study. Winnie turns back around to her, mouths an apology, and points to where her son is, letting her know she is going to talk to him privately. Emma nods her head and motions for her to go ahead, hopefully conveying that she does not mind the sudden disturbance.

Emma can hear voices quietly speaking in the study, but she cannot make out the words. Based on the tone, there is no yelling or arguing, which relieves Emma. Nothing is more dreadful than being in the presence of an argument you're not supposed to hear. Like when a drunk couple yells at each other at the bar or when someone gives a waiter a hard time about their order. Even without it becoming a full-blown fight, there is always still a tinge of awkwardness in the air. Instead of being rude and looking at her phone, Emma eats the cut-up pieces of fruit in the bowl in front of her, despite her full belly. She needs to do something to pretend that she isn't trying to listen in on their conversation.

Soon she hears footsteps come toward her and sees Noah enter the kitchen with Winnie trailing behind him. Emma looks up and stops mid-chew with a piece of watermelon in her mouth, feeling like a deer in headlights.

"I'm so sorry for bursting in like that. I thought my mom was alone," says Noah as he approaches her. He extends his hand, and she stands to shake it. "I'm Noah."

Emma swallows and covers her mouth with her free hand in case there is food in her teeth. "Emma."

She takes a full look at him, finally able to see his face up close rather than from afar. A prickling feeling starts to form down the back of her neck. She's mesmerized by his soft brown eyes framed by tortoiseshell glasses. His short, curly, chestnut hair looks effortlessly styled, though Emma knows what it takes to truly maintain curly hair. She notices a slight dimple on his left cheek when he smiles at her, making her heart melt just a little. Looking at mother and son, she sees the physical resemblance. His physique is not peak athleticism, which makes Emma feel better about her lanky body. He is her dream man. This man screams 'hot nerd', a type Emma always falls head over heels for. Emma's ivory-white skin betrays her as heat forms on her cheeks, showing small pink circles on each side of her face.

She tries to slow her accelerating heart rate, hoping her cheeks don't turn a bright red. Now that she has gotten to know Winnie a bit, she doesn't want to jeopardize the friendship they could have by making her feelings for Noah known. Besides, a cute nerd is almost always taken.

Winnie leans over Noah's shoulder and whispers to him, "She's the one who found George."

His eyes widen. "Oh god, that must have been terrifying. He was such an irritable old man, but I would never wish a death like that on anyone. Neither would I wish for anyone to witness it. How have you been holding up?"

"About as well as you would expect from someone who saw a dead body in a pool of blood," says Emma. "I'm just thankful your mom stepped outside to keep my company. Law enforcement usually focuses more on the dead body than the witness. Oh! Speaking of appreciation," she looks at Winnie, as she remembers the one task her mom gave her, "my parents want to invite you over for dinner as a thank-you. My mom is pretty adamant about her dinner invitations, so I'm afraid she is going to keep on having me ask until you say yes." She looks at Noah, remembering her manners. "You are also more than welcome to join too. My mom loves to host dinner parties, so the more the merrier for her."

Winnie places a hand on her chest, "That's very sweet of her, I'd love to." Winnie looks at Noah. "What do you say? Take a break from grading and have dinner with us?"

"It is a good excuse not to grade papers," agrees Noah.

Emma beams at them both. "Great! We will coordinate a date soon." She looks up at the clock on the wall above them and notices that she has already been here for a few hours. Feeling like she overstayed her welcome, she decides she should head out. "I must get going," she says, even though she does not have any other place to be. "Thank you again for breakfast and for listening," she says to Winnie.

"Would you like to come over tomorrow afternoon for tea and another lesson?" offers Winnie. Noah looks at his mom, confused, and she leans over to whisper, "I'm teaching her French."

He nods in understanding. "You aren't going to get a better teacher than her. She taught me when I was a kid."

"He was my first student…" Winnie looks deep in thought as if she is recalling a memory. She shakes her head as she comes to and laughs. "He was not my best student, that's for sure."

"What do you expect when you try to teach a four-year-old boy French when he knows that the *Teenage Mutant Ninja Turtles* is on TV?" he teases.

Emma laughs at their banter, witnessing how close the two are to each other. A type of closeness that can only exist when they had only each other to rely on.

"There was a lot of bribing with pancakes, that's for sure," says Winnie. She looks back over at Emma. "So, what do you say? Tomorrow, afternoon tea?"

"Sounds great!" says Emma, knowing this is another opportunity to ask Winnie more about her life. Thinking back to their breakfast, Emma realizes how easily Winnie changed the topic of conversation from herself back to Emma. Emma wondered if she was talking too much, not giving Winnie any space to speak, or if Winnie was just being reserved. Either way, Emma has another day to uncover what Winnie didn't tell her.

They all make their way to the entryway, with Winnie and Noah saying their goodbyes to Emma as she puts on her jacket and heads outside.

Remembering her manners, Emma stops and turns around on the outdoor front step. "It was a pleasure to meet you," she says to Noah.

"*Enchanté*," he says with a wink as he closes the door.

Standing on the front steps, Emma reels from the high of the last few minutes of her visit. She stands on the last step in wonder, picking apart every word she said to Noah to make sure she didn't make a fool of herself. Once she convinces herself that she didn't, she starts to make her way back home.

Then she suddenly remembers the bombshell that Winnie dropped earlier.

Stopping in her tracks, Emma turns around and looks at row-house 363. The sadness she felt earlier creeps up once again, but this time in full force. She takes a look around her, watching the people and cars go by, hearing the world move around her. Yes, people move all the time in New York. But the thought of Winnie leaving their small neighborhood feels different than any of the thousands that move in and out of the city on a daily basis. Her neighborhood wouldn't feel the same without her. New York wouldn't feel the same without her.

It doesn't feel right knowing that Winnie may have to leave West 4th Street and I don't do anything about it…

Ideas start to run in her head, trying to come up with ways she can help Winnie not to lose her house. She goes through the conversation they had during breakfast, trying to glean up any possible ideas from there. Emma struggles to find anything helpful until something Winnie said about her financial worries returns.

The book! She mentioned a book she wrote was wrongfully published.

Emma lays out the perfect plan in her mind. One that can help Winnie to keep her house and fix what was wrongfully taken from her.

This is perfect! I can offer to have Dad look into her case and help her get the rights to her book back to her, making her the rightful author. Once the book is under her name, then royalties would come right to her, solving her financial problem in the long term.

Feeling confident in her plan, Emma takes one last look at rowhouse 363 and makes her way home. As she walks along West 4th Street, she thinks back to the Emma that was heading towards Winnie's just a few hours ago. How she initially went over to forget about Friday night and to establish a friendship with Winnie.

And now…

Not only does she want to become friends with Winnie, but she equally wants to help Winnie keep her house. To keep her on West 4th Street, where she belongs.

As she enters her house, Emma thinks about how so much has changed over the course of one weekend. She can't ignore that feeling that the universe has been answering a lot of her calls recently, finally meeting both Winnie and Noah.

Maybe there is a very important reason why this is happening to her now, why it took so long for it to happen.

Better late than never, I guess…

October 2, 1988

My Dearest Mémé,

It always warms my heart to receive your letters, but now it also brings me so much relief to read your words.

I've tried your suggestion to discuss possibly doing volunteer work at the library with Russel, and as I feared, he said that volunteer work is just 'glorified work' and that I 'would be worked like a dog' without getting any financial compensation for it. If you ask me, it's just another excuse for him to get me to do as he pleases. He just doesn't understand that I want something of my own, and he never listens whenever I try to explain myself. He just takes bits and pieces of what I say and twists it around to fit the narrative he has envisioned for us.

As an example, he took what I said about doing volunteer work as me saying 'I want to do unpaid work that will help further my husband's career.' And the next day, he tells me that he signed me up for the wives' club at his company, a 'club' that organizes and plans events and dinners for the company and their clients. (Quite frankly, it's just free public relations for the company.) The worst thing about it is that Russel only signed me up to help him look good to the president and senior principals, not to help me find something to be a part of.

For the few weeks that I've been in this club; I've gone to the mandatory bi-weekly meetings, helped with running errands, and been to three planned events. I'm already exhausted from trying to keep up with all of it. I truly don't know what's worse about this, the fact that everyone must go to every event or the fact that the company convinced the wives to think that they must do this, and if they don't, they will be blamed for the company's and their husbands' troubles.

I feel like I've time-travelled to the 50s...

But I do have some good news: Russel got that promotion at work. I know this comes as a surprise since he has worked there for less than six months; it's still a shock to both of us. But he has been working very hard, and who knows, maybe my involvement with the wives' club helped somehow. Now that he got his promotion, his bosses expect much more from him, which is causing much more stress. The workload is too much for one person to bear. He comes home late every night and works in his study during the weekends to stay ahead. Now I sit around and wait for him to come home, unless I'm at a wives' club meeting or a company event.

I feel more and more like a discarded doll, waiting for her owner to acknowledge and pick her up whenever they have time. When Russel does come home, he is nothing but short-tempered and angry. He takes out his frustrations from work out on me, or the area surrounding him (I've cleaned up more broken glasses than I'd like to admit). I've seen no sign of it improving. The boy I fell in love with in high school slips away more every passing day.

I also noticed that he is starting to drink more. At first, it was only a couple of glasses a night, but now he drinks half a bottle or more a night. Yesterday I discovered empty bottles of whiskey and gin that he hid in the outdoor trash bin, hoping I wouldn't find *it. I'm afraid this won't get better. How can I bring up all my concerns to Russel and show him how much this job not only affects him but also me?*

Why do I have such a terrible feeling that nothing I say will make him see reason?

Ton petit soleil,

Winnie

P.S. Did you know that mixing lemon balm with chamomile and skullcap makes the best tea to help you sleep? I'm calling this one: le sommeil profond.

Chapter Five

Bright sunlight blasts into Emma's eyes as she walks home on West 4th Street. It's like when you leave a dark movie theater in the middle of the day; you forget that it's not night. She wishes that she had her sunglasses for strange times like this in the winter.

She keeps her eyes down at the ground, avoiding 364 at all costs. She feels the frigid air on areas her coat does not cover, and she shivers from head to toe. Thankfully, her walk back home is only a few minutes.

Emma doesn't realize she was holding her breath until she steps foot inside her home, releasing a giant sigh once she closes the front door.

"Emma, is that you?" asks her mom somewhere in the house.

"Yup," she calls out.

She hears footsteps at the top of the staircase, getting close to her. "How was Winnie's?" asks Abigail.

Emma takes off her coat and shoes and places them in their proper home on the entryway's coat tree. "It was surprisingly really good." Emma looks up to where her mom now stands by the upstairs banister. "She's different from other people, but in a good way."

A smile appears on Abigail's face as she makes her way down the stairs to Emma. "Happy to hear you enjoyed it. Did you remember to ask her over for dinner?"

Emma nods and then grimaces. "Which reminds me. Her son was there when I asked, and I felt rude not inviting him too. I hope you don't mind."

Abigail brushes aside a loose strand of Emma's hair that fell out from her braid. "I would have been upset if you didn't. We should have them over this weekend."

"Not on Friday," yells Oliver's voice from the confines of his office.

"Oh! That's right," recalls Abigail. "Your dad has the firm's end-of-the-year charity event on Friday. Let's do Saturday then. I'm dying to meet this woman." Emma follows her mom further into their house, heading into the family room. She plops onto the couch and turns on the TV, changing the channel to HGTV, which she always finds comforting. She tries to unwind and block out certain thoughts. Like batty old man's body. Or the cute dimple on Noah's left cheek.

"You know," says Abigail from somewhere in the kitchen, "it's actually a good thing that the charity event is happening this weekend."

"Why's that?" Emma says loudly for her mom to hear, her head resting on a couch pillow. Once her brain finally caught onto where her mom was heading with this, she bolts straight up from her comfy position. "Wait, you still want me to go to that?" she asks.

Emma can hear her mom typing away on the keyboard at the kitchen desk, responding to emails about the charity event no doubt. "Yes, Ems. We need every Callahan to show up. It is our charity event after all."

Emma rolls her eyes. "You mean *Dad's* event," she mumbles to herself.

"I think getting dressed up and going out will help you, give you a change of scenery," says Abigail as she walks over and sits next to Emma on the couch. She gives her that questioning look Emma is very familiar with.

Emma looks back at her like she just proposed the most ridiculous idea she has ever heard. "Really?"

Abigail reaches over and holds Emma's hand. "I know the past few days have been hard for you. If I wasn't speaking at the university that night, it would have been enough to have just your dad and me." Abigail looks away briefly, glancing toward Oliver's office. "But you know the firm got a massive donation this year from the mayor, making this the biggest charity event to date. Your dad really needs you to be there. He can't show up alone."

Emma always hates going to these events. In her twenty-four years, she has been to more social events than she likes. No matter how much she tells and shows her parents how much she hates being a part of Manhattan society, they still make her come along. She never understood her parents' insistence or eagerness to be all chummy and buddy-like with the billionaires and socialites of the city—until she figured out that it was these billionaires and socialites who were the firm's top billable clients. But what she has never figured out is why her parents still feel like she needs to be involved.

"And…", continues Abigail, "this year's theme is raising money for the future generations of our city. A charter school along with a few non-profit children's organizations were selected as this year's award recipients. There will be music and the Do-nationchallenge to help win more money for organizations in need…". She looks at Emma with the look she gives to guilt-trip her into doing something.

The thought of spending an evening at one of Manhattan's most extravagant hotels with a bunch of middle-aged lawyers in black-tie sounds like the most boring and isolating night of her life. She may be the youngest person at the event, and that could make her feel even worse rather than cheer her up. But Emma drops her head in defeat, knowing that there is absolutely no way she will be able to get herself out of this event, despite recent events. Not when her family's name and reputation need to be upheld.

She sighs. "Fine, I'll go," she eventually says, knowing she never really had a choice. She will try to keep an open mind. Maybe getting dressed up and helping to raise money for important organizations will help her forget things for a while. But that is just Emma's way of deluding herself that she'll enjoy the event.

Abigail's eyes light up like a Christmas tree, a smile of victory on her face, and she pats Emma's leg in approval. "That's my girl."

Mentally, Emma goes through her closet, thinking of what she could possibly wear. She knows she has nothing for this event as she donated most of her formal dresses last year in a form of defiance. Emma knows she must've helped at least five teen girls find a dress for their prom last year. Although Abigail is unaware she has done this, Emma isn't concerned with her finding out as her mom is a strict believer in wearing something fresh and new to an important event, especially when it's for their family.

"Mom…I don't have a dress to wear," announces Emma, knowing there is only one solution to this problem: shopping for a new dress.

"I would go shopping with you later today," says Abigail, thinking. "But I need to finalize the final exams for class tomorrow and prepare my speech for Friday. How about this? We can go to the Tea House for brunch tomorrow and then go shopping in SoHo and the East Village." The Tea House is one of Emma's favorite places in the city (aside from the Strand, of course). Since Emma was a little girl, Abigail has taken her to the Tea House practically every weekend for mommy and daughter time. The number of pastries and finger sandwiches consumed sends her into a food coma every time. Emma knows her mom is using the Tea House as a thank-you for going to the event. But it'll take more than one visit for Emma to feel re-paid, and Abigail knows it.

"Fine," caves Emma, "but I get to pick our pastry tray."

Abigail checks her watch. "I must get back to work. The final exam won't write itself." Emma is left alone in the family room, with Sadie now snuggling behind her curled-up legs on the couch, her fluffy head resting on top of Emma's right hip.

While she mindlessly watches *Property Brothers*, Emma recalls Winnie's suggestion to write a poem, thinking it could help give her more direction on what her unhappiness means and possibly what she truly wants. Anxiety consumes her as she realizes that is a lot to ask from a single poem. But then she remembers what Winnie said. Since she is writing it for herself, it doesn't have to be great; it only needs to feel good to write down what she is feeling.

Wanting to try a therapeutic exercise before she makes a therapy appointment, Emma takes the pen and notepad sitting on the coffee table and stares at the lined paper, hoping for inspiration to hit her instantly. No beautiful words or lyrical sentences pour out of her. Instead, her mind is blank, empty. Because there are no rules when it comes to poetry, she feels lost. All that comes to mind is death, blood, and cute guys with curly hair and glasses.

The events of this past weekend are amplifying her feelings of existential dread and thoughts of the inevitability of death. All she can think to write on is the fragility of life.

That may not be why I'm discontent, but it may help me heal from the events of this past weekend.

She takes the pen and starts writing, not thinking about what the words coming out of her mean but trusting that it will lead her somewhere.

Heart pounds slowly,
dread falling to the pit of your stomach.
Some things seen,
can never be told,
as if later could be understood.
An item,
one we all have in our homes,
can easily be used to end us.
Even in your own home,
you are not safe.
If not there, where can we be?

Emma reads the words in front of her, not quite happy with them, cringing a little. But she feels proud for being able to write something on paper. She can feel the tension that built up inside of her all weekend slowly release, though not quite all of it is gone. Her chest feels a bit lighter. Her breath doesn't feel like it may be her last. She can feel how writing down her unexpressed emotions helps. Maybe Winnie is onto something here.

Once Emma processes the traumatic events of Friday night, and gets through the dreaded charity event, she can focus all her energy on more important things. And nothing is more important than helping Winnie to stay on West 4th Street.

Chapter Six

With today being just as cold as yesterday, Emma can't wait to step inside the warm café that is the Tea House. Her hands are tucked deep in her coat pockets, her ears covered by her beanie. Her nose is starting to run and its tip is turning red—the joys of walking outside in the city on frigid winter days. Her right arm is linked with her mom's left, staying close to her for warmth.

"Do you have any idea what kind of dress you want to wear?" asks her mom, as they walk along East 9th St, always keeping an eye on the world around them.

The beauty of being five-foot-seven means Emma can wear pretty much any dress length without having to get it altered. The only item she has to consider is the color—whether it will clash with her auburn hair. Given she only has five days to find such a dress, she knows she can't be picky.

"I'm hoping to find something in navy. That's always the safest color for me," answers Emma.

"Navy does bring out your beautiful blue eyes," adds her mom.

They stop at the corner, waiting for the pedestrian signal to tell them to cross. Emma turns to look at her mom, doubt in her eyes. "What if we don't find something in time?" At the thought, Emma's mood lightens; if there is no dress then there is no way she could possibly go.

Abigail reaches out and rubs Emma's forearm, reassuring her, "We will, don't worry." Her sudden hope dampens, as Emma knows her mom will ensure she has a dress to wear. The crosswalk signals change, and they start walking along with the other pedestrians.

Emma feels her phone vibrate in her jacket pocket. She takes it out to peek who has messaged her. She unlocks her phone once she sees it's from Astrid, worrying it may be a critical issue at work and they need her help.

`Astrid: Hey! I know you are out for the rest of the year, but I just couldn't wait to tell you this until you got back. I overheard Wyatt speaking to Mika about the Project Manager role, and he told her that he is going to set a meeting with you the week you get back to tell you it's all yours! Happy Holidays and New Year, Boss!! ☺`

Emma begins to feel anxiety and dread. She had hoped that what Astrid said at work last week was just a rumor, work gossip at best. But if this is true, if Wyatt was talking to their VP, Mika, about her filling the position, then she knows she will have to decide about it soon. Much sooner than she wants. She decides to reply now, rather than putting it off till later. It would seem off if she didn't.

`Emma: Omg, that's amazing! Thanks for letting me know.Have a great holiday too!`

Placing her phone back in her pocket, she hopes Astrid can't detect her fake excitement.

"Everything all right?" asks Abigail, sensing wheels turning inside Emma's head.

"Yeah, it's only Astrid with a work question." Emma doesn't say any more, as she isn't sure how to bring up the potential promotion to her parents. How could she, when she isn't sure if she wants to take it?

Out of the corner of Emma's eye, she spots the mom-and-pop bookstore she has always meant to go to. Nestled between a coffee shop and a dry cleaner, East Village Booksellers & Antiques shines, its outside walls painted in a warm burgundy. The display windows are decorated for Christmas and Hanukkah, with tiny cutouts of books hanging on the branches of a three-foot artificial tree and a two-foot menorah. There is something about the sight of this store that compels Emma to go in now. Her lack of desire to find a dress and the shop's unique charm are enough to entice her. She places her hand onto her mom's arm and points to the store, forcing them to stop walking. "Can we stop at that bookstore for a minute?" she asks.

"Ems, we don't have that much time today," states Abigail.

"Just a few minutes to look around. Please?" Emma pleads, trying to mimic Sadie's puppy-dog eyes.

Abigail looks down at her watch and sighs. "Oh, all right. I'll give you ten minutes and that's it! I know how long you can take in a bookshop."

A deep laugh escapes out of Emma as she gives her mom a side hug as they head toward the bookshop. A bell chimes as Emma pushes open the faded red front door; a low gasp escapes her mouth. It's surprisingly large inside, with a high ceiling. There are two floors filled with books, all neatly stocked and shelved appropriately within their genre. Rolling ladders are installed on every bookshelf against the walls. A battered but still charming rug runs across the floor. She's mesmerized and entranced by the endless sea of books around her. If Abigail were to look into her daughter's eyes, she would see that they are sparkling and gleaming.

"Welcome," says a husky voice from above them on the second level. The women look up and see the silhouette of a man, around her parents' age, placing books on one of the shelves. The man walks over to the railing. Moving his wire glasses resting on the bridge of his nose, he tilts his head down and looks at the Callahans. "New books are on the first floor, refurbished and antique books are up here on the second. Is there anything specific you are looking for?"

Emma shakes her head. "Just browsing."

The man nods his head with a smile. "Call me if you need anything." He turns toward the shelf and goes back to what he was doing.

With no real goal in mind, Emma follows her inner book nerd's guidance. The wooden floors hidden underneath the rug creak as she walks along the shelves on the first floor, her fingertips grazing the beautiful hardcover books, some of which are rare print editions. She stops when she sees the title of her favorite book. She picks up the hardcover, tracing the gold engraving that details the outline of ocean waves. When she opens the book, her heart leaps as she hears the faint cracks of the spine. Emma looks up and calls her mom over. "Look," she says as she hands the book to her mom.

"*The Port to Sea*," says Abigail. She too lightly flips through the pages with a smile of nostalgia on her lips. "Little did I know when I bought this for you, it would be the book that sparked your love of books." Abigail closes the book and moves her hands around the smooth engraved surface of the hardcover. "It's such a beautiful edition…"

"Too beautiful to not take home," says Emma. Looking at the figures of the young lovers on the cover, she feels the memory swarm back into her mind—the night fifteen-year-old Emma read and fell in love with this story. Bits and pieces of the epic love story of Madeleine and Beck come back to her, recalling the story of how two people—who were so right for each other—fell in love at the wrong place and time. Younger Emma idolized Madeleine, wanting to be just as fearless and selfless as she was. Hoping that one day she would have her own love story as epic as theirs. Finding a Beck of her own.

All book lovers can recall that one book that started it all for them, the book that hooked them on the high of immersive storytelling. *The Port to Sea* is the book that hooked Emma on that magic.

Relishing the memory and now wanting to re-read her favorite novel, Emma grabs the special edition of the book and tucks it under her arm, planning on taking it home with her.

She heads towards the check-out counter and places the book on the glass top. Looking down, she sees a handful of leather-bound notebooks resting inside the casing, each unique. The one in the middle attracts her eyes the most. The bright red color makes it stand out among the muted neutral-colored notebooks around it. The leather isn't entirely smooth, as compared to the others. This one has a bumpy texture, with deep engraved etchings of a floral design, so deep that it looks like the notebook has veins of its own. The other notebooks are secured by a leather string, wrapped around the torso of the book with a tight knotted bow at the end. The red notebook has a silver lock, making it feel more special than the others. Emma can see the love and passion that was put into making this one.

"I like that one, too," comes a voice in front of her.

Emma jerks her head up and is surprised to see the man is now behind the counter, looking down at the casing of notebooks along with her. So entranced by their beauty, she didn't even hear him come up near her.

"Are these handmade?" she asks, after her heart returns to its regular rhythmic beat.

The man—presumably the shop owner—nods, "You're talking to the maker himself."

"You made these?" Emma asks in astonishment. "They're amazing!" She continues to look down at the case, her eyes still on the bright red one.

"Do you want to see it?" asks the man. She nods her head without hesitation, wanting to feel the leather etchings. "Yes, please," she says.

The man takes out the keys, unlocks the sliding door, and takes out the notebook and places it on the countertop. Emma carefully picks it up and lightly traces her fingers along the deep etchings, treating it as if she is holding onto someone's heart as she knows it took heart to make it. Emma points to the lock and looks up at the man, "Where is the key?"

He reaches back inside the casing and takes out a silver pen. The top is engraved with a swirl design that matches the hole in the lock. The man takes the pen with the tip facing up, places it in the lock, and twists it to the right. Emma hears a slight clicking sound and sees that the lock is now open, releasing the flap that sealed the book shut. The man opens the book to reveal blank, ivory-colored pages inside. "The pen," says the man, holding it up, "is the key, created for just this notebook. They are inoperable without one another. If you lose one, you would be unable to use the other. It's designed to help keep unwanted eyes away." The man leans over and whispers to her as if he is telling her a secret, "The writer cannot write without both their pen and paper."

Emma feels her mother come beside her, peering down at the notebook on the counter. "Oh, that's beautiful," admires Abigail.

"It is…" says Emma as she looks at it, considering whether she should buy it. She wonders if having such a notebook of her own would inspire her to write more. "How much is it?" Emma asks the man.

He eyes her, but not in a 'you're unworthy of it' way, but considering her. "I've always been selective about who can purchase this one. Only someone who truly sees its beauty and will use it as it is meant to be used can own this one-of-a-kind notebook." He looks down at her and smiles. "And I can tell you see how special it is… For you, twenty dollars."

Emma starts at the price. Not for how much but for how little. "Are… you sure?" she asks, astonished. "I feel like I would be stealing it if I paid that amount."

"This one has always had a special place in my heart," the man says, looking proudly at the notebook. "And once I was ready to sell it, I just couldn't give it to anyone who would be willing to pay the price. You see, I made the original leather cover decades ago, and I hadn't met the right person who matches it perfectly. Up until now, of course." The man places a hand on his chest. "It would be my pleasure to see this in the right hands, no matter the cost."

Emma places her right hand lightly on top of the leather cover, caught off guard by the man's words. She looks over at her mother. "What do you think? Should I get it?"

"I know you," Abigail says with a smirk on her face. "If you don't get it now, you'll regret it."

Slightly embarrassed by the way her mother called her out in front of a stranger, Emma hangs her head low with pinkish cheeks. Knowing that her mother is right, a self-deprecating smile forms on her lips. "You're right," says Emma. She picks her head back up, looking at the man. "I'll take it and promise to take very good care of it."

The man nods, elation shining on his face. "I know you will. Is there anything else besides the notebook?"

"Oh, yes!" she says, nearly forgetting about the book tucked snugly in her arm. She places the copy of *The Port to Sea* on the glass top, right next to the notebook. "I'll take this as well."

Picking up the book, the man looks wistfully at it. Emma thinks she sees a hint of sadness in his eyes. But before she can confirm it, his expression changes to a smile. "Exquisite taste," he jokes.

"I read this all the time when I was a teenager, at least three times a year," says Emma, feeling the need to explain why she wants it. "It's amazing how someone could write such a powerful and beautiful love story."

The man nods, his face now stoic. "The author excelled where most could not."

Emma flips the book to face the right side up. "C.K. Rothschild," she reads the author's name aloud, then looks back up at the man. "They never wrote anything else besides this, have they?"

The shop owner shakes his head as if it pains him to do so. "That was the only one."

"Such a shame…" Emma goes inside her purse and takes out her wallet, signaling she is ready to pay. After making her purchases and thanking the shop owner, Emma and her mother have lunch at the Tea House, with not a pastry or finger sandwich left on their platter. Once they've fueled up on food and caffeine, they finally move onto their main goal of dress shopping.

No matter how many stores they went to, boutique or thrift, Emma couldn't find a dress that was the right color or fit for her. She knows she will need to shop around Midtown after her therapy appointment tomorrow. Annoyance knocks at her as she is putting more effort into finding this dress than she'd like.

After their failed shopping trip, Emma walks with her mom back from SoHo to Washington Square Park, where Abigail is a professor of Psychology at NYU. They part ways at the park, and Emma heads toward home to Winnie's house for afternoon tea.

Excitement pulses through Emma's body as she walks west. The added weight in her backpack reminds her that the exquisite red leather-bound book is waiting to be used. She can imagine herself sitting on the window seat in her bedroom, covered with a plush blanket and Sadie curled up by her feet, writing feverishly in her new notebook. Walking down the sidewalk, she can feel her fingertips twitching in her mittens, ready to open those fresh, crisp pages.

As she walks toward West 4th Street, Emma wonders if she will see Noah today. But she remembers that it's the early afternoon on a Monday and school is still in session. She doesn't know how to feel about the hint of disappointment at the thought of not seeing him, so she focuses on what is important—keeping Winnie where she belongs at West 4th St.

I should offer my dad's help to her. If anyone can find any legal loopholes to get the rights to her book back, it would be him…

A feeling of déjà vu comes across Emma as she rings the doorbell, and Winnie welcomes her. Already feeling like she is at her second home, Emma takes off her shoes, without asking this time, and follows Winnie inside. Upon entering the kitchen, Winnie turns to Emma with a grin on her face and waves her hand over the island, as if she is a magician performing a magic trick.

The kitchen island is covered with at least a few dozen jars. Walking closer, she can see that they are all different types of herbs, each lid labeled with masking tape. "Are these all the herbs you use to make your teas?" Emma asks, mesmerized by the number of jars. She stopped counting once she reached twenty-two.

Winnie nods. "I have either grown them myself or purchased them at local stores." She leans over to Emma and whispers, "I will admit, I have ordered some from overseas… Some places grow them better than what I could do here." Winnie turns around and grabs a mug from the counter and pours hot water from the kettle on the stove and hands it to Emma. "I wanted to give you a chance to mix your own. You'd be surprised with how many of them work together."

Emma takes the hot mug into her hands and looks down at the sea of herbs before her. A flush appears on her face and neck, getting overwhelmed by all the options before her. Her eyes start to cross when she reads strange names like tulsi, ashwagandha, and osmanthus.

"What kind of taste are you in the mood for?" asks Winnie, sensing she's flustered.

Emma thinks back to all the scones and sweet finger sandwiches she had at lunch and knows she will get a migraine if she adds any more sweetness into her bloodstream. "Something earthy and calming," she answers. "I had a lot of sugar earlier today."

A laugh escapes Winnie. "Sugar, our biggest vice. Don't worry, I have a sweet tooth myself." She takes out a small mesh tea bag from a drawer and starts scooping up some herbs into it. Once she is done, she seals the bag and places it in Emma's mug of warm water. "Let it steep for a few minutes to get all the flavors."

Emma can already smell the aromas coming to life as the herbs infuse with each other in the water. "Smells wonderful!"

"It's peppermint, jasmine, and green tea. Will clear your head of any incoming sugar headaches in no time," Winnie says with a wink. "Come, let's start a proper French lesson for you." Winnie motions for her to follow her, heading towards the study.

"What about the jars?" Emma calls behind her, looking over at the cacophony of glass next to her. "Do you want help putting them away?"

Winnie, already halfway out of the kitchen, waves her hand in the air. "I'll worry about that later. They aren't going anywhere," her voice echoes in the entryway.

Caught off guard by her laid-back attitude and feeling guilty for leaving this mess behind, Emma hesitantly follows the sound of Winnie's voice into her study. She feels nothing but comfort when she is surrounded by the cozy, chaotic mess of the library. Everything looks the same as when Winnie gave her a tour of her house on her last visit, except for her desk. Before, it was organized and under control, with the books stacked neatly on each side. Now Emma sees stacks of aged papers on the desk, spread out as if the reader left it due to a sudden disturbance.

"Doing some research?" asks Emma, as she gestures at the papers on Winnie's desk.

Suddenly remembering their existence, Winnie walks over to her desk, gathers the loose papers into a single pile, and tucks them safely away in the desk drawer. "Oh, these are old letters that I wrote to my mémé. My pépé gave them to me a few years after she passed. Since then, I like to re-read them every once in a while. It helps me to feel close to her and keep her spirit alive." Winnie looks up at her, giving a shy smile as she takes a seat next to Emma, who is now sitting on her soft leather couch. "I got sucked into reading some earlier and lost track of time."

"That happens to me whenever I read a book. I get so entranced I lose track of time," jokes Emma, taking a sip of tea. "Does it help? Reading through your old letters with her?" she asks, using this as an opportunity for Winnie to talk about her life.

An embarrassed chuckle comes out of Winnie. "I know it sounds strange, but it's really the only thing I have of her. Nowadays it's so easy to have photos and videos of our loved ones, but when I was growing up, taking pictures wasn't the norm. We didn't think we needed to capture every moment all the time. Those letters are the only thing I have left of her."

Emma thinks about how her parents—specifically her dad—constantly videotaped and photographed every moment of her childhood. In her dad's study, she could pull out all the photo albums and videotapes and relive her entire upbringing. Even though she was the primary focus of all of it, there are several videos and pictures of just her parents, grandparents, even her classmates growing up. Which makes her wonder even more about Noah's dad and the lack of photographic evidence of his existence. If he was in Noah's life, even just a small amount, there would have been a few photos with him in it, or at least some with him and Winnie, wouldn't there?

Does Winnie not have any pictures with him? Or does she not show them for a reason?

Emma opens her mouth to ask another question about her family, but Winnie unknowingly interjects before she can, as if she wants to steer away the conversation from her.

"I hope you had enough coffee this morning, along with the sugar," says Winnie. She reaches for her notebook on the side table, opening it to the bookmark where they will start Emma's lesson. "Today's lesson will be tricky. So don't get frustrated with yourself if it is a bit difficult to understand. Everyone always has a hard time with this section, especially those who speak English as their native language."

Emma adjusts her sitting position to face Winnie directly, ready to give her undivided attention. It takes every bit of restraint she has not to grab the merino wool blanket folded neatly behind her on the couch and wrap herself in it like a comfy cocoon. This is what winter does to her—it turns her into a blanket hermit who wants to be a comfy, lazy bum with a book and a cup of tea alongside her. But the last thing she wants to do is fall asleep on Winnie's couch from the warmth of the fire next to her, the softness of the couch, and Winnie's elegant voice speaking in French. Thankfully, the peppermint in her tea will help keep her awake.

"Let's start with the basics," says Winnie as she positions herself to face Emma. She writes down a sentence in the notebook, then flips it around to show Emma. "*Je m'appelle* Winnie," enunciates Winnie, pointing at each word with her finger as she says it out loud. Then she points to Emma, "*Tu t'appelles* Emma." Then she points back to herself, repeating the sentence on her notebook. "Can you take a guess what this means?" she asks.

"You're saying what your name is and what my name is," answers Emma.

Winnie nods enthusiastically. "Bravo! Great job." She flips to a fresh page, then hands her notebook and pen to Emma. "Okay, try writing down what you would say to tell me what my name is."

And the rest of the lesson continues as such, but it's not only Winnie writing down sentences for Emma to absorb. She describes how all nouns are assigned a gender and how that affects how they are written, how some words get trenched together when the beginning of the next word starts with a vowel or a silent 'h'. What perplexes Emma the most is how the sentence structure in French isn't the same as how it is in English. With the English language requiring more words to create a sentence, while the French language uses fewer.

The next time Emma checks her phone, she notices that hours have gone by. She has been listening so attentively to Winnie that she has not been keeping track of the time. Her mind is filled to the brim with information, but she is ready to learn more even though she has reached her limit of new knowledge for the day.

"How did I do on my first lesson?" asks Emma, hoping she didn't disappoint Winnie.

"Honestly, not that bad. You grasped the concepts quite well," says Winnie as she gathers the papers from today's lesson. "Everyone can be a great student and learner," continues Winnie. "The key to being a good one is enthusiasm and an interest in learning the subject in the first place. If you're not interested, then obviously you won't do well." She looks over at Emma and smiles approvingly. "I see that spark in your eyes, your drive to learn and understand. Don't let it fade. I've seen too many who either never find that spark or don't fuel it enough that it dies."

Emma didn't know what the fiery feeling she felt in her core during her lesson meant until Winnie described it to her. Now that she has felt what it's like to learn something brand new again, she wonders how long that passion to learn was dormant in her. She cannot recall the last time she felt so focused and consumed by something.

Emma looks down at her hands in her lap. "I always had that spark as a kid. My parents often brought me to museums to quench my thirst for knowledge." She looks up at Winnie, who looks back at her with sympathy and attentiveness. "I don't know when, or why, that spark died. It was like, one day I just woke up and lost my drive to understand the world."

Winnie sighs heavily and looks out at the window in front of them. "As we get older, we start to see the world for what it is. Not through these rose-colored lenses we had when we were kids. Back then, we thought we had the world in the palm of our hands. That we could get what we wanted if we put our minds to it. But once we get older and start seeing the world for what it truly is—ugly yet beautiful, cruel yet loving—we start to lose the desire to understand the world when most of humanity stopped trying to understand each other."

"Why bother when everyone else gave up trying?"

Winnie nods. "That's why it's so important to keep trying. There aren't enough of us out there to keep that spark alive." After a few moments, a sigh escapes Winnie's mouth, then is replaced by a nervous laugh. "I think I need a drink. Would you like some wine?"

Emma, struck by the hard wisdom of reality and feeling the weight of humanity's shortcomings, wants nothing more than to have a glass of wine to ease her mind. "I would love one."

Winnie gets up from the couch and walks towards the kitchen. "Red or white?" she asks in the foyer, her voice echoing throughout the house.

"Red, please," says Emma. "*Merci!*"

She hears a chortle coming from the kitchen along with the sound of a cork popping, then wine being poured into glasses. Emma looks around the study, taking in the small space, every square inch used by Winnie. Plants hang in opposite corners to liven up the wooden space with some green. Too lazy to get up, yet still intrigued, Emma remains seated on the couch while looking at the bookshelf closest to her. She reads through the titles of Winnie's personal collection, hoping to get a further glimpse into the woman she is spending her time with. Just from this shelf alone, Emma sees titles by classic writers ranging from Mary Shelley to John Steinbeck, poets such as Emily Dickinson and Maya Angelou, even some French works, the titles unknown to Emma. If this is what is on this one shelf, Emma imagines Winnie has immaculate taste in reading materials. Before she finishes studying another shelf, Winnie comes back and hands her a glass of wine and takes her seat back on the other end of the couch.

"I always meant to ask you," starts Emma. "Is Winnie your given name or a nickname?"

"It's actually my given name." Winnie brings her legs up on the couch to a more relaxed sitting position. A position Emma has come to know as the 'story-time' position. She too shifts to get comfy and faces towards Winnie, waiting to hear the story.

"When my grandmother was a young girl, she lived in my hometown of Martigues, as you know. During the Second World War, her family lost almost all of their possessions, either from the Nazis taking them or from her parents selling anything they could to get money and survive. Two of the items my grandmother had left were a teddy bear and a book." She looks Emma in the eye. "Winnie-the-Pooh", she says as she smiles into her wine glass, taking another sip. "It was the only story my grandmother had to get lost in during those dark and scary nights. When she had my mom, she would read it to her every night before bed, keeping the story in the family. When my mom knew she was having a baby, she already knew what she would name it. Winnie if it was a girl, Christopher if it was a boy."

"A family name, so to speak," says Emma.

Winnie smiles as she takes another sip. "In a way, yes, it is."

Emma can feel the first sips of wine make their way slowly down to her stomach, warming up her body even more. It isn't until she has drunk half of the glass that she starts to feel its calming effects. The calmer she feels, the more her body molds and sinks deeper into the couch, not wanting to leave this comfy paradise. Making her so close to forgetting to bring up the one thing she doesn't want to discuss.

Emma opens her mouth, about to tell Winnie about her idea to help her with the house, but before she can say one word, Winnie unknowingly cuts her off. "Have you tried writing any poetry?" she asks.

"I tried," says Emma with no ounce of conviction. "I wasn't too sure what to write at first, but my hand started writing before my brain caught up when I had my pen and paper ready. It's far from being good, not by a long shot. But I think it did help me start acknowledging and processing the feelings I have about what happened on Friday night." A chuckle comes out of Emma, laughing at herself. "I even bought myself a beautiful notebook to motivate me to keep writing."

"I'm happy to hear that it helped you and even inspired you to keep going," Winnie says sincerely. "It will become more intuitive and easier the more you try."

"If only life were like writing poetry..."

"Then I would have saved myself from so much heartache. But I wouldn't be the person I am today," says Winnie with a small smile resting on her face. Emma can see in the cracks of her smile that it may not be that lighthearted as it seems. As if she is trying to mask what she is truly feeling behind that smile.

"I do owe you an apology," says Winnie out of the blue.

"What for?" asks Emma, clueless to what Winnie could think she feels the need to apologize to for.

"For what I shared with you yesterday. About my house and…", she takes a slight pause with a deep breath, "financial issues. It was completely inappropriate and out of line, and I shouldn't have burdened you with my personal worries."

"You don't have to apologize for that," says Emma. She places her hand lightly over Winnie's. "I can imagine how going through all of that is putting stress on you." She looks around the room, taking in the house, the place that has become so much a part of *her* neighborhood for years. Then she looks back at Winnie with a small sympathetic smile on the corner of her lips. "I'll only say this on the matter: I'm truly sorry to hear about your situation. You are as much a part of this neighborhood as this house is. You belong here on West 4th Street."

Winnie lightly squeezes Emma's hand and nods her head, signaling to Emma that she appreciates her words. "Thank you, dear. It means a lot to me to hear you say that."

Blind-sided by her apology, Emma's brain reels to piece together what this could mean. She starts to question if she should still tell Winnie about her idea for how to save her house. Before, she was certain she would tell her, but now she has no idea what to do.

"I do need to ask a favor from you," continues Winnie after a few silent moments.

"Of course… what is it?" asks Emma.

Winnie hesitates and looks down at her wine glass, seeming to be at odds with what she is about to ask of Emma. "You are the only person who knows of this," she eventually says after taking a long breath. "About the book, the house, and the current state of my tutoring business." She pauses and shakes her head. "I haven't even told Noah yet. Until I am ready, I would greatly appreciate it if you don't mention any of this to him."

Emma nods. "Of course. I won't say a word of this to him," she says without hesitation. The favor seems simple enough to agree to since Winnie didn't mean to tell her in the first place. It makes nothing but complete sense to Emma that she should keep it to herself until Winnie is ready to share it. Besides, this isn't any of her business to share. Even if Winnie didn't ask her to keep it between them, she wouldn't have said anything to Noah.

But the more Emma thinks about the apology, and now this favor, the more she starts to wonder why Winnie felt the need to say anything to her at all.

What strikes Emma the most is that Winnie hasn't told this to anyone. Not even her son. Why did no one before her know about what happened to Winnie's book, or what's going on with her tutoring business? Is she embarrassed by what's happening? Ashamed? Could it be that she doesn't want to worry Noah about her financial issues? But if her situation is *that* dire, wouldn't she want her son's support? Not have to do this all on her own?

Maybe there is a reason why she feels like she must do this on her own...

If pride is keeping her from asking for help, Emma is reluctant to tell Winnie about her idea. The last thing she wants to do is make her feel even more embarrassed by offering her dad's help. But she also knows she won't be able to live with herself if she doesn't do anything to help Winnie.

I can't do nothing when I know I could help her find a way to keep her house...

As Winnie cleans up after their French session and wine time, Emma mentally runs through her options, all leading to one big obstacle: time. If Winnie only has until the beginning of summer to figure out something before resorting to selling the house, Emma needs to decide now about what to do.

Emma thinks back on the past few days as she has gotten to know Winnie and realizes just how much she has already done for her, someone she just met. Not knowing before how to repay Winnie for her kindness, generosity, and friendship, Emma suddenly realizes that this is the ultimate way to thank her and show how much she means to her. Emma looks at Winnie as she tells Emma a funny story about one of her students, her smile and laughter lighting up the room. Seeing that look on her face, Emma knows that she can't tell Winnie just yet about her idea. There is a chance her idea won't work, and the prospect of seeing Winnie heartbroken and in pain, all because of her, makes her certain that she must find out first if Winnie's case is solid before telling her. The worst thing to be given is false hope, and Emma knows that is all she'd be giving to Winnie now. She needs to know her idea is foolproof before presenting it to Winnie.

The only hiccup Emma can see is the possibility that her case can go to court. That can drag this on for months beyond the summertime, leading her plan to be ultimately useless if Winnie can't keep her house. Emma hopes that having her dad and his firm help Winnie with this case will increase their chances of having this not only be resolved outside of court but in a timely manner that they can meet her summer deadline. Emma mentally crosses her fingers that Winnie has a strong case, needing all the odds to go in their favor.

And to figure this out, I'll need the name of her book.

December 7, 1988

My Dearest Mémé,

I too thought about reaching out to Gracie for help. Not only as my close friend, but also as Russel's sister, she may be able to make him see how his job is changing him. But every time I pick up the phone, I hesitate to dial her number as I think about how Russel would react if he knew I brought our troubles to her. You know how he likes to keep everything private. So no, the option to call Gracie for help is impossible, despite my good intentions.

Besides, I fear that my time to have that discussion with Russel has passed.

Due to his charming personality, the company moved him up to be the Department Head (client-facing), and we've had to host a few dinners at our house for the company's top priority clients. Which now puts even more pressure on me to ensure everything goes smoothly. If the table isn't set properly, or the veal isn't cooked correctly, the relationship with the client could be at risk.

Mémé, some of these clients are more than a bit questionable. Who shows up to a house dinner with several of their employees, all with scars on their faces and hands? I've seen Scarface and know what men who look like that truly are. I'm starting to question the morality of the company and wonder at what lengths they would go just to get a high-paying job. I know that the architecture industry in this city is highly competitive, but I never would have thought the company would make partnerships with questionable people. I can't get over how everyone glosses over their methods, not realizing how callous and unmoral they are. But I guess morals don't matter as long as they keep getting their fat paychecks every other week.

It doesn't help that these new clients drag Russel to fancy gentlemen's clubs and bars. Not only is he staying out late and drinking more, but he's also started gambling. He has lost $7,500 so far. I'm scared he is now in too deep. His vision of being a senior principal is just within sight, and nothing will make him step away from it. Nothing.

As for me, I took your suggestion and have started journaling. You are right, I miss writing, and even if it's just a short poem or a few thoughts and feelings, it does make me feel better to be connected to something that I once loved. Reminds me of who I am and not what other people want me to be. After pretending for so long, you forget that person isn't the real you.

Despite the falling temperatures, I've been keeping up with my daily walks around the East and West Villages. It's truly the simplest things that make the biggest difference in your mood and outlook.

On my walk back home from a meeting with the wives' club yesterday, I stopped at Tompkins Square Park to finish reading Beloved (which I highly recommend you read), and the most unusual thing happened. It is very common in this city for others to share a bench, but this is the very first time that my bench mate struck up a conversation. The nicest man talked with me for more than an hour about books; he asked how I was liking Beloved. Talking to him reminded me of you; it almost felt like being back home. I learned that my bench mate is not just an avid reader like me but also is a collector of rare first editions, and he refurbishes damaged books to donate to underfunded libraries and schools.

You have no idea how wonderful it was to discuss literature with a like-minded person. It has been so long since I had such an engaging conversation that I wish there was a way for me to see him again. Maybe if I go back to the park at the same time all week, I can possibly run into him again? Us New Yorkers have our routines and habits, and something tells me that visiting this park may be his. Let's just hope that the club meetings finish on time so I don't miss my chance. Fingers crossed!

Ton petit soleil,

Winnie

P.S. Thank you for giving me the recipe for la femme forte. You were right! Ginger root with green tea helped with my menstrual cramps. Merci beaucoup!

Chapter Seven

The subway car speeds north, forcing the standing passengers to sway with the uncontrollable jolting. Emma stands by the door while holding onto one of the metal railings, trying not to get nauseous while looking at her phone. She's scrolling on Bloomingdale's website to see if they have something she likes before shopping at the department store in person. So far, nothing she sees piques her interest.

Before heading out to do her errands today, Emma had the time to discuss her idea with her dad. If she has to hunt down the name of Winnie's book, she wants to know if there is a chance that this plan could possibly work. 'In theory, it could' is all her dad said, but he needs to know the name of the book and its publisher to do some further digging to confirm if Winnie has a solid case. Once Emma finds out what he needs, her dad is more than willing to help Winnie out with her case. Emma just has absolutely no idea where to start.

A notification pops up on her phone screen. It's a follow-up email from the therapist she met with a few hours ago. Emma eventually decided she wanted to see a therapist about the incident; with her parents supporting her decision wholeheartedly. With the help from her mom, Emma got a referral to a therapist from one of her colleagues at NYU. Emma figured it wouldn't hurt to try therapy out with Dr. Priya Varman by going for one session.

With shaky fingers, Emma opens the email from Dr. Varman, reading through the list of coping mechanisms they discussed she could try. Emma takes a breath as she looks back up at the unique characters in the subway car with her, considering which one she should attempt first. Eagerness runs through her as she re-reads the third mechanism on the list, sensing that is the one she'll ultimately decide to try out first. When the subway reaches her stop at Lexington Ave and 59th, Emma walks across the busy platform and climbs up the stairs to the street. Her mind goes back to the part of her session where Dr. Varman explains how she can use this mechanism, wanting to recall her exact words.

"Have you tried your own methods of processing?" asks Dr. Varman. Her iPad has been tucked away at least thirty minutes ago when they finished completing her new patient form. For the majority of the session, the surprisingly young-looking therapist has kept her eyes on Emma, giving her undivided attention.

A small smile appears briefly on Emma's lips as Winnie's suggestion comes to mind. "I've been writing poems, nothing great, but something to express my feelings. I think they have been helping."

Dr. Varman nods encouragingly. "That's a great idea. Writing is a great form of release." She pauses, thinking for a second. "I have an idea, and it may sound a bit… out there."

"Okay…," Emma says cautiously but curiously.

"After you write these poems, instead of keeping them in a journal or stashed away in your desk drawer, I would like you to burn them."

"Burn them?" Emma repeats, making sure she heard her correctly.

Dr. Varman laughs lightly, knowing her suggestion is a bit out of the norm. "When you write down your feelings, you are cementing it physically in addition to it being stuck in your head. If you burn the poem once you've written it, it will also be a literal release of what you were feeling. Shredding it is also an option." Dr. Varman shrugs. "You don't have to do it; it's only a suggestion. But sometimes physically destroying something that is haunting us can help us to release it emotionally too."

As Emma now opens the heavy glass door of the department store, the familiar scent of Jo Malone hits her nose, she feels confident that this is the mechanism for her to try first. For no other reason than to listen to her gut tell her this may be the catalyst to help her move on from that dreadful night.

A few hours later, Emma stands before Winnie's front door.

She didn't plan on visiting her after her shopping errand. But she was walking home on West 4th Street, and after her second failed shopping trip, the turquoise blue door was like a magnet. After she rang the doorbell, Emma considered that Winnie may not be home or she could have company over. Her heart skips a beat at the thought of someone else being here.

What if Noah is here?

Relief courses through her when the door opens, halting the first worry she had but not quite stopping the second.

"Well, don't you look adorable!" welcomes Winnie in her typical cheery and exuberant fashion.

"You don't think I look stupid?" asks Emma, adjusting the black felt beret on her head that she purchased at a thrift store after her trip to Bloomingdale's. A consolation gift for her failed shopping trips.

"With that face, you can wear anything," assures Winnie. She stands aside to leave space for Emma to enter her house. "Come in! I just made some tea."

A trace of disappointment runs through her as she walks into the kitchen, neither seeing nor hearing the presence of a certain man.

"I hope you don't mind my surprise drop-by," says Emma as she takes a seat on the kitchen island's stool. "I was on my way home and thought I'd say 'hello.'"

"You are always welcome here, Emma. I'm happy you stopped by," says Winnie as she pours Emma a cup of tea.

Emma takes the freshly brewed tea and takes a sip, her mouth getting hit with the flavors of lavender and ginger. "This is amazing," she says.

"I call this mixture 'anti-seasonal depression'. It helps me get through the dark, cold winters. Considering how cold and bleak this afternoon turned out to be, I thought you and I earned a cup."

Winnie takes a piece of cheese and a cracker from her cheeseboard on the island and nibbles on it. She points to the beret on Emma's head. "I wore several of those in my younger years. Have your lessons inspired you to wear one?"

"No, this was purely coincidental," says Emma with a smile as she touches the side of the beret again, feeling slightly self-conscious. "I was out in my last desperate attempt to look for a dress, and I came across this in a thrift store. My dad's law firm hosts an annual holiday charity event, and my mom thought, with everything that happened this past weekend, that I could use a little dress-up and get into the holiday spirit by going with him this year. I couldn't really say no since this year's charity event is to help children's organizations in the city."

Winnie makes a face. "A charity event hosted by a law firm? Sounds like a boring night to me."

"I've been to far too many of them. They were terrible as a kid, but thankfully they changed it up a few years ago. Instead of the standard charity event where people just donate cash and offer a raffle for some mediocre prizes, they made it into a competition. The more challenges a team wins, the more money you accrue. If your team wins the game, you donate the money you earned to an organization of your choosing. The team wins bragging rights and a trophy, naturally. Give people booze and something to compete for, and they'll let loose and go crazy."

"That's an innovative way to fundraise," says Winnie. "Get people involved, make it fun, and still raise a lot of money for the charities. Wish someone thought of that in my event days."

"Thank you. My dad actually co-created the event."

"How do they get funding?" asks Winnie, intrigued.

"Each challenge in the competition has a sponsor, like Spotify, Saks, or even a person like the mayor, which is how they get funding for the prize donation money. The event itself is funded by the price of the ticket to attend. I'm not sure how much it is nowadays, but I heard it's like attending the Met Gala—*very* expensive."

"And that is why you need a dress. Black-tie, I'm assuming?"

Emma sighs and places her head in her hands, leaning her elbows on top of the marble countertop. "I can't re-wear a dress I've worn previously as that's a no-no in the socialite world. Trying to find one that fits and looks good on my body in a matter of days is like finding a needle in a haystack. As the daughter of one of the partners, I can't show up underdressed."

Winnie taps her fingers against the countertop, her head resting on one hand, mimicking Emma's relaxed, yet defeated, body language. "Black-tie… and a color that will complement your gorgeous hair…" Then suddenly Winnie stands up straight. "Oh! I got it! Follow me." Quickly she makes her way out of the kitchen.

Puzzled, Emma follows Winnie to the unseen section of her house, the second floor. As she thought, the upstairs is just as charming as the first floor and even cozier. A lilac blue and white floral wallpaper runs along the hallway walls, with white wooden trim running across the top and bottom corners. Winnie too has her own built-in bench that is underneath a full spring line window. The soft cream cushions and pillows make Emma want to curl up and take a nap in the sun on the bench.

They make their way into Winnie's bedroom; Emma feels like an intruder walking into a sacred personal space so nonchalantly. The calm blue and white colors in the hallway continued into the bedroom, extending the calm and cozy aesthetic Winnie has in mind for her house. Politely, Emma lingers in the middle of the bedroom as Winnie heads to the walk-in closet—a rare feature to exist in any historic rowhouse— and turns on the light, disappearing into the abyss of the closet.

Emma stands awkwardly in the room, not sure where to stand or sit as everything feels off-limits in this intimate space. Her eyes trail across the room, making note of the neatly made off-white bedding on the queen-sized bed, the few pieces of artwork hanging on her walls, and the dust-free white vanity with neatly organized perfume bottles and lotions. Not a thing is out of place. Not a single speck of dust or fingerprint left on any surface. The room doesn't feel complete, yet it also doesn't feel bare. Reserved without feeling cold. Still giving the feeling of being lived in while not giving away too much detail about the person. A stark contrast to the first floor of the house.

Her gaze moves towards the window as the sun breaks through the overcast sky, sending the last ounce of sunlight through the bedroom window. Drawn by the sight, Emma walks to the window, feeling the warmth of the sun hitting her face. Looking down, she sees a small backyard, a notorious feature of city rowhomes. Below is a set of iron table and chairs residing next to several empty planters. Emma envisions them in full bloom with flowers during the summertime. Off in the far corner by the wooden fence is a small garden of hardened soil with dead grass underneath a few inches of snow. She assumes this is where Winnie grows her herbs to make her teas. The space reminds her of the small backyard they have at home, making the most of the little space they have.

"Ah! Found it," exclaims Winnie inside her closet, bringing Emma back to the room.

Emma turns around and sees Winnie coming toward her holding a hanger with a silk navy dress hanging on it. Upon closer inspection, her eyes widen, taken aback by the delicate and beautiful material. She reaches to touch the silk fabric of the dress, then stops, worried about how unclean her fingers may be. From top to bottom, the dress is navy silk, with slim spaghetti straps, a V-neck, and a floaty but still fitted ball skirt. As if Gwyneth Paltrow's Oscar pink dress and the black silk dress Natasha Richardson wore in *The Parent Trap* had a baby. Emma is awestruck by it.

"This is beautiful," she finally mutters.

"I had to go to a fair share of black-tie events myself during my youth in the nineties. Still have all my dresses, even though it's been twenty-five years since I last wore one." Winnie hands the dress over to Emma. "Wear it for your event."

Emma retreats a step. "Oh no, I can't wear it… it's too gorgeous."

Winnie lays it on top of the bed. "We have the same physique, and it will look amazing against your hair and complexion. Besides, it's just going to sit in there until I croak; then Noah will donate it to Goodwill."

"Are you sure?" Emma says hesitantly.

Winnie places a hand on Emma's shoulder. "Of course, dear. It will make me happy to see someone wear one of the dozens of dresses I have collecting dust." She motions to the en-suite bathroom next to her closet. "Go try it on."

Emma firmly holds onto the hanger, looking at the dress from top to bottom. "Okay, if you insist...", she says, heading to the bathroom. Carefully, she puts on the dress, not wanting to get deodorant or sweat marks on it. The back is just low enough for Emma to be able to zip it up herself with ease. Glancing up at the mirror, Emma can see that the dress fits her like a glove, as if it was designed for her.

A gasp escapes out of Winnie as Emma heads back into the bedroom, with a hand covering her mouth in awe. Winnie places her hands on Emma's shoulders and guides her to the full-length mirror next to her vanity. In the sunlight, Emma can see the sleek shine and hues of deep blue in the dress. Running her hands over the silk material, it feels smooth on her skin, making Emma feel like she is wearing a flowy nightgown rather than being confined in a tight dress. The color doesn't clash with her skin tone or her hair color at all.

"This fits you perfectly," says Winnie, her eyes looking at Emma's in the mirror.

Emma turns around to face her, the movement causing the skirt to sway gracefully in a motion she has seen only in movies.

This dress makes me feel like a princess.

"Are you sure I can wear this to the event?" she asks Winnie one last time.

Winnie runs her hands along Emma's upper arms, a victorious smile on her face. "Absolutely."

Emma releases a breath she didn't realize she was holding—relieved to have found a solution to her dress problem but now uneasy from Winnie's generosity. This is the second time she has helped her in her time of need. "Do you have a garment bag I can use to carry this home?"

"Oh! Yes, silly me," says Winnie, shaking her head as she heads back inside her never-ending closet, coming back out with a garment bag. She helps Emma to secure the dress carefully in the bag after Emma changes out of it. "Would it be weird for me to ask if I could get a picture with you in it on the night of?" asks Winnie.

"None at all," says Emma. "It's the least I can do, truly. But I don't think I have your cell number."

"Well, we will have to fix that then," says Winnie. After exchanging numbers, the pair decide to have another French lesson to learn the very basics of greetings. This time, Winnie has Emma writing down the words, as repetition, both verbal and written, can help the brain digest information to stay in one's memory.

"It's the norm for students these days to memorize just what is needed for exams and to pass a class, which is not how you are supposed to learn," says Winnie in her tutoring voice. Her critique of the education system slips out, as it has in every lesson Emma has had so far. Emma doesn't mind at all, as in the few years she had since graduating from high school, she too had realized how flawed and convoluted the system is.

"It would also help if the American education system had you kids start learning languages at a very young age, as that is when our brains most easily learn another language. I learned English along with when I was learning French, still just a mere toddler, and because of that I know both fluently," she says, starting to go off topic.

"Who taught you? English, I mean," asks Emma, hoping this could be another small breadcrumb needed to get to know more about Winnie, who she is, and how she became the woman she is today.

"My mémé did. She was very adamant about me learning both languages when I started speaking. She even did the same to my mother when she was the same age."

"Do you know why she was so adamant about it?"

Winnie takes a sigh, thinking. "I never really knew why, but I think it had to do with the war. Once she and her family realized what was going to happen to France, not only was it too late for them to flee, but they knew only French and were limited in reaching out to other nations like England or the States for help. If I had to guess, I think she didn't want my mother and me to have the same limitations she had."

"Was she in Martigues during the war?" asks Emma.

She nods her head. "She and her family stayed, fought till the very end to defend their home." Emma waits for Winnie to speak, unsure whether she will share more or if that is all she will share about her family.

"Marvelous woman, my mémé," says Winnie, eventually breaking the silence. "So selfless and brave. I aspired to be a woman of her caliber."

"I would say you are," says Emma. "I can vouch that only a selfless woman would do what you did for me on that night. Not many people would've done that."

Winnie gives a slight titter. "I am not as bright as her, that is for sure." She lifts her mug to take another sip of her tea and finds that it is now empty. "Do you want another cup?" she offers to Emma.

"Yes, please," says Emma, handing her empty mug to Winnie. She uses this time as an opportunity to walk around her study, hoping to gather some more visual clues about her. The bookshelves are filled with all types of books in various genres. On each shelf, Emma finds another book she wants to add to her TBR list. As she approaches the last bookshelf, a well-worn folder in the bottom left corner catches her eye. Bending down, she picks up the folder nestled in between the last book and the wall of the shelf. Delicately, she opens it and finds five pages of loose paper, yellowed from time, with red and black pen markings all over. She sees that the words on the pages were originally typewritten. There are a few traces of typed words that haven't been scribbled to bits with the markings. At first, she thought that the notes on the side were made by one person, but with another look, she can see that there are two types of handwriting. One is asking the other their thoughts and suggestions in black, while the other responds in red. Emma flips through the other pages and sees that they are marked the same.

She is unable to determine what the content and annotations mean as the cursive is difficult to read, aside from one note in red on the bottom of the last page.

My love, this is a wonderful start. Thank you for entrusting me to read your story and give you feedback. I cannot wait to see where this story goes. Forever yours, O. June 1, 1989.

The sight of the pages and the note leads Emma to have one clear, heart-racing thought:

This must be from Winnie's book. A few pages from possibly the first version of the manuscript.

Before she can take another good look at it, the clanking of the tea kettle echoes in the kitchen, awakening Emma back to the moment. Reminding her that Winnie can come back into the study at any minute, catching her snooping into her study. She places the pages back into the folder and slides it back into its hidden spot, exactly as she has found it.

"The poetry writing still going well?" asks Winnie when she comes back with two full mugs of herbal tea.

Sitting in her spot on the couch as if she never left, Emma takes the mug from Winnie. The mention of poetry not only reminds her to try out Dr. Varman's suggestion when she gets home, but also that she has a brand-new notebook at home waiting to be used. She intends to write poems in it, but she will also jot down everything she can remember from those pages she just found.

Now she's itching to get back home to do just that.

Back home, Emma stands outside under the night sky on their back patio, with the metal garbage bin in front of her. In her right hand is the poem she wrote about George's death, and in her left is a matchbox. She releases the paper into the empty bin, then strikes a match and drops it. The paper slowly starts to burn, turning yellow, then brown, until it becomes burnt pieces of ash. Emma doesn't take her eyes off the small fire, watching the once white paper turn into black specks. She already feels a heavy load lift off her chest. A foggy, deep breath escapes out of her as she closes her eyes, physically trying to eliminate the incident from her mind. After a few freezing minutes out in the cold night air, once the smoke from the burnt papers subsides, she heads back inside, wanting to write something entirely different in her notebook.

She sits on the built-in window seat in her bedroom, with Sadie comfortably lying right next to her. Her new red leather notebook is open on her lap, ready to be written in. She fidgets with her pen, tapping it rhythmically on the clean page, trying to remember everything she read earlier in the note on the bottom of the manuscript page. Two very clear pieces of information stand out to her, enough to narrow down her search of the book. With the pen securely in her hand, she writes them down, along with some notes:

Who is 'O'?

The note had affectionate words like 'love' and 'forever yours.' Could this be Noah's dad? Or an ex-boyfriend?

June 1989: This could be the year she wrote the book. Could the book have been published in the early to mid-90s?

Emma re-reads what she just wrote. The anticipation that had been pulsing in her veins since she left Winnie's slowly dwindles. At first, Emma thought the note would provide her with more clues about Winnie's book. But now, as she stares at all she could remember, the note looks to provide little insight. In a desperate attempt, Emma grabs her phone and starts to Google 'books that were published in the early 90s'. She knows that search is useless, as hundreds of books were published in that timeframe. When she doesn't know anything like the book's genre or what it is about, how on earth could she find the name of this book?

Tired and discouraged, she locks her phone and plops it on the seat cushion. The loud thump and bounce of the phone force Sadie's head to perk up from her nap, annoyance in her eyes from being awakened. Emma scratches her ears, giving her a kiss on the top of her fluffy head. "Sorry, Sades. Didn't mean to disturb you."

Emma massages her own forehead with her free hand, hoping to prevent any potential headaches from forming as the wheels turn. Her head perks up as an idea sparks, proving that all might not be lost just yet.

The date may be useless, but 'O' may not…

A new plan starts to form in her head, thinking that if she can find 'O', they can possibly help her find the book since it looks like they helped Winnie when she was writing it. Emma starts to list names that begin with O, even searching Google for help. Her heart stops for a moment when she sees her dad's name, Oliver, listed as the top 'O' name in a baby name website.

Her thoughts suddenly fall deep into a spiral of what-if scenarios and hypotheticals in her brain, all leading her to think one simply ludicrous—yet still possible—thought that her dad could be the 'O' she is looking for. The only connection she can think of between her dad and Winnie is that they live in the same neighborhood. But that doesn't mean that they knew each other in the 90s. Emma knows that it is nonsensical, even laughable, that it could be true.

But even in the largest cities, worlds are still very small...

Shuddering at the thought, Emma shoves it away, wanting to cleanse its existence from her body. Exhausted from the day and herself, Emma closes the notebook, puts her phone away, and cuddles with Sadie. Soon she realizes that what she needs right now is time to escape, to not think about dead bodies or house-saving plans, for just a little while.

Grabbing *Pride and Prejudice* from her night table, she reads the last remaining chapters so she can move onto her next re-read: her favorite love story.

Chapter Eight

Caught off guard by the sight of the woman staring back at her in the mirror, Emma cannot believe that it is actually her. She is in awe of what less than an hour of doing hair and makeup can do.

Her mom helped her style her hair. Her loose waves hang in a half-updo, the hair by her temples twisted to meet on the back of her head. Her makeup is simple: pink blush to bring color into her face, mascara to show off her long lashes, and a thin line of black eyeliner to bring out her blue eyes. Winnie's dress shines in the light as Emma twirls, amazed at how perfect it is. Now she is all ready to go to the charity event.

In the days since Emma burned the poem in the garbage bin, images of George's dead body have appeared less in her mind. She can see the clear hues of ocean blue in her eyes again. Her eyelids have stopped drooping, her big eyes no longer small slits just big enough for her to see. She knows her trauma will never leave her, but for the first time since that night, she believes that it won't haunt her forever.

Emma hears her mom's footsteps coming back toward her bedroom. Glancing over at the door, she sees that her mom is holding a delicate necklace in her hands. Upon closer inspection, Emma sees that it is a lariat-styled diamond necklace, with half a carrot cut of diamonds dotted along the cable chain. It styles perfectly with the V-neck of Winnie's dress. "This was a wedding gift from my grandparents," says Abigail as she comes behind Emma and clasps the necklace on her. They both look at her in the full-length mirror before them, in complete astonishment. Abigail places her hands on

Emma's shoulders, smiles at her over her shoulder, and kisses her on the cheek, "Now your outfit is complete. You look beautiful, Ems."

"It's not too much?" asks Emma, with worry in her voice.

Abigail shakes her head. "Not at all. You should see how everyone has stepped up their attire since the last time you went. It really is like going to the Oscars."

Emma knows that not only must she look the part of the daughter of one of the partners, but she must act the part too, as the elite society of New York City will be there: the mayor, the governor, editors of magazines and publishing houses, celebrities who primarily reside in the city. Having been to all of the previous charity events and being one of the main coordinators of the event, Abigail is obviously better suited for the role as Oliver Callahan's plus-one. Emma knows her mother should go instead, leaving her to stay home in her comfy clothes and work out how to track down a book without knowing its title or find a person knowing only their supposed first initial. But there is no way that could happen; her mom is the keynote speaker at an NYU psychology conference tonight, leaving her to be Abigail's fill-in.

Sensing her nerves, Abigail rubs her hands over Emma's exposed upper arms. "You're overthinking it. You've been to several of these events. You know how it all goes; you do your rounds and talk to all the major clients, and you can let your dad worry about how the whole event goes. You will not be there as my replacement. Once you've done your rounds, you can enjoy the rest of the night like any other attendee, trying to raise money for the organizations. I know doing this is a headache and a half, but we want you to have fun too." Abigail gives Emma an encouraging smile. "And you are going to have fun, so allow yourself to try, okay?"

Emma nods. "Okay…"

Abigail turns Emma around, looks her in the eye, and gives her a mischievous wink. "Now go kick some ass and raise the most money of the night."

The Plaza Hotel, famously displayed in *Home Alone 2,* is still just as extravagant and elegant now as it was then.

The whole hotel has been secured off for this event. No one is allowed to enter the building without an invite. The plush red carpet that always covers the stairs to the entrance has been extended to cover the black-and-white marble sidewalk. A divider has been put up to block off the entrance; security details have been put around the perimeter to ensure the safety of all attendees. Across the street is the southeast corner of Central Park, freshly covered with a light layer of powdered snow.

Lines of cars wait behind them as attendees start to arrive. Looking through the car's tinted window, Emma watches as the firm's two other partners get out of their vehicles to walk down the red carpet and pose for the handful of photographers camping on the left side. It's been years since she last attended one of these, but she doesn't remember the event ever being *this* big. She never posed for pictures on a red carpet before. Nervously, she gulps down her reservations. Now that she is here, all dressed up and ready, she knows she has to go through with it. Besides, making her parents upset would be much worse than what is waiting outside.

Oliver's hand rests lightly on top of Emma's. She turns to look at him, all dapper in his wrinkle-free black tuxedo. "Ready, Ems?" he asks with a grin on his face.

Her dad loves this event; he wouldn't miss it for the world. It's his pride and joy. One of his greatest achievements is creating this event years ago, and it has become the city's annual must-attend event. This event is his firm's Christmas. He and his other partners developed it so well that they had to hire a team to plan and run the yearly event. Once they finish one event, the next day, they start planning and organizing next year's.

Emma musters the most enthusiastic smile she can. "Ready," she confirms.

Or as ready as I'll ever be.

They're one of the very first attendees to arrive. As one of the hosts of the event, it is crucial that her dad, and Emma by extension, arrive early. The event planners took the decorating seriously, as they even ensured the hotel's lobby and hallways are in theme. Fairy lights twinkle from the ceiling, as fake snow stacks an inch high on the side of the red velvet carpet leading to the ballroom where the event is taking place. Emma knows that every square inch of the massive ballroom is decorated in holiday décor. Her breath is taken away as she enters the ballroom, amazed by the transformation into the wintery wonderland she magically stepped into. Fake snowflakes hang from the crown-molded ceiling, twinkling along with the ornate crystal chandeliers, illuminating the low-lit room. Faux trees surround the perimeter of the room, covered in fake snow and glistening white lights. Black iron light posts are scattered around the room, along with wooden benches. The whole room looks like Central Park in a winter wonderland.

For the first few hours, Emma walks around the whole ballroom with her dad, greeting and making small talk with the major clients as well as the big donors for the event. One after the other, face after face, the conversations start to blur and merge with every new conversation Emma gets into. She can barely remember what she has said and to whom, or what they've told her. When she finally completes her responsibilities as a Callahan, she nudges her dad, engrossed in a conversation with one of the biggest tech moguls in the world, and lets him know using a few hand gestures that she is heading to the bar.

As she makes her way to the bar, she grabs a glass of champagne from a server's tray and takes in the whole scene unfolding around her. The room has come to life with thousands of New York City's socialites. She hasn't been in a room with this many people since her college graduation.

As she sips on her champagne, she hears Frank Sinatra's sultry voice singing along with the live jazz band. Looking around the room, she tries to find a face that is either familiar, not famous, or at least the same age as hers. Despite all the conversations she had in the past hour and a half, there is not a single person she could hang out with and enjoy the rest of the night. Upon this realization, dread consumes her. Anxiety sweat creeps up into her underarms. Another nightmare of hers is being at a crowded social event and not having a single soul to talk to. Unfortunately for her, that nightmare is now becoming her reality.

'Have fun!' Yeah, right. Thanks, Mom.

Emma gulps down the rest of the champagne and walks over to the bar to find something stronger. "Can I have an amaretto sour?" she asks the bartender once she reaches the corner end of the bar.

"I thought that was you," says a familiar voice.

Emma turns around and is surprised to see Noah, dressed in a fresh black tuxedo, looking like James Bond. Well, maybe if the nerdy tech guy that supplies Bond with his gadgets donned a suit.

"Noah?" she says, perplexed. "I didn't know you were coming tonight. I mean," she takes a second to collect herself to prevent humiliation, "your mom didn't tell me you were invited."

He flashes a smile that would break any girl's heart, showing off that left dimple Emma has not forgotten about. "Well, technically I wasn't," he says, then clarifies once he sees the puzzled look on Emma's face. "The charter school I teach at is one of the organizations that is being awarded with a donation. Our vice principal was supposed to attend tonight, along with our principal, but she unfortunately is suffering from food poisoning. They called me in as an emergency backup."

"And you happen to have a tuxedo ready at a moment's notice?" she uncharacteristically asks, feeling the champagne's effects. She surprises herself with the boldness of the words that just came out of her mouth.

Noah takes a sip of his dark brown drink and laughs in his glass. "It's actually my roommate's. He's a pianist for the New York Philharmonic."

"Amaretto sour," cuts in the bartender, placing Emma's drink on the bar. She mouths a thank you to him and lifts her drink, about to take a sip.

"Cheers," says Noah, lifting his glass up in a toast. Emma raises her glass to meet his, then takes a sip, the bittersweet and nutty flavors of the drink swimming down to her stomach.

"How did you manage to score an invite?" asks Noah, with no ounce of judgment in his voice, just pure curiosity.

"My dad is one of the name partners of Kratz, Callahan, and Howard, so I get a free invite."

Noah leans in with a shy smile. "So, we both managed to snag an invite by association."

A titter comes out of Emma. "There's no way I could have afforded a ticket on my own. Besides," she turns around to look at the party before them, "this isn't really my crowd."

"Wealthy celebrities, politicians, and businesspeople aren't your type?"

Emma shakes her head. "Not at all. I'd rather be with my dog Sadie, eating some ramen on my couch." She looks over at him. "I was strongly persuaded to come tonight. Believing it would help to forget all that happened last Friday."

Noah nods, understanding. "Besides, you get to help organizations in need and have free food and drinks, of course. How have you been since that night?" Noah asks as his face turns serious.

Emma sighs and takes a long sip of her drink. "If only I hadn't seen his body in that way, then maybe I wouldn't be so scarred from it. I keep getting these images in my head from finding his body. They're haunting me." She looks down at her drink, swirling her thin straw around the rim of the glass. "There are times I'm scared it will never stop." She doesn't know why she is telling him this, spilling out her inner thoughts and feelings to a stranger at a charity gala, no less. Yes, he may be Winnie's son, but Emma has never said more than a few words to him. Winnie may have raised Noah to be polite, but that doesn't mean he wants to know the true details about her trauma. There is just something about the Reynards that makes her want to spill her guts to them.

Noah turns around, leaning his arm against the black wooden bar. He takes a sip of his drink and waits a moment before he responds, thinking of the right words to say. "When my dad died," he finally says, "it felt like the whole world came to an end. I was only eight, and at that age you don't really understand death. It felt like everything was engulfed in flames. Then a few short weeks later my great-grandma, who was like a grandma to me, had a stroke and passed too. I didn't know how to go on with life after losing two people I loved dearly."

Emma's grasp on her drink loosens, the glass about to fall completely out of her hand from being stunned. Luckily, her reflexes kick in before it could drop to the floor. She didn't expect him to meet her on her level of openness and share with her a traumatic time in his life. She assumed his dad and Winnie were separated. The last thing she would ever think was that he had passed. Now that she knows what happened to him, Emma feels like cold water has been splashed on her face, unexpected and jarring.

Noah turns to Emma and looks into her blue eyes with a small smile on his lips. She hopes that her shock is not lingering on her face. "But I had my mom," he continues, "so resilient and brave. She picked up the pieces and showed me that tragedies happen and that we cannot let them define us. Still to this day, I don't know how she did it: raising me, trying to teach me about grief and death while also grieving herself. She did it all on her own, no friends or family stepping in."

The life Winnie's had so far... I never would have imagined so much pain and loss for such a generous and lively woman.

Noah looks down at his glass in his right hand, moving it in circles to swirl around the ice cubes inside. Emma doesn't speak just yet, sensing that there may be more he wants to say. "We all are different as human beings," says Noah, as he looks back up at her. "We process emotions and events so differently from one another. But we all can heal and persevere. It is all just a matter of time, which is the one thing we can't control." He looks directly into her eyes, which have not drifted away from him. A smile filled with encouragement shines on his face. "One day you will be able to not think about George and his death, just like how one day I was able to not think about my dad's and my great-grandma's. Just be patient with yourself."

"I'm so sorry to hear about your dad and great-grandma, Noah," Emma finally mutters. "Your mom never told me about them."

Noah shrugs. "I'm not surprised. She barely talked about my dad after he died, and I stopped bringing him up as I knew she was so heartbroken by it. By the time I thought she was doing alright again, too much time had passed, and I was frightened I would be bringing up her pain again. I can't even remember the last time we ever talked about him. It could have been at his funeral actually…". Noah downs the rest of his drink, placing the empty glass on top of the bar. "She still brings up my great-grandma from time to time. My mom was very close to her. My great-grandma was more of a mom to her than her own. But, like my dad, I don't remember much of her."

Emma stands next to him in silence, trying to process everything Noah said. She tries to envision Winnie as a grieving wife and granddaughter with a young child. Being so heartbroken by the loss of her husband that she couldn't bear to mention him again, not even to her child. Emma cannot imagine what it must be like to lose the love of someone's life and the one person who was like a mother to her so close together, all while raising a child on your own. Slowly, the door containing answers of who Winnie Reynard is starts to open, but ever just so slightly.

"Do you have any memories of your dad?" asks Emma, intrigued by the mysterious man that was Mr. Reynard.

Noah shakes his head; Emma can see a mix of pain and sadness in the corners of his eyes along with another emotion that she cannot pinpoint. "A lot of my memories of him are foggy. Only little snippets come into mind, like how he liked to drink whiskey after work in his study or how we would go boat racing at Central Park." A small smile rises on his face. "He and my mom were so happy and in love. The kind that makes anyone both nauseated and envious. They were high school sweethearts, you know."

"What was his name?" Emma asks, wondering if he could be the mysterious man who wrote the note and helped edit Winnie's book.

"Russel," answers Noah.

Okay… the first initials don't match, but that still doesn't rule Russel out just yet. 'O' could have been a nickname Winnie called him by.

As Noah orders himself and Emma another drink, she observes him, thinking back to how he described his mom and their family's story. Emma gets the impression he's intuitive and observant, and wonders if he has already figured out the state of Winnie's tutoring business and that she may have to sell the house, even though she never said a word of it to him. The two of them seem so close, having gone through hardships that bond people together, which makes Emma question even more why Winnie hasn't told him anything yet.

The sound of a fingertip tapping onto the top of the microphone can be heard from the ballroom speakers. Everyone turns their attention to the stage where the jazz musicians are playing, and Emma sees her dad on stage along with his other partners, Tyrell Howard and Eugene Kratz. Tyrell is in the middle, standing behind the microphone.

"Welcome to Kratz, Callahan, and Howard's annual give-back charity event, everyone!" shouts Tyrell. The room roars with professional applause, not too loud or rowdy. "According to the latest survey from the youth advocates and Citizens' Committee for Children," he continues once the cheering dies down, "only forty-two percent of NYC children who need or want mental health services receive it. Less than fifty percent receive extracurricular support. The children of our city feel that their biggest challenges they face today are education, mental health, economic security, public safety, and public health. Let that sink in for a minute…"

The statistics Tyrell shared don't shock Emma, but hearing what concerns children have breaks her heart. These are children, young kids, asking for help, saying what they need, but she knows the city and state will only do so much to help them.

"The children of our city need help," continues Tyrell, "and I am happy to announce that this year's recipients of our give-back donation of $500,000 will do just that. Our first awardee is Westview Charter School." Another polite applause echoes. "A school founded and run by a diverse board of educators who strive to help underprivileged and minority children in the five boroughs receive a better education."

"Our second recipient is A Brighter Day." More hands clap. "A non-profit organization dedicated to providing mental health awareness and free services to young children who need it."

"And our last recipient is No Hungry Nights, a non-profit organization that provides breakfast, lunch, and dinner to schools across the city to ensure no child ever goes to school or comes home hungry. Each of these organizations strives to help our future generations by ensuring that every child has the foundation they need to excel." Tyrell raises his glass of champagne. "Let's raise our glasses to the honorable and selfless work of these organizations and toast to their continued success." A roomful of arms lift with glasses in their hands, and a low murmur of cheers echoes throughout the big ballroom.

"Now let's get the party started with our annual do-nation challenge," continues Tyrell. "You know the rules: Teams of two will compete against one another to accrue the most money in ten challenges. Only those who place in the top three of each challenge will receive a monetary prize that will be added to their overall score. For each round, first place will win $50,000, second place $30,000, and third place $15,000. Those who place below will accrue $5,000 to their amount. The team that wins the most money will pick an organization of their choice—this does not have to be one of tonight's recipients—to receive their total earnings and take home our beautiful crystal trophy. The money earned by the other teams will be evenly distributed amongst our three chosen organizations. Even if you don't win, you will still be greatly contributing to a great cause." Tyrell motions his arm to the table to his left, where a head-sized Tiffany crystal sphere blob resides. Emma has never understood the design of the trophy or what on earth it represents. It was designed by a New York abstract artist, and abstract it truly is.

This time, a rowdy applause booms in the open space. Everyone loves a competition, and everyone loves an ugly, expensive trophy, especially the rich socialites of New York.

"The competition will start in ten minutes. For those who want to participate, find a partner and register your team in the back by the bar." He points to where Emma and Noah are standing but off to the left side. They both look over to their left and see three associates standing together with cheerful smiles on their faces and iPads in their hands. "Don't worry about keeping track of your score; the team will also keep a record of that too." Tyrell leans closer to the mic and whispers into it mischievously, "Now let the games begin."

In an orderly fashion, everyone moves around, trying to find a partner. But not just anyone; they want someone who is in it to win it, who has the skills they lack, the dream team that will take that trophy home with them tonight. Winning the crystal trophy is the socialite's version of winning an Oscar; it comes with prestige. There is even a wall at the offices of Kratz, Callahan, and Howard showcasing the winners of the previous years. In no way does Emma want to participate just to win the trophy. She wants to feel useful, to do something that she knows will benefit the city, something she hasn't felt since she did volunteer work during college. Knowing that one of the organizations is a non-profit dedicated to helping kids with mental health, and after everything she's recently been through, Emma feels that this is a clear sign for her to act. She wants to help these organizations as much as she can, win or lose.

"I heard about the Do-nationchallenge," says Noah, breaking Emma from her running thoughts, reminding her that he is standing beside her. "And once they told me I was going to be here tonight, I knew I was going to win it for my kids. It's been years since they've gone on a proper field trip. Can you imagine? Being at a school in the capital of the world, and not having enough money to send a class of fourth graders to the Museum of Natural History? Stupid budget cuts," Noah shakes his head slightly, staring out into the distance. "Even with the money that was already donated to Westview tonight, I know it's all going to the major reconstruction that is desperately needed for the building and to finally update the archaic computers we have. The other teachers and I have tried so many times to run fundraisers and there was always something that came up that took priority to receive the funding..." He motions his arm to the room around them. "But this—this will finally allow the school to send the kids to as many field trips as we like, on top of providing them with the supplies and books they need. I know this sounds very much like a white savior complex, but I'm being given a chance to get the funding we need. I can't not try. I'm going to compete and win this for my kids."

Emma can't imagine the frustrations the teachers at Westview must endure, forced to work with what they are barely given.

"The fact that we still can't provide every child with the education and accessories they need to excel, reminds me how easy everything was for me. How a lot of it was just expected and handed out," says Emma, speaking aloud her thoughts. She looks around at the faces before her, knowing many went to expensive private schools and Ivy League colleges and now have executive-level jobs, some of which were simply handed to them. Her parents are nowhere near the super-rich of NYC, but Emma knows that she is still in a circle of New Yorkers who are lucky and privileged.

Noah gestures toward the crowd. "Just look at the people who are here with us. They are the ones who have all the money to donate and fund such an event. Then think of the majority of the people in this city; it's the backbone that keeps it running and operating. Those are the ones who barely see any differences made despite how hard people work for change. Things do change in this city, but it only changes for those who can pay for it. Which is why I'd rather be paid less and work for a school like Westview. Everything the school does is for the kids. Not for rich, entitled parents. Not for a board who only cares about their Ivy League statistics. But for the kids."

Emma turns to look at Noah. She can see his passion for his students, noticing his immediate, unfaltering action to help those who aren't as privileged. Sensing her eyes on him, Noah looks back at her with fiery passion in his eyes. "Do you want to help me win this for the kids? Be my partner?"

Emma dumbly nods her head, mesmerized by the sparks swimming in his eyes while also relieved she doesn't have to worry about finding a partner, not realizing she is subconsciously responding to him. The grin on his face sends a wave of giddiness and warmth throughout Emma's body. She cannot recall a guy ever smiling at her like that.

Noah turns around and motions to the bartender. "Two shots of tequila, please." He looks at Emma over his shoulder and winks. "For liquid encouragement." He hands her the small glass of tequila that is more than just a shot, both gulping theirs in one take.

Emma coughs in disgust. "Oh god, that's terrible."

Noah laughs at her and offers his right arm to her, letting her place her hand on the crook of his elbow. "Come on, partner. We need to give these billionaires a run for their money."

January 29, 1989

My Dearest Mémé,

The worry you poured into your last letter struck a chord in me. I've known for far too long that I was being passive and allowing things to happen to me, but your words awakened in me the realization of what I need to do, despite being afraid of what could happen afterward.

I spoke to Russel about my worries and brought up the matter of his drinking and gambling delicately. At first, he was receptive to seeing how we have been spending a lot of money to accommodate his clients and explained to me that he can get carried away when he is in his 'client mode', as he likes to phrase it. I thought we were finally starting to get to a point where we can discuss as life partners what his job is doing to us. But as soon as I asked about the background of his questionable clients, a switch flipped inside his head and we lost all the progress we had made.

He went on a rampage, accusing me of wanting him to fail in his career, saying that I was doubting him and his judgement for what is best for us and our family, even questioning my loyalty and devotion to him as his wife. No matter how I tried to calm him down and make him see that I wasn't trying to do any of those things, he wouldn't listen to me. After that argument, I couldn't help but think back and wonder if maybe he was right. Maybe I did want him to fail in his job at this company so we can start fresh elsewhere. Maybe I did doubt him and his judgement; I questioned everything down to who his clients are without any solid proof. But one thing I can confidently defend is my loyalty and devotion to him and us. I have always stood by his side and did everything he asked without a fuss; everything I did was for him. How dare he question my loyalty to him!

We haven't talked since that argument. He suddenly has been busier than usual with more clients, and Gracie came up to visit us for a few weeks. With her staying at our house, it's been harder for us to have any private moments. Oh Mémé, I cannot lie to you, there were several times I have almost broken down in tears, wanting to confide in Gracie about what is going on with us. But replaying our argument in my head compels me not to. It's hard keeping up a façade with her. Gracie is my childhood friend, I always tell her everything, but as Russel's sister, where does her loyalty lie? Will she side with me or with her brother, her family? It hurts me to keep things from her and I worry that she senses that I am keeping things from her too. Mon dieu... I already feel like I'm losing my only close friend.

The only person I truly have is you. Ma mère would be aghast to know the things I write to you, thinking I'm being selfish.

My daily trip to the park is the only thing keeping me sane. Thankfully I ended up running into that man again. We talked at the park for over two hours. Fossettes—my nickname for him as he has the cutest dimples I have ever seen—and I have arranged to meet every Tuesday afternoon at the park to talk about books and life. On every Tuesday, he brings me a single lily flower, as he knows those are my favorite.

One afternoon we ended up talking all about Martigues. Since he has never left the States, he was intrigued to hear all about my other home. On our last visit, he even surprised me with a first edition of Winnie the Pooh, as he remembered its importance to me and our family. I have never treasured a gift as much as that book. (And before you ask, yes, he knows I'm married.)

I've only known him for a few weeks, and he already knows everything about me. And yes, I mean everything. What I like, what my passions are. This includes my writing.

One Tuesday afternoon, I went to the park early to finish writing a poem, and I simply lost track of time. Fossettes caught me off guard when he showed up and asked what I was writing, even wanting to read it. I was hesitant at first to let him, but I couldn't say no to that smile. I couldn't tell if he said he liked it just to be nice, but then he asked to read the rest of my work. Mémé, you have no idea how uncomfortable it is for someone to read every short story and poem you ever wrote right in front of you. Je pense que j'aurais pu mourir d'humiliation.

He's been telling me frequently how good my works are and was shocked to hear that I am not taking my writing seriously. Every day since he first read that poem, he has encouraged me to go further with my writing. He truly thinks that I should write a book. Un livre!

What do you think, Mémé? Do you think I should do it? I could write during the quiet times when I'm at the park, so Russel would never know about it.

I anxiously wait for your next letter.

Ton petit soleil,

Winnie

P.S. I've snuck in a new ingredient into our tea inventory: whiskey.

Chapter Nine

Emma's heart beats rapidly, sweat gathering in places she does not want it to. "We have to what?" she asks, out of breath. The rules of the second challenge come back into her mind with bits and pieces missing. All she remembers is that they have to pop the balloons; the rest has completely escaped her mind. She looks to Noah, her eyes pleading for help.

"We have to pop the balloons," he says with embarrassment in his voice.

"Yeah, I got that part."

"But the catch is that we both have to touch it and pop it… without using our hands." He looks shyly at her. Emma's eyes shoot wide open once it connects in her head. They will have to get close to each other. *Very* close.

"On the count of five…," says the announcer's voice. "Five…"

Emma looks down at the balloon in her hands, then at the pile beside them. She curses in her head silently, wishing that she hadn't signed up for this, knowing that this challenge with a dress like hers is a recipe for disaster.

"Four…"

Think of the children, Emma.

"Three…"

Fuck, fuck, fuck.

"Two…"

Oh, why did I look into Noah's eyes!

"One! Go!"

And off the teams go, rushing to meet in the middle of the dance floor, working together to pop their balloons with a different body part for each balloon.

"Left foot!" exclaims Noah once they meet in the middle. Both press their left foot on top of the balloon, instantly deflating it. "Right foot!" *Pop*. "Left knee!" *Pop*. "Right knee!" *Pop*. "Left elbow!" "Right elbow!" "Butt!" This one made Emma give Noah a disgruntled look, but she still complied.

"How many do we have left?" she asks, hoping it is fewer than what she thinks.

"Just two more," says Noah. "Back! We can use our backs!" *Pop*.

The list of parts already used runs through Emma's head, realizing what areas are left for them. Blood drains from her face, anticipating the humiliation. Reading her face, Noah reluctantly holds their last balloon. They both look over at the other teams and see that they are ahead, but not for too long. He looks at her and shrugs his shoulders, silently asking for consent.

Emma takes a deep breath.

It's for the kids, Emma.

Before she knows it, she reaches for the balloon in Noah's hands, places it onto his chest, and thrusts her chest to his, causing the balloon to pop instantly.

"Winner!" she hears one of the associates yell as they yank Emma's and Noah's arms into the air. She can feel the blood rushing back to her face but then remembers that they now have added $50,000 on top of the $15,000 they won in the first challenge of the treasure hunt around the Plaza.

We got this. We may actually win this!

In between the next few challenges, both Emma and Noah take more shots of liquid encouragement. Once they get to the dance challenge, any reservations they had in the first two rounds go out the window. Emma gets the sense that they are both feeling ease with each other and now are enjoying themselves, taking away the pressure of what would happen if they don't win.

"I hope you know how to do most of these dances," says Noah. "I never took ballroom dance lessons."

Emma, really feeling the liquid encouragement, shrugs her shoulders with confidence. "I have not, but thankfully I've watched enough *Dancing with the Stars* with my mom to know what each *should* look like."

A laugh escapes from Noah while he shakes his head. "Just don't stomp on my feet."

A mischievous smile creeps up on Emma's lips, and she places a hand on his bicep. "I don't make promises I can't keep."

One by one, each remaining team comes onto the dance floor, dancing the style assigned to them. The best rendition of said dance takes the top prize. Luckily, Emma and Noah were given one of the easy ones: the waltz.

"Just follow my lead," Emma whispers to Noah, with his hand on her waist and the other holding her left hand, while her right hand rests on his shoulder. Once the band starts playing music, they float along the dance floor in harmony. Their bodies communicate to each other silently. Listening, moving with and against the other, as if they are one being. With not a foot stomped on, they take second place, losing to a couple in their forties who have obviously taken couples' dance classes for date nights.

With the extra $30,000 they won from that challenge, Emma and Noah are now in third place. With one challenge left, they need to win first place to beat the top two teams and win the whole thing.

"The final challenge for tonight will be very familiar to most of us," says one of the associates on stage. "So far, we have tested you on your dancing ability, physical ability, and trust you have with your teammate. Now we will test you on your knowledge." Voices erupt in pleasure, all of them thinking they too are smart enough to answer any trivia questions the firm created. The associate raises her hand. "That's right, we're going to be testing our final three teams to a game of pub trivia. You know how the rules go, we give you a handful of categories with several questions. Each question the team answers correctly will add the monetary value of that question to their overall score. Whoever wages their answer for the final question smartly will win the do-nation and gets to donate their total monetary winnings to a charity of their choice and take home the crystal trophy!" Some jeers and snickers can be heard, presumably from the teams below third place who are disappointed they can't pull off a Hail Mary and win it all. The three teams in the top look at each other, assessing who is their threat. Emma and Noah are the youngest, competing against a pair of retired basketball players and a CEO of a Fortune 500 company and his wife. With age on their side, the other teams may have an advantage, knowing more about history and pop culture events of the past.

Emma finds her dad off to the side, watching along with the other partners. Knowing his daughter, Oliver motions for Emma to take a deep breath. He then mouths to her that she's got this, with an enthusiastic grin on his face, even though that is the last thing she feels about this last challenge.

"Do you think we have a chance?" Emma whispers to Noah, looking away from her dad and toward their opponents.

Noah doesn't shrug or show any kind of hesitation, trying to keep a poker face. "Depends on what kind of categories they have. If it's anything related to sports or before the year 2000, we could be screwed."

Knowing this time they can't rely on liquid encouragement, Emma tries to hype herself up, finding it much harder to do without the help of tequila or vodka. "We can do this," she says to herself, but loudly enough for Noah to hear. "We got this far. Besides," she looks at Noah, "think about the smiling faces of your kids when you can finally take them on a proper field trip."

Noah looks down at her and smiles, nodding. "You're right. We can't give up just yet when we are this close to the finish line."

"My name is Janelle, and I will be your host for this last challenge," continues the associate on stage. "Teams, please make your way to the podiums on the dance floor."

As Emma and Noah make their way to the floor, they can see three legitimate podiums standing six feet apart from one another. On top are iPads with a stylus they will use to write their answers. In front of the podiums are blank screens, which will show their answers to their host and the 'audience' during the game. The stage has been cleared of the band, replaced by a projector screen, displaying what the category and questions are.

Emma and Noah take the podium on the left, the basketball players in the middle, and the CEO and his wife on the right. Emma feels herself sweating again and hopes she has not ruined the dress with perspiration stains. She takes a sip of water from one of the glasses placed inside the podium, trying to calm herself.

Don't think about the crowd. Don't think about the number of eyes watching. It's just a fun game of pub trivia.

"Before we start, let's introduce our teams." Janelle comes down from the stage, microphone in her hand, and walks toward the closest podium. "Team One, please give your names and the charity you are playing for."

Laughter rumbles in the room as everyone knows who the CEO and his wife are. A charming smile rests on his face as he leans over to the small microphone fixed onto the podium, "My name is Mark Gordon." Then his wife leans forward. "And I'm Camilla Gordon, and we are playing for our charity Tree2Tree, which helps combat deforestation."

An applause cascades around the room. "Thank you, Mr. and Mrs. Gordon, and good luck." Janelle makes her way to the middle podium. "Team Two, please introduce yourself and the charity you are playing for."

The podium and mic look tiny compared to the tall basketball players standing behind it. The two men look like giants trying to fit inside a tiny house. "Hello," says the first player, his muscles showing in his perfectly tailored suit as he leans forward. Cheers roar from the women in the room, a catcall whistle echoing throughout the place. A smile of modest cockiness comes onto the player's face, knowing how good-looking he is, and how well-loved he is by the people of this city. "My name is Brandon De Fuentes."

The other player, just as equally muscular and well-loved as Brandon, leans forward toward the mic. "And I'm Tarek Jones. We are playing for Hoops for All, the charity organization that provides basketball equipment to underprivileged areas across the country." A loud applause roars throughout the ballroom.

"What a fine-looking team, I might add," says Janelle, while fake fanning herself. "Thank you for participating, and good luck."

She makes her way to the last podium, to Emma and Noah. "Team Three, please introduce yourself and your charity."

Noah makes the move first to speak, speaking clearly into the mic, "I'm Noah Reynard."

"And I'm Emma Callahan," says Emma, a bit too nervous and weakly. Unlike the other two teams, a very faint and modest applause is heard.

"And the charity you are playing for?" asks Janelle

"We are playing for the fourth-grade class at Westview Charter School," says Noah.

This time, a respectable applause echoes throughout the ballroom.

"Thank you," says Janelle, eyeing them both as if they are outcasts crashing the event. "And good luck." In a way, they are outcasts. The majority of people in this room are famous or well-known in the five boroughs. And here they are, two nobodies in their mid-twenties competing in the top three teams, about to possibly win thousands of dollars and a crystal trophy.

"Now that we've met our teams, let's begin!" cheers Janelle.

The screen changes, displaying what their first category of the game is: Business & Industry.

"Shit," mutters Emma after reading the categories, hoping it would have been something she knows well.

"Shit, indeed," agrees Noah, sounding deflated that the category is not one of the main school subjects.

Emma and Noah nearly skate by the first round, answering half of the questions correctly while the other two teams get nearly two-thirds of them right. Then the game gets heated as the value of the questions in the next few categories double as the game continues on, upping the value of the final questions to ten times the original amount. Thankfully, the categories for the last few rounds are on topics they both know well: American History, Literature, and Recent Movies. This gives them the momentum they need to catch up to the other teams, but they're still in last place by a narrow margin when they reach the final question of the game.

"Before I read our final question," says Janelle, "let's see where the teams stand with their total scores from the last two rounds. Team One has a score of $52,600, Team Two has a score of $62,600, and Team Three has a score of $49,000." A respectable applause then carries throughout the ballroom.

"The final question is a wager," continues Janelle. "Teams can wager up to the exact amount they have or lower. If they get the question right, the wager will be added to their score. If they get it wrong, the wager will be deducted from their score. Teams, please keep in mind, you do not have to double wager; you can wager a small amount and still win. Your final category is, 'Name that Writer'. You will now have thirty seconds to write in your wager."

Emma's heart skips a beat at hearing the category, knowing that this will be an author. She prays that it is something she has read. As soon as the clock starts ticking, Emma quickly tries to calculate their options. All of them leading her to the same result: They don't have enough to win. She knows the other two teams will double wager; it would be ridiculous not to. But considering Emma and Noah's track record of questions answered correctly, the question is if they should take the same risk as well. "What do you think we should do?" Emma asks Noah.

"We have to double wager," says Noah, thinking the same thing she is. "If not, there is a high chance we will lose anyway. We might as well put it all in, increase our chances of beating them if we know it and they don't." Noah takes the stylus and writes out $49,000; he takes a quick look at Emma for confirmation. As soon as she nods her head, he hits enter.

Emma didn't realize her hands were shaking by her sides until Noah takes one into his, giving her a reassuring squeeze. "Hey," he whispers to her, "we did the best we could."

"But the kids," she whispers back.

"If we lose, we will find another way to get them to the planetariums and museums." He looks down at her and gives her the most heart-melting smile of both defeat and gratitude, making her heart soar out of her chest.

"Okay, all final wagers are in," says Janelle as the timer rings, breaking up their moment and forcing their hands to separate. "Your question is: This famous American author once wrote, 'They say love takes your body, mind, and soul. But in truth, I've never truly felt mine until I laid eyes on you.' You have thirty seconds to answer."

The notorious ticking Jeopardy song starts to play, distracting Emma from concentrating on the question. She reads it once more in her head, the words sounding familiar, but the writer doesn't yet come to her.

"Do you have any idea?" whispers Noah.

Emma waves and shushes him, re-reading the quote again and again.

I know this. I know who wrote this. But who is it?

She can feel the time ticking down, getting closer to the thirty seconds being up. Then it suddenly hits her.

It's the book that has been on her mind for weeks. The only book she read more times than she would like to admit. It's the book that convinced her that true love and soulmates do exist. She grabs the stylus and furiously writes down the name and hits enter, with only three seconds left to spare.

Noah's left eyebrow perks up, asking silently how confident she is in her answer.

She gives him a knowing smile and nods her head. Deep down inside she tries hard not to already celebrate. Even if she is right, the others could have double-wagered and gotten it right as well.

"Let's start with the leaders of the board, Team One," says Janelle. The board changes to their answer, "You said, 'Jane Austen'. I regrettably have to say that is incorrect." A unanimous 'oooh' echoes throughout the room, the whole crowd circling around the dance floor, caught up in the moment to find out who will win. Emma can hear the CEO's wife snicker at him for putting down the wrong answer.

"Depending on what you wager, it may take you out of the lead. Let's see how much you wagered." Both Emma and Noah hold their breath, hoping to see that Team One did as they thought and double-wagered. The screen changes again, showing a neat $4,000 on the board. "Only $4,000! Which leaves you with a final score of $48,600. You may still be able to win this!" Relief spreads across the CEO and his wife's faces, optimistic that they can still end up winning this.

"Team Two, let's see what you put down." Emma anxiously looks at the board, crossing her fingers underneath the podium. The screen changes. "You said, 'John Steinbeck.'" Laughter comes from the crowd as everyone, including the basketball players, knows that is the wrong answer. "I'm sorry guys, but that is also incorrect. Let's see how much you wagered." The screen changes to '$62,600.' The crowd lets out a loud "Ah" of disappointment. "With a double wager, that leaves you guys with zero." The retired basketball players give a shrug and a grin of 'we didn't know any better' to the audience, mocking themselves for losing all they've earned. The players clap each other on the back. Emma can hear them agreeing that they're just surprised to have lasted this long in the do-nation.

"Let's see what Team Three wrote down," continues Janelle. Emma grabs Noah's arm, holding onto it to keep herself steady. She barely lets out a breath, waiting to hear the words to let her know whether she can rejoice or not. The screen changes, and she sees her messy handwriting back at her. "You said, 'C.K. Rothschild.'" The crowd is silent, equally on the edge of their seats as Emma and Noah are. Emma can sense that Noah too is holding his breath.

"That is correct!" exclaims Janelle. Relief and triumph course through Emma in a tidal wave, with shock coursing through her in its aftermath. She can feel her body release all the tension that it had been holding. Emma doesn't need to wait for any confirmation to know that they've just won the whole thing.

"Let's see how much you wagered," says Janelle. The screen changes, and they see their double wager staring back at them. "A double wager!"

Janelle's voice, along with the noise of the now-boisterous crowd, is muddled in Emma's ears as their final earnings are announced. Emma looks up at Noah in disbelief; they are equally shocked. In those few seconds, all she sees is amazement and wonder in his eyes, astonished at what they were able to pull off. It isn't until Emma hears who Janelle is about to announce the winner that she tunes back to her surroundings.

"The winner of this year's do-nation with a final donation amount of $98,000 is... Team Three! Congratulations to Emma and Noah!" The crowd finally cheers loudly for them, despite them being the clear underdogs of the game. In the distance, she can see her dad visibly cheering much more exuberantly than his other two partners. When his eyes catch hers, the only thing he mouths to her is 'I told you so' with a wide grin of overconfidence on his face.

Emma turns back to Noah and yells out a cheer as they hug in a tight embrace. The sound of the commotion from the crowd feels thousands of miles away. In this moment of celebration, it is only the two of them. When Noah pulls away, his hands resting on her shoulders, looking at Emma as if she's one of the seven wonders of the world. "You did it," he says joyously.

Emma shakes her head. "No, *we* did it." And before she can go in for another hug, they are dragged up to the stage, where the associates and the partners are now standing. Spotlights are now focused on them. Emma silently prays that she isn't as visibly sweaty as she feels. One by one, they shake the hands of the partners. When Emma gets to her dad, instead of a handshake, she gets a hug. "Congrats, Ems!" he says into her ear.

The next few minutes go by in a blur. Before she knows it, the crystal trophy is in her hands, and they all gather for pictures. The partners then present to them a check written out to the school for $98,000. Once off the stage, the other teams shake their hands in congratulations, and other members of the crowd join in. They have brief conversations with the mayor and the principal of Noah's school, and once it all dies down, they feel like they can finally breathe and take in what they just pulled off.

"Emma!" comes a voice from the crowd.

Emma turns and sees her dad walking toward them, without the other partners. This time she knows he is coming as Oliver Callahan, her dad, not Oliver Callahan, the partner of the firm. "Congratulations, sweetheart," he says as he gives her another hug. "Your mom will be so excited to hear you won this year's do-nation." Once they pull away from their hug, Oliver looks over at Noah and extends his hand once more. "I don't think I've properly introduced myself. I'm Oliver, Emma's dad."

Noah takes his hand and shakes it. "Noah. Pleasure to meet you, sir."

"Noah?" Oliver repeats back to himself. "Are you the same Noah who is joining us for dinner tomorrow night?"

"Indeed I am."

"Ah! How wonderful! We can all celebrate together then." They hear Oliver's name being called by someone off in the distance, most likely another socialite he has yet to make his rounds to. "So sorry," he says to them, "duty calls." He leans over to give a kiss on Emma's cheek. "Congrats again! Go and celebrate! I hear the drinks are free." He gives them a wink and then gets submerged into the crowd.

"That gives me an idea," says Noah, now holding onto the crystal blob that is their trophy.

"And what idea is that?" asks Emma.

Noah wiggles his eyebrows and charms her with a smile that shows off his left dimple. With butterflies fluttering in her stomach, she knows she would say yes to just about anything he suggests.

"You'll see," is all he says.

Chapter Ten

The night sky is clear, for once.

Usually, the smog from industrialization prohibits New Yorkers from ever seeing the stars or a clear sky. It's always dark with a slight haze. But tonight, there is no haze or smog. It's just the jet-black sky and the twinkling of the stars.

The temperature is still the same freezing cold. Luckily, Emma has Noah's jacket to keep her warm, as well as the bubbles from the champagne they snuck onto the rooftop. Getting access to the roof was quite easy; no one questioned whether they were guests, and at this late hour of the night, all the hotel residents were either snuggled in bed in their room or still out gallivanting in the city. The fire exit door leading to the roof was already ajar, kept open by a brick, most likely by one of the staffers who likes to sneak up for a smoke break.

Considering that the champagne was already free, and that the egress to the roof was already open, they technically haven't done anything bad, easing Emma's guilt-prone conscience.

Emma and Noah sit side by side on a raggedy bench, with their crystal blob of a trophy in between them, passing the bottle of champagne between each other. Their knees are touching, and their hands linger for a moment whenever they pass the bottle. These slight physical touches electrify Emma, heating her up even more than the suit jacket and champagne have. She wants to close the gap between them but is terrified to do so.

She can already feel that she is past the buzzed phase and getting closer to being drunk. She cannot remember the last time she drank so much, but she knows she needs to limit herself before she gets sick. Even knowing she will have a bad hangover tomorrow, it feels worth it.

"I can't believe we did it," says Noah. He reaches into his pants pocket and takes out the freshly written check made out to the school. A chuckle escapes his mouth as he holds up the check. "This small piece of paper will change so many lives." He looks over at Emma, giving her that smile. "All it took was having the right partner, acting like buffoons, and beating out a Fortune 500 CEO and two ex-NBA players. In all seriousness, thank you. You are the reason why I have this in my hands."

"Just so you know, I did it for the kids," Emma says teasingly.

"Oh! Not for me?" Noah places a hand to his chest, as if Emma struck him with a knife, then giggles like a child, the alcohol clearly affecting him as well. "You should stop by my classroom next week," he says after they've stopped laughing. "You can meet the kids, talk about the do-nation, and let them see the trophy. I think the kids would really like to meet you."

Whether it is from the alcohol, the high she is still on, or her blooming crush on Noah, she doesn't spare a moment to respond. "I think that's a great idea. I would really love that."

Noah's cheeks start to turn a deep pink, either from the cold air, the alcohol, or from blushing. "Awesome," says Noah as he sheepish-ly looks down at his feet with a grin on his face.

They both stare at each other for what could have been minutes or hours. But it is not an awkward stare; it is as if they are both seeing each other for the first time, taking in the presence of each other.

Eventually, a puzzled look comes onto Noah's face. "Has anyone ever told you that you look like Jolene?"

Emma shakes her head. "Should I know who Jolene is?"

Playfully shocked, Noah places a hand on Emma's arm. "You don't know who *Jolene* is? Don't steal my man, Jolene? Have ivory skin and bright auburn hair, Jolene?"

Then it suddenly clicks in her head. "Ah, you mean Dolly Parton's Jolene? No, no one has ever said that to me. I've been called Princess Merida more times than I'd like to admit, though."

Noah scrunches his face in disagreement. "You may have the same eyes, but your hair is completely different. Hers is more of a lion's mane of flaming bright red hair, while yours is tamed, lighter, elegant like a sunset. You definitely have the same bravery as Merida, I will give them that."

Emma doesn't know what to say. No one has ever said such wonderful things about her and directly to her, especially someone of the opposite sex to whom she is indeed attracted. Bravery would not be on her list of her personal characteristics. She cannot even recall a situation where she's been brave in her life.

"I don't know about that," she says with a snort. "I don't think I have any ounce of bravery in my body. I'm more of a passive, go-with-the-flow kind of gal."

Noah grabs the bottle of champagne, taking another sip. "Could have fooled me. You have to have some bravery to do what you did down there. And you did help when you sensed something was wrong on the night George died. Not everyone would have done what you did."

"I would say that was more stupidity than bravery on my part," Emma retorts. "I mean, everyone knows not to go through open doors that strange men have run frantically out of. That's like Scary Movie 101 on what *not* to do."

"It may have been slightly foolish, but it still shows you have compassion and courage to help someone in need."

Emma's cheeks blush as she smiles sheepishly instead of saying thank you, feeling too self-conscious to accept those kind words said about her. She leans back on the bench, resting her head on the wall behind them, and looks up at the stars. "Did you know that it was a burglary gone wrong? George died because someone broke into his house when they didn't think that someone was home. Can you imagine? Simply being in the wrong place at the wrong time or having just really bad luck."

She can feel Noah shrugging, as he too leans back and looks up at the sky. "It really isn't like how they show it on TV; the real reason why the victim died is usually less exciting than what we have envisioned. It's scary to think that something like George's death could happen to any of us." Noah looks over at Emma. "I mean, look what happened to you: it was just a normal Friday for you, and fate just happened to make you the person who had to suffer through that." It's certainly an empathetic remark, but Emma wonders if Noah is talking more from personal experience rather than making a simple observation. Maybe thinking about his father's death, leaving Emma to wonder if his dad died suddenly, or even tragically, like George did.

Emma feels her head start to throb from all the drinks she has had, and it becomes clear that having a deep conversation about her trauma is not a good idea. Instead, Emma changes the subject to a random thought that occurred due to thinking about death while also not having her usual filter activated, thanks to the alcohol. "In my next life, I want to be a dog."

Noah turns his head to look at her profile, looking amusingly perplexed. "How come?"

Emma shrugs nonchalantly. "I would be pampered my entire life, and the only thing I would feel is unconditional love." She turns to meet his gaze. "Who wouldn't want that?"

Noah smiles. "A sociopath, when you put it that way."

Suddenly, Emma giggles as if Noah said the most hilarious thing in the planet, the alcohol clearly doing its work on her. Noah too starts to laugh along with her, caught up in her contagious laughter. Tears of laughter flow down her cheeks, and she fans her face to dry them.

"I'm not sure why I'm laughing," she says in between gasps. "Nothing we said was funny."

Noah lifts the now-empty champagne bottle from the floor, examining it. His eyes bulge in shocked horror. "We're drunk," he proclaims. They look at each other and burst into laughter once more. Without even realizing it, the gap between them closes, the side of their bodies touching slightly. Emma lays her head on top of Noah's shoulder, laughing with happy tears. Oxygen fights to get into her lungs as she tries to take giant gulps of air.

"I like you, Emma," says Noah once they collect themselves.

"I like you too," replies Emma.

"I'd like to see more of you."

Emma lifts her head from his shoulder and looks at him with a teasing smile on her face. "You're in luck, you get to see me tomorrow."

Noah nudges her knee with his. "Not just tomorrow. But after that, too."

"Oh," is all she can reply with, surprised by his interest in her, something she has never experienced before.

He leans his head slightly toward her. "Is that alright?"

"Oh, yes! Sorry…" A nervous blush forms on her cheeks, and Emma silently curses herself for being embarrassing and awkward, even while drunk. She looks over at Noah and sees she is not the only one with pink hues on her face.

Noah peers up at her and gives her that smile she is starting to crave. "Good."

A phone dings, breaking up their moment. Emma knows the sound did not come from her phone; she always leaves it on vibrate, and there is no one who would be texting her this late at night. Another ding chimes, and she realizes that it is coming from her, specifically the jacket she is wearing.

"Um… I think it's yours," she says, nudging Noah on the arm. She flips over the lapel of his jacket, revealing the hidden pocket on the right side. Noah grabs for his phone and looks at who texted him.

"Oh, it's just my mom," he says while unlocking his phone screen, laughing to himself, then places it into his pants pocket. "She has a habit of sending me pictures of baked items she is trying out. Doesn't matter if it flops or not, she still sends me a report." A laugh escapes his mouth as he shakes his head. "Tonight was raspberry cheesecake, and she managed to burn the top while the inside stayed soggy."

"Oh my god, I completely forgot!" exclaims Emma as she rushes to stand up.

"What?" asks Noah frantically.

"I promised your mom that I would send her a picture of me in her dress." Emma reaches for her clutch and takes out her phone.

"Wait, that's my *mom's* dress?"

Emma nods. "She was kind enough to let me wear it tonight since I had no other options…"

"Wow… I… can't even imagine her wearing something so…"

"Revealing?"

"I was going to say glamorous," he says with that smile and left dimple showing. "Come, let's send her a picture of us with our lovely new trophy. She'll get a kick that we both were here tonight." Emma puts her phone in selfie mode and places it on the bench. She sets the timer for ten seconds and rushes to stand next to Noah, with his left arm cradling their trophy and his right one placed around her waist. She leans into him and hopes that he doesn't feel her erratically beating heart.

Of course, it is in this perfect moment that her brain betrays her by sparking a thought that makes Emma's stomach turn. Instead of thinking about how he is just inches away from her and his hand is now resting on her waist, she thinks about how she knows what his mom is going through and he doesn't. Emma doesn't like to keep secrets, and now that it looks like she will be seeing more of Noah, she doesn't like that she knows something that could also affect him in some way. But she knows that this isn't her secret to tell, no matter how much she wants to. If it weren't for all she had to drink, her stomach wouldn't be feeling this unsettled and queasy.

Before she knows it, the flash flares, and the picture is taken, blinding her for a few seconds and jolting her away from her trance. They both head toward her phone, checking to see if it looks presentable to send. "Let's hope we don't look as drunk as we feel," says Emma, as she opens her Photos app. "You know what," she says as they both look at the picture, "we actually look pretty good." Emma looks over her shoulder and didn't realize how close Noah was to her, practically resting his head on her shoulder. She notices how easy it is for them to enter one another's personal space, as if it's almost instinctual behavior.

"Is it okay for me to send it to her?" she asks.

He nods. "Can you send it to me too?"

"Is this your way of asking for my number?" she asks teasingly, feeling bold by his sudden proximity.

"Maybe…" he says, shrugging like a child caught snacking before dinner.

Emma takes his phone and adds her number to his contacts but saves it under a name she hopes he finds charming and witty.

He laughs out loud once he sees what she entered herself as. "That's a good one." He texts her so she has his number. "I don't know about you, but I'm freezing my butt off. Want to head back inside?"

Eagerly, she nods and follows him as they make their way down the stairs, the heat from the building slowly warming up her body once more. Emma finds her dad back in the ballroom and gives him the head nod, signaling to him that they can go home. Noah helps her carry her things to the car waiting for them by the Plaza's entrance and even helps her to get in the car, saving Winnie's dress from being damaged by her drunken negligence.

"Goodnight, Mr. Callahan," says Noah as he leans toward the open passenger window, peering in to see Oliver sitting on the other side.

"Pleasure to meet you, Noah. See you…" Oliver looks down at his watch, "later today actually. Congratulations again on winning."

Noah looks down at Emma, "Good night. Thank you again for being the best partner."

Emma tries to contain her drunken thoughts and the blush forming on her cheeks, as the last thing she needs is to embarrass herself, and in front of her dad too. "Anytime, partner," is the best she could come up with. She leans her head against the closed window as the car drives down the street, hiding her grinning face from her dad. In so many ways, this night went much better than she thought it would. Looks like she'll have to thank her mom for making her go.

As the car hits the first stop light, not even a block away from the Plaza, Emma feels her phone buzz in her hand. Looking down at the screen, she sees a text from the person she was hoping it would be.

1:34 a.m.

Noah: :)

Emma: I can still see you! The Uber hasn't gone that far yet lol

Noah: Just wanted to make sure I had the right number. You could have given me a fake one.

Emma: I'm def too drunk to come up with 10 random digits. You think too highly of my intoxicated brain :)

Noah: I hope I'm gonna remember your contact name in the morning…

Emma: Nah, you won't be able to forget that, drunk or not lol. How many other Jolene's have you met in your life?

Noah: You are the first…

Emma: HA! Case proven

Noah: Smh

2:05 a.m.

Noah: I hope our hangovers aren't too dreadful tomorrow. I don't want to show up at dinner feeling and looking like utter death.

Emma: At least we will both feel like death together. You better take good care of our trophy! Make sure to make it the highlight of your place. In its full blobbiness glory.

Noah: It's an ugly monstrosity that needs to be hidden from humanity. I noticed you left it for me to take home, thank you very much. I see how the parental rights of our trophy are going to be, Jolene : (

Emma: Us Jolenes only take your man. That trophy is all yours to keep :)

Noah: LOL. Goodnight, Emma. I'll see you tomorrow :)

Emma: Sweet dreams Noah.

March 19, 1989

My Dearest Mémé,

I'm happy to tell you that I am now more than halfway through the first draft of my story.

I've been falling into bouts of losing confidence in myself. Despite your words of encouragement and Fossettes', I still have trouble thinking that I'm good enough for this. It's also been hard to find the time to write. I wish I didn't have to spend so much of my time at the club or prepping/hosting a dinner party at home. It's all so repetitive, over and over again, not one is any different than the last. Mon dieu!

Every time I slip on that housewife persona, I feel the life draining out of me. My patience is getting so thin with the club, the company, even Russel—especially now that I have found something of my own to be proud of. I still don't think it would be a good idea to tell Russel about the story I'm writing. It would only lead him to be outraged that I'm not giving all my energy to him and the club.

I know you must be wondering what on earth the story is about, since I'm writing it so feverishly. Well, it's about true love. As I suspect you must be wondering if this story is based on true events, I must say that it is. It's a story based on my own life.

As you have cautioned me in your last letter, I fell right into my own trap and fallen hopelessly in love with Fossettes. I think I've been falling since I first laid eyes on him. But I knew when he gifted me the first edition copy of Winnie-the-Pooh that there was no doubt about the unconditional love I have for this man.

This isn't just some distraction since my marriage is falling apart. No. I know that what I'm feeling is real, as this is very different from when I 'fell' for Russel. Night and day, as you would say. Nothing has ever felt so right in my entire life, and I can't allow myself to let this slip away.

I know you must be on the edge of your seat, wondering if I took any action on my feelings. Initially, I listened to what you said to me a few months ago, to give my marriage with Russel time to get back on course. But now... how can I wait, after finding out what true and unconditional love feels like? I took that step, or really, that jump. You know how writers describe love as this out-of-body, almost ethereal, feeling? An electrical shock that both jolts and warms you at the same time? That's exactly what it felt like when Fossettes finally kissed me a few weeks ago. I've been feeling that high every day since.

I know I should feel guilt and shame for cheating on Russel. But the man I once loved disappeared ages ago. It was the moment he decided that his career was worth forsaking this marriage that ruined us, not the moment I fell in love with someone else.

I know that Fossettes is just as serious as I am about us, without a doubt. I've started to look up divorce lawyers. Yes, Mémé, it is that serious that I am looking for a divorce attorney. Just know that I am not rushing or acting without reason nor am I being pressured into leaving Russel. All of this is my doing and my idea alone. You raised me to not be foolish and naïve, so I discuss all of this with Fossettes, and we have come up with a plan. Our first step is to get an attorney and file the papers. I will keep you posted on this, as I know that there are a lot of things that can possibly go wrong.

Ma mère called me the other day. I am not at all surprised my parents are moving back to France. I knew by the sounds of their voices when we talked last year how homesick they are. It's just fitting that they decided to do this now. If they had decided to do this five years ago, I would have been going with them. I even thought about flying out there with them so I could see you. But of course, the week that they are leaving, Russel and the company have a big dinner party that is only with the top architects and their top clients. As I need to be on my best behavior until the divorce papers are filed, I need to do my part and be there. But I truly want to see you. I too miss Martigues desperately. How does September or October sound for me to visit?

Missing you and our Côte Bleue.

Ton petit soleil,

Winnie

P.S. Fossettes suggested I should add cardamom with black tea, cinnamon, and honey. It's such a wonderful spicy kick to it! I'm now calling it 'Sweet and Spicy.'

Chapter Eleven

Emma wakes up the next morning with a raging hangover. Her head throbs, and her body feels heavy and stiff, every cell in her body aching. Too afraid to move her head, Emma lies still on her bed like a zombie. She wants to move her hair away from her face, but it will hurt to move her arm. Her bedroom door opens wider, with small patters of pawed feet clacking on her floor. She suddenly feels extra weight on her back.

"Sadie..." she groans into her pillow.

She feels Sadie's snout nudge the back of her head. Groaning, Emma finally moves, and when she turns over to face Sadie, she is instantly met with kisses on her face. She wipes her wet face with her raggedy t-shirt and stares up at her ceiling. Slowly, the events of last night come crawling back into her mind, and with each one she falls further into disbelief. Drunk Emma is fearless and not bashful, especially around men she is very much attracted to.

Her heart rushes in her chest in a panic as she is reminded that he will be coming over tonight. To her house. To have dinner with her and her parents.

Emma grabs one of her pillows and plops it on top of her face. "I can't believe he is going to be here tonight with my parents. How is hungover me going to be able to handle this?" she says to herself.

She hears a whine coming from Sadie and looks down at her, lying on the foot of her bed. Emma reaches down to scratch Sadie's head. "If only I were you. Then all my responsibilities would only be looking adorable and being the best cuddler ever."

Emma looks at the time. Even though she could lie in bed for a bit longer, she decides to get up and take a hot shower to wipe away the alcohol sitting on her pores. Once freshly clean, her wet curls set, she heads downstairs to get something into her system.

She can hear her mom in the kitchen, preparing for the meal she will be making for their dinner party tonight. At the top of the staircase, Emma can hear the clanking of pots and pans being moved about along with faint grunts coming from her mom. In the kitchen, Emma makes herself a cup of coffee with the Keurig, even though what she really wants is a cup of Winnie's French press coffee.

"Your dad told me you won the competition last night. Sounds like you ended up having fun then?" says Abigail as she peers her head out from the bottom cabinet, with a hint of 'I told you so' in her voice, just enough to rub it in without being too in Emma's face.

Emma leans against the countertop next to where her mom is kneeling and takes a sip of coffee. "Yes, you were right. I ended up having fun."

"Noah was there too?" asks Abigail, a bit too curiously.

"Yeah, he teaches at Westview Charter, one of the schools that the firm selected for their donation. He ended up going as one of the representatives of the school."

"What a small world… Him showing up at your dad's event, you being there too. Life works in strange ways, especially here in New York." Abigail leans out from the cabinet with a deep pan in her hands. "Ah, found it."

"You're making your famous mascarpone pesto pasta?"

"I mean, everyone loves pasta and pesto, right?" Abigail asks.

"Mom, I am sure they will love whatever you make."

"Do you mind stopping at Neal's and getting us a bottle of Chardonnay?"

Emma lifts up her coffee mug. "Once I feel slightly less hungover. Noah and I may have taken some shots of tequila during the competition and drank a bottle of champagne to celebrate our win." Her face contorts into a wince, preparing herself for the lecture she will get from Abigail.

But instead, Emma sees a grin forming on her mom's face. "I'm happy you two had a good time. Sometimes we need to let loose. Are you hungry? Do you want me to make you some eggs and toast?"

Just the thought of food makes Emma's stomach churn. "Eh, maybe by lunch I can eat something."

"You still think the pasta is a good idea?" Abigail asks again, second-guessing.

Emma laughs. "Yes, I promise it will be more than fine."

Abigail nods to herself. "Oh, and I can make some chicken for protein and get a fresh loaf of baguette at Whole Foods… Or maybe I should do ciabatta…" she continues to say to herself in deep thought, with her hand pressed to her cheek.

Emma shakes her head but understands her mother's uneasiness. She knows she would be overthinking just as much if she were to host.

But in a way, I am hosting the dinner too.

Suddenly, her anxiety creeps up, a feeling she knows too well. She wants her parents to like Winnie and Noah just as much as she does, as they are people she wants to have in her life. She hopes that Winnie and Noah enjoy her family's company too.

Oh god, what if my parents and Winnie don't get along?

No, Emma, we must not think of the worst-case scenario first. They will all like each other and tonight will be as amazing as I hope it will.

Before she can second-guess herself further, she pushes away her thoughts about tonight. She tells herself she won't even allow herself to think about it until the Reynards are actually at their front door. That way, she must go through with it.

It will all be fine…

She repeats that in her head several times as she goes about her day. While picking out her outfit in her room. *It will all be fine.* Walking over to Neal's Wine Shop to get a bottle of Chardonnay. *It will all be fine.* Even when she is sitting on her built-in window bench, with her new notebook on her lap, trying to write another poem but coming up empty. *It will all be fine.*

But will it? Frustrated and annoyed at herself, Emma slams the notebook shut and rubs her forehead to prevent a migraine from forming.

She feels her phone buzz by her foot and grabs it. Her face lights up after seeing who it is.

Noah: How is your hangover treating you?

Giddiness suddenly sweeps over her, and she finds herself smiling uncontrollably.

Emma: As long as I don't move my head too quickly, I'm all good.

She sees the three dots pop up after she hits send. A green flag. Nothing is worse than someone who feels like they must wait a certain amount of time to respond to someone, especially someone they are into. Either Noah doesn't care to follow those rules, or he doesn't like her in that way. Emma hopes that it is the former. She feels her phone buzz and reads his text.

Noah: I have not left my bed at all today…

He sends her a picture, a clear view of their crystal trophy resting on top of his nightstand, the afternoon sunlight directly hitting the backdrop of the trophy, giving it a halo glow. She is already typing away her response, forgoing the need to orchestrate a reply that sounds cool, witty, or flirty. For the first time, she doesn't overthink it.

Emma: At least you are in good company.

And if she thought that her heart was thumping, then it fully jumped, leaped, and soared out of her chest once she read his instant response.

Noah: I will be later. ☺

He is flirting with me, right? Or am I reading his friendliness as something else?

Before she could doubt even more, Noah sends another message clarifying what she was thinking.

Noah: I meant by seeing you later.

She giggles to herself, feeling foolish for doubting and now at ease with herself once more. Noah's act of reassurance shows her that he is being open about his interest in her. Something she never has experienced before. Usually, it's coy indifference; don't say too much too soon or you will scare them away. But this time, it's nice to know someone has the same amount of interest in her she has in him from the get-go.

Her lingering nausea and migraine from her hangover eventually disappear in time for the dinner. With an hour left until their arrival, Emma sits and waits for them to show up.

It will all be fine.

Chapter Twelve

The night is not going as planned.

Of all nights, tonight is the night that Sadie decides to jump on the kitchen island and steal the whole baguette that Abigail bought at Whole Foods, leaving Sadie to lie motionless on the living room floor, her gluttonous belly swollen. The vet said she will be all right, just wait for her bloated belly to subside and make sure she still behaves as she normally does.

On top of that, Oliver was called into the office to help clean up a mess in a case one of his associates is working on. For the past hour, Emma has been looking at the time. As it gets closer and closer to seven, she wonders if her dad will make it back before Winnie and Noah show up. It doesn't really matter if it's just Emma and Abigail; she doesn't think the Reynards' would mind. But it feels off to her if her dad doesn't show up to a dinner her mom and he are hosting.

Before she can send her dad a quick text about his ETA, the doorbell rings.

Crap.

Emma and Abigail make their way to the front door, opening it with a gust of cold air hitting their faces. Emma puts on a smile, trying to hide her slight apprehension, not letting the Sadie incident or her dad's delay ruin what could be a perfectly good evening. Once she opens the door, they see Winnie standing in the middle of the top step, with Noah lingering behind on her left. A white box rests in Winnie's hands, showing she knows the rule to never show up empty-handed when invited over to someone's home.

"Welcome," says Abigail, "please come in." Emma gives them both a hug as they enter her house, then introduces them to her mother and vice versa.

Emma tries to calm herself. Seeing Winnie and Noah in her house causes her heart to beat rapidly. She takes an unnoticeable breath to calm down and smiles at them both. "I can take your coats," she offers. "And please don't worry about your shoes. We don't mind if they are on or off." She sneaks a look at Noah and feels at ease once more. The smile on his face is enough to give her some encouragement.

"I brought dessert," says Winnie. "I hope you all like cheesecake."

"What New Yorker doesn't?" says Abigail as she takes the box from Winnie. "Thank you. That was very sweet of you. I'll go put this in the fridge." Abigail makes her way to the kitchen, leaving Emma alone with the two of them. She suddenly feels like a child, waiting for her parents to come back to the checkout line at the grocer when they ran off to grab eggs. She has never had her own company over as guests. Although this is her mom's idea and her parents' house, she still feels like she is the true host of this dinner, being the bridge between the two parties.

"Would you like anything to drink? We have wine, soda, or water?" she offers.

"Oh, wine would be lovely," says Winnie. "Noah, would you like one too?"

Remembering the night they just had, Emma already knows he will say no.

"Water would be great, thank you," he says.

Emma motions for them to follow her as she heads further into the house. They take a seat in the family room, while Emma gathers the drinks.

"You didn't mention that Noah was cute," whispers Abigail to Emma in the kitchen.

"Yea, he is..." she says, blushing while uncorking the wine bottle.

The pinkening of her cheeks does not go unnoticed. "Oh, you like him!" exclaims Abigail.

Flustered, Emma shushes her mom to keep her voice down, which makes Abigail giggle in giddiness, excited by the news of Emma's crush on Noah. "Mom, please… They might hear you," Emma peeks at the family room, checking to see if they are indeed listening. So far, they are good.

Abigail presses a finger to her lips, trying to contain her excitement. "I'm sorry, I can't help myself." She takes a deep breath to compose herself. "We will definitely be talking more about this later. Come, we need to go back before they start to wonder where we went off to." The two walk back to the family room, Emma carrying a glass of wine and a cup of water.

"I hope your journey here wasn't too hectic," jokes Abigail, taking a seat opposite the Reynards on the loveseat.

"We did hit a bit of traffic along the sidewalk," says Noah, carrying on the joking theme of the conversation, making the others laugh out loud.

"I'd like to apologize for my husband's absence on his behalf," says Abigail. "He got dragged into a case at the firm and hopes to be back any moment to join us."

"That's alright. Sometimes when duty calls, we can't say no," says Winnie as she takes a sip of wine. She looks around the family room, taking in her surroundings. "You have a lovely home, Abigail. You picked the right neighborhood, too."

"West Village is the best village as we say," jokes Abigail.

"Speaking of our village," says Winnie, "did you see on the news that the police charged the man they arrested on that night?"

Emma shakes her head. "I didn't hear that, but it's a relief to know they were able to charge him."

"Well, thank goodness," says Abigail. "We can finally put this whole thing behind us and bring some peace back to the neighborhood."

Just as soon as it was brought up, the death of George Krueger is pushed aside, stamped with a red 'closed' on its case folder. Soon enough, everyone in the neighborhood will have forgotten all about it.

Emma is ready to push it aside herself.

Abigail turns to Emma. "Why don't you bring out some bread and cheese for us to munch on? And check on the pasta too, please."

Emma nods and stands up.

"I'll help you," says Noah, standing up to join her.

A shy grin rests on Emma's face, as she tries to contain it from being visible to everyone. "Thank you, I'd appreciate the help."

Abigail gives her a wink and an excited smile as Emma turns around.

If Noah doesn't know that I like him, then definitely by tonight he will. Hell, even Winnie will know too. No thanks to Mom.

"I don't know about you, but this feels a little weird," whispers Noah as he follows Emma to the kitchen.

"I know, right?" Emma grabs the oven mitts and takes the bread out of the oven, placing it on the island to cool off. "At first when my mom suggested dinner, I thought, 'Yeah, sure, why not?' But after last night, having you both here feels off-putting." She looks up at Noah and gives him a reassuring smile. "Don't get me wrong, it's not that I don't want you here. It's that having you here, with my mom and your mom…" She leans in closer and whispers, "Feels like we're doing a meet-the-parents kind of situation."

Noah raises his left eyebrow, giving her that smile. "You caught me. My plan all along was to ask your father for your hand in marriage tonight."

A snort comes out of Emma's mouth, making Noah laugh with her. Playfully, she punches him in the arm. "Oh my god, please don't say that out loud. My mom will take you seriously."

Feeling their mothers' eyes on them, Emma and Noah look over at them in the family room, forcing them to look away as they were obviously talking about them too. The women soon restart their lively conversation, looking like they are two friends catching up.

"Do you think they heard me?" asks Noah, as they cut the toasted baguette into small pieces.

"Probably not. But by the looks they just gave us, something tells me they were already plotting." Emma doesn't hear Sadie's paws tap along the kitchen tile, forcing her to jump in alarm when she feels her cold, wet nose nudge her on the arm, her way of asking for food.

"Sades, no. Your stomach literally was about to explode an hour ago. How can you be hungry after eating a loaf of bread?"

Emma looks up at Noah when she hears him giggling. "What's so funny?" she asks, laughing along with him. She can't help herself when she sees him smile and laugh; it forces her to do the same thing.

He shakes his head. "Nothing, it's just cute how you talk to her like that."

Emma tries to contain her blushing cheeks as they head back to the family room with their version of a charcuterie board, not wanting to give substantial evidence to support Winnie and her mom's romance conspiracy on her and Noah. Although they are right that a potential romance is blooming, whatever this is with Noah has barely begun, and the last thing Emma needs is meddling mothers secretly planning a wedding.

I just hope tonight doesn't end up being a turn-off for Noah.

Conversations start flowing, an ease spreading among all of them, as if they have done this before. Abigail thanks Winnie several times for looking after Emma, Winnie makes a few remarks about psychology that spur a lively dialogue between her and Abigail, and Noah charms Emma's mom with compliments and jokes. Before she knows it, Emma is calm, enjoying herself and feeling hopeful that the night will end successfully. She feels stupid for being worried that the night could turn sour.

It isn't until her dad comes strolling into the house from the office that the night takes a strange turn.

When Oliver steps into the family room to say hello, Emma notices a shift in Winnie's expression. It is barely noticeable, but Emma can see the quick panic inside Winnie's eyes and her smile quivering into a tense frown. Just as quickly as the expression comes, her face shifts into a forced smile. Emma quickly looks over to Noah to see if he noticed as well, but he is already standing up to greet her dad. She looks over to her mom and sees that she is in the kitchen, checking on the food. Leaving Emma to be the only one who could have noticed it.

Emma starts to doubt herself, questioning if she made up the quick change in Winnie's face once she saw her dad. She looks over at Winnie, now shaking hands with her dad, and does not see any of the panic or tension she thought she saw before. Emma decides to brush it off and blame it on her imaginative mind for the sake of the rest of the night.

"Everything alright?" Emma asks Oliver, as they all make their way to the dining room to have dinner.

Oliver nods curtly. "Oh, you know, just some good old Wall Street lawsuits."

Abigail plates the food in pasta bowls, with a small side salad next to each bowl. The sight of the green pesto and sundried tomatoes makes everyone's stomach rumble in hunger. There is truth to how presentation is equally as important as the taste of the food. Abigail is even using their best kitchenware tonight.

"This looks wonderful," says Noah as they all take their seats. Emma lingers behind, allowing the guests and her parents to take their seats first. Winnie sits next to her mom at the end of the table and beside Noah, allowing Emma to take the seat opposite Noah and next to her dad on the other end of the table.

Emma steals quick glances at Winnie during dinner, analyzing her every move and facial expression. A little pin-prick feeling stabs the bottom of her stomach, her gut telling her that something is off, but she cannot figure out what. She thinks back to the look Winnie had when her dad finally arrived, wondering what could cause Winnie to change her expression for a split second.

For most of the meal, Noah and Oliver discuss Westview Charter and how he plans to use the money, leaving Winnie and Abigail to chat between themselves on the other end of the table and shutting Emma out of either discussion. She tries to listen to either conversation as she eats her meal silently.

"So, Oliver, what kind of law do you practice?" asks Winnie, once both separate conversations come to an end. Emma tries to contain her slight shock; this is the first time since they sat down that Winnie talked directly to her dad.

"I mainly deal with corporate law," replies Oliver, "but as technology has grown to be a much more complex system in our lives, exposing the grey area of law that does not protect citizens' rights, I am focusing more on privacy law."

"Do you handle cases that deal with people making deepfakes of celebrities or political leaders?" asks Noah, intrigued.

Oliver nods while taking a sip of beer. "That's exactly the type of cases we are branching into. Photoshop, deepfakes, those are all new issues that everybody will deal with in one way or another. As technology advances and becomes more complex, so does the law in having to ensure the protection of people's privacy and safety."

"Did you start out in corporate law?" asks Winnie. Confused, Emma tries to understand Winnie's sudden interest in her dad's law career. She's been disengaged during the entire dinner besides talking to Abigail, so why does she decide now to speak up—and about her dad's career of all things?

"No, I started as an associate in the nineties at a firm that handles family law," says Oliver.

Winnie nods and looks down to resume eating the rest of her meal. She quickly flips back to the quiet version of herself, making only a few comments here and there to Abigail. Emma takes a mental note of the strangeness of that whole interaction, wanting to get Noah's perspective on it. If he thinks the same as she does, then something must have happened during dinner to make Winnie act so unlike herself.

Before the conversation transforms into an awkward silence that would make every inch of Emma's skin crawl, she decides to further discuss the events of last night, hoping to create a lively end to the dinner.

But as Emma describes their narrow victory, she notices that Winnie's responses are short or timid. She says barely anything to further the conversation, only contributing when it's expected of her to respond. A completely different person is sitting with them compared to the Winnie who was chatting chummily to Abigail not too long ago. Emma looks at her parents; they don't seem to notice Winnie's strange behavior. But how could they? This is their first time meeting her. Regardless, it is still a strange way for any guest to behave with their hosts.

Emma glances at Noah, and his eyes finally meet hers. Her eyes quickly dart to Winnie and back, silently asking him what is going on with her. He looks puzzled, not about what Emma is asking, but about not knowing why his mom is acting this way. He lightly shrugs, barely noticeable to anyone else. Emma can feel the tension in her stomach start to loosen; someone else has noticed the same thing she is seeing. It's all not in her head.

When they all finish eating, Emma volunteers to clean up the dishes. Noah, as if reading her mind, offers to help her.

"Am I the only one who noticed how your mom completely changed during dinner?" whispers Emma while she washes the dishes in the sink, handing them to Noah to dry. "Did my mom or dad say something that could have upset her?"

Emma feels Noah shaking his head. "I'm just as lost as you." Noah pauses, drying the plate he is currently wiping down. Emma takes a side glance at him, seeing that he is staring off into the distance at the plate, as if he is lost in thought. Then suddenly he shakes his head to himself, pushing aside whatever he had going on inside his head briefly.

"What?" asks Emma.

"It's just that she seemed totally normal earlier. Then once we sat down to eat, it's as if a different person was sitting with us," says Noah.

"I was thinking the same thing," says Emma. She lets out her frustration on the pasta bowl she is cleaning, scrubbing hard to wipe away the remaining pesto sauce on the surface. "I've been thinking back to tonight's conversations, and nothing is coming to mind that seemed to be a sensitive topic. If someone said or did anything that upset her, I want to know so I can apologize. But I can't do that if I don't know what caused it."

Her fingers are starting to prune and her fingernails are weakening from the intense scrubbing. The sound of the running water puts her in a trance, sending her deep into the abyss of her mind to put together a viable explanation for Winnie's sudden change.

She lists out what she does know, the evidence she has. It's indisputable that Winnie was her usual self when she arrived and while chatting in the family room. All Emma knows is that the shift started when her dad got home.

Her dad… Oliver… O…

Emma drops the dish to the bottom of the sink, splashing soap bubbles and water onto her jeans and sweater. It was just a silly idea that had no validity at all—just her imagination running wild. But the actual possibility of her dad being 'O', sends her into a shock. Winnie and her dad not only may have known each other in the past, but they may have been romantically involved too. Emma shakes her head to herself, not wanting to believe that the world can be this small and coincidental. She wants to believe that this is what happens when you read too many books; you come up with wild, outlandish ideas where you lose yourself, all for it to end up being so far from the real truth.

But can my dad really be 'O'?

It takes her a second to realize that she feels a slight pressure on top of her hand. Looking down, she sees Noah's hand resting on top of hers, signaling her to stop. Stop cleaning. Stop thinking. "I promise there was nothing either you or your parents said that was uncalled for," says Noah.

Emma looks worriedly at him, wanting to believe that all of this could just be from some misunderstanding. "You promise?"

He nods. "I know how close you two are getting and how important you are to each other. I would let you know if there was anything said or done that could jeopardize that."

A sigh escapes out of Emma's mouth as she looks back towards the dining room where she hears low voices talking. "So, how do we figure out what has agitated her so much?"

"Only one way to find out," says Noah.

Emma looks back at him with a quizzical look on her face. "And what's that?"

"We ask her ourselves."

May 11th, 1989

My Dearest Mémé,

Everything has gone terribly wrong.

First, the law firm I mentioned in my last letter declined to work with me before I even stepped foot in their building. Just from hearing my name and Russel's, they didn't want to get involved with my case. They told me that we are prohibited from working with any law firm besides the one my husband's company has on retainer. How can I go to his company's lawyers and ask them to help me divorce my husband, who is their priority client? I can't! The company designed it so that the wives truly are stuck, left defenseless, and helpless.

But that is not the worst of it. Not even close.

Last week, Russel was on a work trip to Los Angeles. He was supposed to be gone all week. Using this time of having a truly empty house and thinking it was safe, I brought home my manuscript pages. Oh Mémé! I was foolish! The one time I let my guard down, everything exploded into a million pieces.

Russel came home from his trip three days earlier than planned. I was meeting with Fossettes in the middle of the afternoon, wanting to get his opinion on an idea I had for my story. Naturally, it was during that time that Russel came home, finding all my manuscript pages that I carelessly left out on the dining room table.

Mémé...he read <u>everything</u>.

It was easy for him to connect the dots of what's been going on. The pages had Fossettes' comments all over them, even his endearing notes of encouragement. Reading those comments, along with the theme of my story, provided no doubt that I've been having an affair.

Russel played clueless when I got home later that evening, so I had no idea that he had found them. Then a few days later, he confronted me and told me that he knew about Fossettes and me. Once he read those pages, he hired a private investigator to follow me. Foolishly, I thought I had just lucked out with him not seeing the pages. But no—my dumb; foolish self went back to the park and Fossettes' place like an idiot. I led him right into everything, handing it to him on a silver platter. Now Russel knows <u>everything</u> about my affair.

And my story? Russel burned all the pages. All of my work... my love story... is now gone. Forever.

He was so enraged when he confronted me, Mémé. But the saddest thing of all was that he was more worried, even terrified, about the company finding out than what this would do to us. He's convinced that this would diminish his chances of making senior principal. 'If I never knew what my wife was doing right under my nose, then how are they going to believe in me as a partner, Winnie?' When he yelled that at me, that was when I knew that his career, the company, will always be the priority. It was never me. Not our marriage. I was always a pawn in his game to convince the company that he is principal material. And that required him to have a loving and devoted wife.

Oh, how I desperately want to be encircled in Fossettes' comforting arms. But Russel demanded that I put an end to it. Even threatening to 'have him dealt with' if I ever see him again, never mind trying to run away with him. Russel will never admit it, but he needs me. He needs me to continue with his game. He will do whatever it takes to make sure that he gets what he wants, even if that means threatening me.

Now I have no choice but to do what Russel wants. To protect the love of my life, I must leave him and never see him again.

I mailed a letter to Fossettes this morning, breaking things off with him. I couldn't risk seeing him one last time, as that would only lead to devastation. To protect Fossettes, I had to make him believe that I never loved him, that our love was only a phase, a meaningless fling. I had to make him think that I decided to go back to Russel, that I realized I was making a mistake for leaving him and our marriage. I even made up a story about how we reconciled, and that Russel promised me that he would be a better husband. I told Fossettes all these cruel lies just so I knew that he would never try to reach me.

Breaking his heart and mine is the only way to protect his. And I would do anything to ensure his safety.

Oh Mémé...

I have truly lost everything I have ever loved. Everything but you.

Ton petit soleil,

Winnie

P.S. Do you have a tea blend that can cure a broken heart?

Chapter Thirteen

Emma feels a small hand pulling on the sleeve of her cardigan. In fact, it's the sixth small hand that's been on her arm, shoulder, or hand within the past hour. But there is something about this one that feels slightly different from the others. Peering down to her left, Emma sees a young girl with fiercely determined, yet patient, brown eyes staring up at her.

"Yes?" asks Emma.

"Can I hold the trophy, Miss Emma?" asks the young girl.

It isn't until now that Emma registers why this one felt different. This young girl wasn't one of the many in Noah's class who made a beeline to the trophy once Noah presented it to the class. Instead, this girl waited patiently on the side as the rest rushed to be the first ones to hold on to it.

Emma looks over at the rest of the class in the reading corner, huddling around Noah as he is re-telling them the story of their victorious win once more, even having some of the kids re-enact the challenges. Then she looks back down at the young girl who didn't follow the rest of the class to the reading corner but instead came up to Emma.

"Of course you can," says Emma. She reaches behind her to grab the trophy from Noah's desk and hands it to her.

"Thank you," says the girl as she rotates the blobbed figure, looking through each surface area of the translucent crystal.

"Don't you want to act out the story with the rest of your classmates?" asks Emma.

The young girl shakes her head as she flips the trophy completely upside down. "I was cast as Annie in this year's school play." The girl looks away from the trophy and toward her classmates, the room filled with boisterous laughter as the kids act along with Noah. The girl looks back up at Emma with a knowing look. "It wouldn't be fair for me to take the spotlight in the reading corner *and* be the lead role in *Annie*."

"That's very noble of you," says Emma, shocked by this young girl's self-awareness.

"My mommy says that arrogance won't get you anywhere in life. If I want to be a leader when I grow up, I'll have to learn to let others do things, even though I know I would be best for it." The young girl places the blob back onto Noah's desk and extends her hand out to Emma. "I'm Nia. Hall monitor, point guard, and the lead in *Annie*."

Emma takes Nia's hand and shakes it, surprised by the girl's firm grip. "I'm Emma. Friend of your teacher and co-owner of this wonderful trophy," she says as she places her other hand on top of the blob.

Nia leans forward to Emma, standing on her tippy toes as she whispers into her ear, "Don't tell Mr. Reynard, but the trophy is mad ugly."

A loud snort comes out of Emma, which she quickly tries to contain. Knowing she made Emma, the adult, laugh sends a wide grin onto Nia's face. Emma instantly smiles back at her, giggling along with their little secret. "Yes, it really is mad ugly."

"Can we keep it?" asks Nia.

"Oh, I don't know. You'll have to ask Mr. Reynard about that."

"Ask me about what?" asks Noah as he and the rest of the class make their way back to the front of the classroom, their re-telling concluded.

"Nia was asking me if the trophy can stay here in the classroom," says Emma. She raises her eyebrows, hoping to signal to Noah that this is a way out from having either one to keep the blob. The class goes into a cheerful uproar, as if they heard that the class is having a pizza party or no homework for a week.

"Oh! Can we, Mr. R.?" asks one of the boys behind Noah. Several 'yeah, can we?' soon echo across the room, the kids unanimously agreeing that this is the best idea ever.

Noah looks back at Emma and shrugs his shoulders. "Oh, I don't know. I really wanted to keep this," says Noah, going along with the charade. Boos can be heard around them. A wide smile shines on his face, along with that dimple, "What do you think, Miss Emma?"

Emma can feel the many eyes on her, feeling like she is in the spotlight. To the kids, she is their only hope to keep it. But little did they know, it was already theirs from the moment they first showed it to them. "Well, we did win this for them," she says to Noah, but loudly enough for the kids to hear. "So, I think it should stay here."

The class booms with cheers and jumps of glory. Emma laughs at how simple it is to make these kids happy. Yet she's also relieved to know that she doesn't have to worry about bringing the blob home with her. Looking at the clock on the wall, Emma knows she has exceeded her visit. The kids will need to get ready to pack up for the day soon. She looks over at Noah, gestures at the clock, and points to the door, signaling that she should go.

Following her point, Noah nods and turns back to the class. "Okay, class. It's time for Miss Emma to go." A wave of 'no's and 'aw's erupts. Noah, being used to the class's frequent displays of disappointment, ignores them. "Let's all give her a big 'thank you' for stopping by today."

The kids give her the loudest 'thank you', warming her heart. It is one thing to win the competition for them, but another to be able to learn the names and see the faces of the kids of Westview—it feels much more real to her. Seeing their excitement when Noah told them about the trips the class will get to go on and the class projects they can now do, it is unlike a feeling she has ever felt before. Knowing that she helped to be able to give these kids that joy—it is easily one of the best feelings in the world. If only she knew how to translate this feeling to her professional life. To utilize her access to billionaires and Fortune 500 companies to help those in need. But how?

Knowing she won't figure this out now, she gets ready to leave. As Emma puts on her hat and coat, a small hand shoots up into the air. "Yes, Carlo?" asks Noah.

"Will Miss Emma come with us to the planetarium?"

"That's a great question and a wonderful idea, Carlo," says Noah. He turns back around to look at Emma with a grin on his face. "Would Miss Emma like to come with us to the planetarium?"

Emma doesn't need to look at the dozens of doe-eyed kids. She doesn't even need another second to think. She already has her answer on the tip of her tongue. "I would love to."

The kids cheer once more. Never has she remembered a time when anyone, much less a group of children, was this excited that she would be joining them somewhere. Shaking her head in disbelief, she laughs to herself as Noah walks her to the classroom door. Emma can easily see why Noah would become a teacher. Just by being in these kids' presence, any sour mood she is in would be instantly lifted. If only she could have an instant mood lifter like that in her job. Emma turns back around once she is under the door's threshold and leans against the frame to take one last look at the class.

"I did mean it when I said that you are more than welcome to come with us," says Noah, leaning against the opposite side of the doorframe.

Emma moves her gaze back to Noah, searching those warm brown eyes. There's a look in them that she can't quite read. But if she had to guess, maybe it's happiness or even a look of captivation. The thought of her being the reason sends a rush of blood to her cheeks. Annoyed at her brain's betrayal, she looks down at their shoes, hoping the pinkened hues will die down in a second or two. "And I meant it when I said I would love to join you," she says to him, once she feels her cheeks are no longer cherry red.

A contagious grin spreads on Noah's face, looking like a kid on the last day of school before summer break. "The school's administration will need to approve it first for you to chaperone the trip. I'll give them a call now, and you can stop by on your way out to fill out the forms. You're heading over to my mom's after this?" he asks.

Time stops completely as dread instantly rushes from her head to her toes. For the past hour and a half, she had completely forgotten all about their plan. She and Noah decided that she should be the one to bring up Saturday night's dinner to Winnie since she is the bridge between the Reynards and the Callahans. Since she already had plans to stop by Winnie's today for another lesson, they figured there would be no better time to talk to her. Although Emma wishes she didn't have to do it, especially all alone, she knows that she must. For the sake of her endlessly ruminating imagination and her friendship with Winnie, she has to find out what happened.

Unable to say a word, she only nods.

Noah places a hand on her shoulder, comforting her in the manner appropriate for the audience around them. "There's nothing to worry about. I promise," says Noah.

But the voice in the back of her head yells otherwise.

Please, oh, please. I hope I am so wrong about the real reason why.

Fidgeting with the flap of her mittens, Emma walks along the sidewalk to Winnie's house. It's a cloudy, moody Monday afternoon, as if the city itself is brooding over the start of a new week. Not even one cloud breaks up to show the sun, making Emma believe that snow is soon approaching. She checks the weather app on her phone, confirming there may be a small dusting later.

Emma can feel the blood pulsating in her hands as they hold onto the garment bag with the dress borrowed from Winnie; she nearly forgot to stop by at home to pick it up. She can even hear the thumping of her heart beating in her eardrums. As the least confrontational person on the planet, this is extremely out of Emma's realm. She would much rather avoid it at all costs. But this is Winnie, not some random person she'll never see again. If someone said something during dinner that upset her, Emma needs to find out what was said and by whom. If it happens to be about her potential past relationship with her father, she'll just have to worry about it—and its destruction to her plan to save her house— until then. But for now, Emma will bury that theory in the ground until she no longer can.

Emma pauses as she reaches the top step at Winnie's front door. Closing her eyes, she takes a full, deep breath. "I can do this," she says out loud. "I can get to the bottom of this. Just ask, that's all you have to do. Just ask." She rings the doorbell. Suddenly, all the courage she had built up quickly dissipates, petrified of what she knows she must do.

"Door's open," yells Winnie from inside the house, knowing very well that Emma is at her door.

Emma takes one last breath before she heads inside, not knowing what Winnie's behavior will be like when she walks in, dreading what the outcome of her actions will be.

The warm air smells like lavender and chamomile, as if Winnie already knew Emma needed to reduce her anxiety. Already feeling at home, Emma takes off her hat, coat, and shoes. She places the dress on the entry hall hook and heads towards the kitchen, knowing that is where Winnie will be. With each step she takes, she feels her stomach fall deeper and deeper into itself, and every movement feels like it's happening in slow motion. She forces a smile on her lips when she sees Winnie, sitting on the banquet table reading the *New York Times*.

"Dreadful day out, isn't it?" asks Winnie, as if the events of Saturday's dinner never happened.

When Winnie speaks like her normal self, Emma's body resumes its normal speed. "Yeah, it looks like we are supposed to get some flurries later."

"At least you don't have to travel far," jokes Winnie. She points to the tea kettle on the stove. "I made a big batch of chamomile, would you like a cup?"

Needing to relax, Emma graciously accepts a cup as she takes a seat across from Winnie. As she sips the steamy tea, Winnie looks at her as if she can read her mind, that she knows what she is going to ask her.

"You don't have to be nervous around me," she says.

Oh god, she knows.

Not knowing how to reply, Emma acts clueless instead. "I don't?"

"Just because my son is smitten with you, that doesn't mean we still can't be friends." Seeing the surprised look on Emma's face,

Winnie laughs heartily and places her hand on top of Emma's. "He can't stop gushing about you," she says. "I should have known that you two would make a great pair. I don't know why I didn't think of that sooner."

Caught off guard, Emma tries to wrap her head around the bombshell she dropped. "I'm sorry, Noah talks to you about me?"

"Oh! We don't talk behind your back, if that's what you're thinking." Winnie says to quickly reassure Emma. "We only had one discussion, honestly. He wanted to make sure it was okay with me if he asked you out, that's all."

A giddy smile spreads uncontrollably on Emma's face. She's been hoping that Noah would ask her out, but in the back of her mind, she doubts everything. Even hearing that her wish will come true, Emma feels like it's just a dream. "He's going to ask me out?" says Emma in disbelief, meaning to say this in her head rather than out loud.

The pink hues on Winnie's face drain to an ashy white. "Oh crap, he didn't ask you yet?" Emma shakes her head. Then Winnie shakes hers in disbelief. "He told me he was going to do it soon. I guess I assumed he would have done so the second after our conversation ended." She grimaces. "I'm sorry, I didn't mean to ruin it for you."

Emma places a hand on top of Winnie's. "Honestly, it's okay. It's best for me to know ahead of time, actually."

Winnie's face contorts into an expression of heartbreak and dread. "Oh no, you are going to say no. He was so sure you felt the same way as him." Winnie pulls her hand away, tapping her fingers onto the table. "If I had known how you felt ahead of time, I wouldn't have encouraged him."

Cringing at her word choice, Emma rushes to clarify. "No, I'm sorry, I didn't mean it like that. I really like Noah. *Really* like him. Of course I would say yes." She takes a deep breath, giving herself time to best describe her feelings in words. "I usually don't handle surprises well, and even though he has made it clear that he likes me, it still would have been a big surprise. So, a heads-up actually works in my favor. That way I don't embarrass myself in front of him." Looking down at her hands, Emma can feel her cheeks pinkening with embarrassment. Never before has she confessed her feelings to the mother of the guy she likes without telling him first.

Winnie gives her a sympathetic smile and shakes her head in disbelief. "Emma, dear. There is nothing you could do or say that would be embarrassing to him. In fact, that's part of why he likes you. Your facial expressions show as clear as day what you are thinking, while your quick-witted remarks give anyone with a humorous bone in their body a good laugh." Winnie raises her hands in defense at the incredulous look on Emma's face. "Those were his words, not mine."

Distracted by this whirlwind of information, Emma nearly forgets about the main goal of her visit today, making her start to wonder if Winnie had done this on purpose. Did she reveal this information first thing so that Emma would be too sidetracked to bring up the events on Saturday night? Even if that was Winnie's true intention, Emma knows she can't leave today without getting some answers from her. Putting her foot down, she knows she must get out of her own ways in order to get to the bottom of this. Which means she'll need to be assertive.

"May I ask you something?" asks Emma, shifting the spotlight to Winnie.

"Of course," responds Winnie in a heartbeat, thinking it would be about Noah and not about anything else.

Emma looks down at her lap and takes a deep breath. *It's now or never.*

"I couldn't help but notice that something seemed off at dinner on Saturday," she finally says. Once those words are spoken, she lifts her head and looks Winnie in the eye. "And I've been racking my brain since then to figure out if there was anything that we said or did that could have unsettled you so that I could apologize to you on my family's behalf. If there was anything at all that we were not aware of, please tell me as I do not wish to unsettle you again."

Winnie leans back in her chair and nods while looking out the kitchen window, knowing that her actions the other day did not go unnoticed. She looks back at Emma. "I had a feeling you'd noticed. You're intuitive in that way." Leaning forward, Winnie places her hands on top of the kitchen table, tapping her fingers and thinking of what she wants to share with her. "It wasn't anything you or your parents said or did, I promise."

"Then what was it?" asks Emma, leaning forward to the edge of her seat.

Winnie takes a moment, a moment too long for Emma to handle. "It was seeing your dad," she finally says.

Emma's heart drops what feels like a thousand feet to the floor. She's nothing but shocked by Winnie's omission. Why would Winnie have had that reaction to seeing her dad?

Dad has to be 'O' then…

"My dad?" she barely gets out, trying to act dumb when she just connected the dots all on her own. "Have you two met before?"

Winnie nods. "Briefly, decades ago." She takes a deep breath, continuing to tap her fingers against the table. It would be a few minutes later when she looks at Emma, ready to explain it all to her. "Back in the nineties, I reached out to the legal firm your dad worked at to help me with a case. He, on behalf of his firm, rejected my request for their representation. Seeing your dad after all these years, it caught me off guard and brought me back to that messy time in my life."

"That's why you asked him those questions about his work history… You wanted to make sure it was really him," mutters Emma, processing Winnie's explanation. Looking down at her lap, she tries to put the pieces together. Emma desperately wants to believe Winnie's explanation as it means that her plan could continue. But there's a feeling in her stomach telling her that something isn't quite right. Maybe Winnie cannot tell Emma about her past romantic ties with her dad and instead gave her an explanation that isn't quite a fabrication but a white lie to cover up the real truth.

What is it they say about lying? Stick to some forms of the truth to make it believable?

Emma sees the cracks in Winnie's explanation. She didn't share what type of case she needed representation for, or why they would have rejected her as a client, making her believe even more that Winnie isn't telling the whole truth.

Not knowing their whole history, Emma wonders where this leaves her plan to save Winnie's house. She can't make that decision unless she knows exactly what happened between her and her dad.

There's only one person who could still tell her the truth. The one person she knows who would tell her the truth if she asked.

I'll have to talk to Dad. There's no way around it.

"This all makes sense now," Emma finally says, deciding to accept Winnie's explanation for now until she could get confirmation from her dad. "I thought we did something to offend you, but I'm glad to hear it wasn't because of that."

Winnie places a hand on Emma's hand. "No, dear. I promise it wasn't like that."

"How has the poetry been treating you?" asks Winnie as she removes her hand from Emma's arm, changing the subject.

"It has helped to process my emotions," says Emma, "putting it all into perspective. I still haven't had my 'A-ha' moment of clarity of what to do with my life, but I didn't expect that to happen after writing a few poems down in a notebook."

"That's what writing is all about," says Winnie, "letting your emotions and feelings flow out of you instead of being balled up inside, festering and brewing until it turns into something darker." Winnie speaks with a hint of regret in her voice, making Emma wonder if the regret she feels is tied to how her husband died.

"It sucks not knowing what I want or how to make it feel right," says Emma. "If anything, George's death and the poems have helped me to realize how boring and stagnant my life has been. I mean, at any time, something could happen to me, and I wouldn't even realize what I have taken for granted all this time. All because I never tried to do something out of the ordinary. I have no passions or hobbies. I'm just Emma, who loves to read and be a homebody with my dog. And I'm only twenty-four."

Winnie gives her a look of disbelief. "That doesn't sound like the Emma that Noah told me about. The Emma who stepped out of her shell to help him to win that money for his students. The Emma who still has a passion to learn way after her school days. The Emma who befriends a stranger she met under morbid circumstances. You have so much to give, Emma. You don't even see it yourself. *You* have changed; *you* have come out of your shell. As long as you are open to all the possibilities, you'll find what feels right to *you* in your own time." A thought comes into Winnie's head, forcing her to get up from her chair and head toward her study. She motions for Emma to follow. "Come."

Cautiously, Emma follows her to her study and stands in the middle of the room as Winnie looks for a book on one of her many shelves. "Ah!" says Winnie, finding what she is looking for. She stands on her tiptoes to grab a book on the topmost shelf and hands it to Emma.

"*The Little Prince*?" asks Emma, reading the title of the book aloud. She flips the old, musty book over, seeing the yellowing pages on the edges and hearing the deep creaking of the spine that may be older than herself.

Winnie nods encouragingly. "My grandmother used to read me this all the time growing up. When you're a kid, you miss the larger picture Saint-Exupéry is conveying with this grand idea of a prince from an asteroid travelling all over the universe hiding it from plain sight. But you'd be surprised with the metaphors and allegories contained inside. Have you ever read it?"

Emma shakes her head. "I don't think I ever have."

"Even better; you can read it with fresh eyes. The story shows how narrow-minded we become when we get older. We lose our sense of being open to new possibilities." Winnie looks over at Emma. "Maybe it can help you open your mind to new possibilities. Either way, it's a good book everyone should read at some point in their life."

A timer dings somewhere in the kitchen. "Oh! The cake must be ready," says Winnie as she rushes out of the study, leaving Emma in the study with the book in her hands.

"Cake?" asks Emma, confused. But then she remembers how, on the night of the charity event, Winnie sent pictures of her trials and errors with a raspberry cheesecake to Noah. Emma lingers in the study while Winnie investigates the status of her cake, holding the copy of the *Little Prince* close to her chest.

"I'm trying out a new recipe for Noah's birthday," Winnie says loudly enough so Emma can hear her. Emma hears her opening the oven and sliding the rack out to retrieve the baking dish. "Don't tell him, I'm surprising him with a marjolaine cake. I just hope that I made the ganache right."

Alarms ring in her head after hearing that Noah's birthday is coming up. She tries to think if he ever said anything and realized he didn't. "I didn't know his birthday was coming up," Emma yells loudly enough for Winnie to hear. "When is it?"

"January 12," replies Winnie. "Born on a miserably cold morning."

Before she forgets, Emma takes out her phone and adds Noah's birthday to her calendar.

"You should come over for his birthday dinner," says Winnie as she re-enters the study. "I think he would really like that." Before Emma can agree to the invite, Winnie asks her another question. "Would you like to stay for dinner?"

Checking the time on her phone, Emma sees that they spent their entire lesson time talking about her life and the events of Saturday night's dinner, coasting right around to dinner time. Feeling terrible for wasting Winnie's time, she apologizes for her own oversight. "I'm so sorry, I didn't realize I was rambling so much and completely overtook our lesson time."

Winnie smiles and gives her a nonchalant wave. "It's alright. You know I don't have you over just to teach you French. I also enjoy your company. That means sometimes we can get sidetracked and talk instead of learning how to say, 'I'd like an iced coffee' in French."

Emma gives her a smile, appreciating her understanding and the words about their friendship. "Thank you. I would love to stay for dinner, but I promised my mom I'd help her wrap Christmas presents tonight."

Winnie places a hand over her mouth. "Crap, I completely forgot to do that. Thank you for reminding me! It's crazy how Christmas feels so far away, and then suddenly it's only three days from now." She places her hand on her head, scratching as she thinks. "I won't be able to meet for a few days after Christmas. I need the time to get next semester's lesson plans organized and you'll be going back to work soon after. Darn, I wish we were able to have more time before your vacation time is up."

Seeing how panicked Winnie suddenly looks, Emma wonders if it's not just wrapping presents or creating lesson plans that has her worried. Maybe her financial situation has her worried about Christmas and Noah's birthday. Emma knows that it won't help Winnie much in the long term, but she hopes that this semester is better than the last, if it could delay her selling the house for a little bit. But looking into Winnie's eyes, Emma has a hunch that this coming semester will be worse than what she hopes, reminding Emma once more how important it is for her plan to work perfectly.

"We can figure out a new schedule for us to meet after the New Year," reassures Emma. "For now, let's enjoy the holidays and the weird limbo period between Christmas and New Year's where life just seems to come to a halt."

Winnie walks towards her with open arms, giving her a hug. "Oh, have a wonderful Christmas, dear."

"You too," replies Emma over Winnie's shoulder. Emma hopes this hug can make Winnie feel the reassurance and support she is trying to send to her. Letting her know that she is not alone, that she has others who will help her in a moment's notice. But Emma knows this hug means to her, marking the end of her adventures at Winnie's.

She knew once she went back to work and Winnie's semester started, they were bound to face issues with their schedules. Emma can envision their friendship gradually drifting apart. At first, they would try to make it work; Emma would stop at Winnie's during her lunch hour, or Winnie would let her know of a last-minute cancellation with one of her students, giving them an opportunity to meet. But after one or two weeks go by, they both would get swept up with other things and their sessions will be pushed to a later date, until one day it has been three weeks since they last met and it would hit Emma that she hasn't seen Winnie in a long time.

Emma has endured this specific scenario too many times before. Thanks to her freshman semester of college and her times at summer camp, she knows when something will not continue. She hopes she will be proven wrong this time.

As she gathers her things and heads outside, she feels her phone buzz in her coat pocket. Her face lights up when she sees that it's a text from Noah.

`Noah: Do you have any plans after Christmas?`

Oh my god, is he going to ask me out on a date? A real, true, proper date?

Emma tries to contain her sudden giddiness and moves her fingers at lightning speed as she drafts a response. This time, she reads it over several times to make sure she isn't being cringy and doesn't sound too eager or too indifferent.

`Emma: You mean other than eating Christmas leftovers for days on end and binge-watching all the holiday movies in my pajamas? Then I'm free.`

She hits send before she doubts herself and takes twenty minutes to find the perfect thing to say. Noah responds before she can take her phone away.

`Noah: Perfect! Meet me at the entrance of the Plaza on Friday at 8 p.m.`

`Emma: Are you going to tell me what we are doing?`

`Noah: Nope, that is a surprise : ) Just dress warmly.`

Chapter Fourteen

Christmas comes and goes in a flash, as holidays tend to.

Thankfully, it was a quiet holiday compared to the days Emma has experienced over the past two weeks. After having her mom's world-class Christmas breakfast, the family opened presents by the tree, and Emma curled up in her pajamas with Sadie while watching holiday movies all day. It was exactly the relaxing day she needed.

The next day, she's getting ready for her date after spending hours trying to find the best outfit to wear. Emma's delayed the conversation with her dad as much as she can. Eventually, she decides to have their talk after Christmas. If there is any bad news, she'd rather hear it after her favorite holiday than before. Now that Christmas is over, there is no longer an excuse. Emma thinks back to Winnie's explanation and wonders if it's true. Wouldn't her dad recognize her too? Even when Emma mentions her name whenever they discussed her potential case, there was zero recollection. If she believed Winnie a little bit and in her own stomach-turning theory, she can't help but think that her dad may have always known the name of the book. He just couldn't tell her without revealing their intimate history. So instead, he had her hunt for it because he knows she would never find it. But if she can't find the name of the book, there is no case and no way to help Winnie. But Emma hopes that she is reaching, so much so that she'll laugh about it at some point. Even with their history, bad or good, Emma would like to think that her dad would still help Winnie. But there really is only one way for her to find out.

All set for her date, Emma lingers outside her dad's office. She can hear him typing away, catching up, and annotating his cases that will resume after the New Year. Emma waits to hear the typing subside, a signal she learned as a kid for when she can interrupt him during his office time and lightly knocks on the door while entering.

"What's up, kiddo?" asks her dad as he glances up from organizing his paperwork in his briefcase.

"Can I talk to you about something? And please, I just need the truth," asks Emma, closing the door behind her.

"Of course," says Oliver, his eyebrows pushed inward with concern and curiosity.

Emma releases a breath, letting the question flow right out of her. "Did you know Winnie before Saturday night?"

"By 'know,' you mean…?" asks Oliver, waiting for Emma to finish the question.

"As a friend? More than a friend? A client?"

"Possibly as a client, but I've had hundreds of them over the years."

"So, you don't remember her at all? She didn't stand out for any reason?"

"No, Ems. Should she?" he asks, slightly more alarmed now.

So, Winnie was telling the truth about how she knew Dad…

Relief washes over her as the truth comes out. A smile forms knowing that her dad and Winnie didn't have any kind of past that could ruin her plan. But now this leaves her with one problem. If her dad didn't know Winnie before Saturday and Noah's dad died over fifteen years ago, then there is no way for her to find who 'O' is. No way for her to find the name of the book. It didn't occur to her that there could have been a negative outcome. She's been so focused on not wanting her dad to be 'O' that she didn't think about what it would mean if he wasn't.

How is she going to find 'O' now? And how is her plan going to work if she can't find them?

Defeated and feeling foolish, Emma grabs her things and makes her way to the Astor Place subway station, taking the 4-express line to the Lexington Station on 59th Street. Standing in the jostling subway car, Emma feels naïve to think her plan could have worked in the first place, that she could have found a way to fix all of Winnie's financial problems. Now that there no longer is a plan, there is nothing she can do to help Winnie stay on West 4th Street. She will have to sell the house in the summer.

As she walks along the busy street towards Central Park and the Plaza, Emma decides to push this all aside. She's about to go on her first date with Noah, and ruminating on a silly plan that was doomed to fail from the beginning is not what she wants to occupy her mind with.

Glancing up, Emma sees the night sky is cloudy, as if it may snow at any moment. She even sees the glamorous yellow lights of the Plaza's awning illuminated in the distance. Hoping to distract herself, Emma people-watches as she makes her way closer to the hotel. Couples and fellow New Yorkers are sitting on the stone benches placed along with the Pulitzer Fountain that resides just in front of the hotel. A pair of siblings are making a snowman on the lawn by the fountain. Emma takes in the sight of the hotel as a hazy memory of *that* Friday night springs into her mind, shuddering once she recalls the dreadful hangover the morning after. If she squints her eyes, Emma can make out the outline of Noah's frame right underneath the hotel's awning. Knowing he is already there waiting for her puts her at ease.

"Came back to the scene of the crime, I see?" asks Emma while she walks the few feet closer to him, making Noah turn in surprise and flash that smile upon hearing her voice. Emma slowly feels the warmth return to her body just from the sight of that left dimple alone.

"Couldn't resist it," smirks Noah as the glow of the hotel's awning creates an ethereal warmth on his skin. Suddenly, Emma has an instant urge to be close to him, run her fingers through his curly chestnut hair, wrap her arms around his torso, and feel his body heat. She even surprises herself with the thought that she jolts like lightning struck her body.

I want to kiss him. Right here, right now.

She looks into his eyes and sees that he is waiting for her to respond. Mortified by her distracting thoughts, Emma hopes that he is not able to read her face this time. "Huh?" she asks, hoping he doesn't take offense to her not paying attention for a brief second.

Noah chuckles; thankfully, he finds her trailing mind endearing. "You hungry?"

"Starving," responds Emma.

"Good, I booked us a table at a place with the best view of the city."

She looks down at her attire: jeans with a striped wool sweater and boots. A sense of dread follows as it dawns on her that she is not dressed for such a place. "I don't-" she starts.

"You are dressed perfectly, I promise," he reassures. Noah extends a hand, and after a few heartbeats, she takes it, leading her towards the hotel.

"Wait, we're eating in the hotel?" asks Emma, bewildered.

He looks down at her and winks. "Shhh… It's a surprise."

Emma leans closer to him and their enclosed hands as they walk into the hotel lobby, feeling very much out of place. Walking into the Plaza in a magnificent gown as Oliver Callahan's daughter for a charity event is starkly different from walking in as Emma Callahan in cozy winter attire on a date with a charming guy. She follows Noah to the elevators and waits for the next one to open. Upon entering the elevator, Noah presses the button for the nineteenth floor. It doesn't take Emma too long to register where they are going.

Are we going back to the roof?

Once they reach the floor, he leads her to a nearby staircase, a very familiar one. They proceed up two flights of stairs until they make it to the rooftop door. Noah beams at her as he holds the already-ajar door open for her. Emma's breath is taken away once she steps outside. Gone is the bleak and bland seating area of the rooftop. Before her is a row of fairy lights hanging above the bench, a plush red blanket spread out to make it cozy. Next to the bench is a portable heater, an insulated bag, and a Bluetooth speaker that's quietly playing music.

"You set this up?" murmurs Emma.

Noah nods. "I would have done more, but there was only so much I could fit in my backpack before I looked too suspicious."

Emma is utterly speechless, completely caught off guard by his thoughtfulness and the amount of effort it must have taken him to set this whole thing up. Instead of taking her silence for what it truly is—genuine astoundment—Noah mistakes it for awkward disappointment. "If you don't like it, we can always go someplace else," he says before Emma speaks, trying to salvage the date. "The idea seemed much better in my head."

Emma squeezes his hand reassuringly and looks into his eyes. "No, I absolutely love it."

Hope sparks back into his eyes. "You do?"

She nods with the biggest grin on her face and looks back over at the 'table'. "This is the sweetest thing anyone has ever done for me. It is the perfect surprise, thank you." Emma gestures toward the insulated bag on the bench. "What's on the menu for tonight?"

Noah leads her to the bench, motioning for her to take a seat. He places a blanket on her lap and proceeds to take out the items contained in the bag as if he is doing a show and tell. "First, I got us a toasted focaccia bread to start, as everyone loves bread, and a bottle of sparkling water. Then I got us Sole Toscano's famous mushroom risotto. To finish it off," he takes out two thermals, "I got hot chocolate and chocolate-covered strawberries."

Noah has already won her heart just by bringing bread and chocolate, the two food groups she cannot live without. Her eyes fixate on the bread, watching in a daze as Noah opens the container, letting the warm steam trail into the cold air. Her stomach growls as the scent of garlic hits her nose. Noah offers her a piece first, then starts munching on one himself. Snuggled in the blanket, they both sit and take in the sight of the overcast, dark city sky while Ed Sheeran's voice sings quietly from the speakers.

Consumed by the comfort and warmth from the blanket, toasty bread, and the portable heater, Emma is itching to rest her head on his shoulder, wanting to bridge the gap between them. But her anxious brain warns her not to. The last thing she wants to do is overstep and make things uncomfortable so soon into the night. For now, she shifts on the bench so that she is a bit closer to him.

"I know the first thing you do not talk about while out on a date is mothers," says Noah, breaking the brief silence. "But I am dying to hear what she told you about Saturday night. Did she share anything?"

Emma takes a sip of the sparkling water he poured for her in a cup, wondering how much she should tell him. But there may be something in Winnie's explanation that Noah can provide insight into. "She did, but…," she pauses, reluctant to finish her sentence.

"But what?" he asks.

She glances at him. "I don't know if it's the truth."

He looks at her quizzically. "What did she say?"

Emma looks away and takes in the city before them. The hazy sky. The lit-up offices and apartment windows. Sirens ringing in multiple destinations. Car horns echoing up against the concrete walls.

"She said that it was from seeing my dad," she says eventually, still not looking at him. "Back in the nineties," she continues, "your mom reached out to the law firm my dad worked for, hoping they could help take on a case she had." Finally, she turns to him. "My dad was the one who rejected her on his firm's behalf."

Noah nods his head slowly. "And seeing him after all this time was probably a surprise to her."

Emma nods too. "I didn't ask her what the case was about. I had a feeling she was being vague for a reason, so I didn't press. Do you have any idea what it could have been about?"

Noah places his cup of sparkling water on the ground and brushes his focaccia-greased hands on his pants. He looks down at his hands as he speaks. "The case could have been about my dad's accident."

Emma patiently waits for him to continue. She has wanted to know how his dad died since he told her he passed the night at the gala. Winnie never mentioning her husband dissuaded Emma from asking her. And in the few times Emma has been with Noah, it wouldn't have been appropriate or sincere to ask him about it. But now that Noah brought him up, there seems to be no better time to finally ask. Emma reaches out to place her hand lightly on top of his. "Was the accident how he died?"

Noah reaches for her hand, holding onto it fully. He only nods to answer her question.

"If you don't want to talk about him, we don't have to," says Emma, reassuring him that she won't pressure him to talk about it.

He brushes his thumb across hers, giving her a smile, which she can read only as appreciation. Appreciation for being empathetic. Appreciation for being there to listen. "My dad was an architect," he finally says. "He worked for one of the country's best architectural companies. He was one of the top architects in the city at the time, the peak of his life, one would say." Noah stops, taking a breath before continuing. "He was on site at this fancy new apartment complex they were building in the Upper West Side. It was a windy day, and one of the cranes on site was swaying. He was on one of the exposed floors, one that didn't yet have windows and drywall installed on the outside. Due to a big wind gust, the crane hit one of the floors of the building, along with my dad."

A gasp escapes out of Emma's mouth, horrified by hearing the words said out loud. She sits in stunned silence next to him, her hand still in his, but unable to look him in the eye. She had hoped it was a car accident. But this. This is something you pray for someone to never have to go through.

"It wasn't until I was thirteen and knew how to use the internet that I found out the true details. He died right on impact," continues Noah. "Knowing he didn't suffer helped in a way. To know that he wasn't in pain or agony. It took me till then to realize why my mom never mentioned the accident or him. How do you tell your eight-year-old son that his father was crushed by a crane?" He shakes his head in disbelief. "To lose someone you love like that, I know that it devastated her. I never had to ask her to confirm that."

No wonder she never brought him up. I would lose my mind having to re-tell that story.

Emma's heart hurts. For Noah, and for Winnie. He lost his father too young while she lost her husband too young. Now knowing her tragedy, Emma marvels at how she persevered. Raising her son as an only parent, continuing to live life without the one person she thought and vowed would have been by her side until their nineties. Thinking back to the note from 'O' on the manuscript page, and now understanding the kind of relationship they had, Emma feels with certainty that 'O' has to be Noah's dad. Who else could it be if not the love of Winnie's life?

Emma secretly hoped that Noah could provide her with information on who 'O' could possibly be, and even though she got an answer she didn't want, at least now she knows who 'O' is and that her search for the book is futile. As much as it breaks her heart, Emma will have to adjust to the fact that she cannot help Winnie and rowhouse 363 will eventually be put up for sale.

"So, your mom was seeking legal counsel against your dad's company and the crane contractors, then?" asks Emma, going back to the reason why they were discussing the death of Noah's dad in the first place.

Noah nods, "I guess she did. I never knew she sought out legal counsel for the accident. I only know about it from one of the articles about his death. There was a one-liner that briefly mentioned something of that sort. It never ended up going to court, though. I assumed some kind of settlement was agreed upon between my mom and my dad's company."

But why would my dad's firm decline to represent her? Even if it were just a consultation, it would have been an easy case for them to take and get payable hours on.

Knowing how much it took for him to share this with her and wanting to show how much it means to her that he did, Emma places her free hand on top of their conjoined hands. He looks up into her eyes. A smile of thankfulness slowly forms on his lips. It's barely noticeable, but Emma can see his dimple faintly. "Thank you for sharing this with me," says Emma. "I'm sorry about what happened to your dad and that you didn't get to grow up with him around."

Noah squeezes her hand back. "Thank you."

"You know," starts Noah after a moment of silence. Glancing at him, Emma sees he is thinking deeply while also feeling hesitant, as if he is unsure if he wants to speak what he is thinking out loud. "I've always had this gut feeling that my dad isn't my real dad," he finally says. He looks at Emma with a perplexed look. "Now that I've said it out loud, it sounds crazy, doesn't it?"

"What makes you think that?" asks Emma, surprised by Noah's disclosure.

He emits a nervous laugh. "It was never *one* thing that made me think this. It's a bunch of little things that paint a certain picture once you put them together. Or perhaps the picture I'm imagining isn't what I think it is." He runs his hand through his hair, trying to gather his thoughts. "I'm sorry, this is too much and too strange to talk about on a first date."

Without hesitation, Emma places a hand on his upper arm, looking toward his face that he's now hanging low to hide. "It's okay, you can talk about it. I promise this isn't ruining anything at all."

"You sure?"

Emma nods, giving him a reassuring smile. "You've listened plenty to my strange thoughts. Besides, it may help to get this off your chest."

"Okay," agrees Noah. "We will speak of it this only once, and then that's it." Emma mimes crossing her heart on her chest, her way of sealing a promise that she has done since she was a young girl. "Well, as I said, there are these little things that I could never get out of my mind. Like how my mom has green eyes and my dad had blue, but I have brown eyes. Looking at basic biology and genetics, the chances of me having brown eyes are slim to none. There is also the fact that as I've gotten older, I've never seen any of my dad's physical characteristics in myself. I see a little bit of my mom, but my dad, I see none of him in my face. But the one thing that I always think back on was when we changed our name."

"Changed your name in what way?" asks Emma, confused.

"Our last name," clarifies Noah. "After my dad died and my great-grandma a few weeks after, I vividly remember that my mom changed our last names to her maiden name. I wasn't always a Reynard. Until I was eight, I was Noah Peterson."

"How come she changed back to her maiden name?" asks Emma.

"She tells me it's to honor my great-grandma, but wouldn't she want to keep my dad's last name to keep *his* memory alive and have me carry on the family name?"

Emma considers the evidence that Noah presented to her, thinking about how they all might fit to prove his point. All of them are valid, but she doesn't want to think that Winnie could keep such a secret from Noah and continue to tell him such a heavy lie for all his life. She wants to believe and keep on believing that Winnie would never do such a thing, that the person she envisioned in her head for years is the real her. But what does Emma know about her? Her character? Who was Winnie when she was Emma's age? She doesn't know who Winnie *really* is and what her life has been like, though she now knows what happened to Noah's dad. Because of that, Emma can't definitively dispute or shut down Noah's gut feeling, and that scares her the most.

"Have you ever asked your mom about it?" she inquires.

Noah shakes his head. "How could I? Not after everything that happened to Dad. I just couldn't bear to ask that and hurt her even more by doing so."

"If it's any consolation, there are times when someone doesn't look anything like a parent. I have red hair, but my parents have brown. And the chances of me having red hair are small."

Noah nods and laughs to himself. "Like I said, it was just a feeling I had. I never found any other reason to think that it could be true." He sighs. "I first got this idea shortly after he died, and if we psychoanalyze it, my younger self probably came up with that in hopes I still had a living father out there." Emma gives him a sympathetic smile.

It didn't occur to her at first how all of this changes her plan. With this new information, Emma realizes that there is still a chance 'O' can be out there, alive. And that maybe, just maybe, 'O' could also be Noah's real father. A bit of hope emerges once more. If Noah is right, then that means 'O' is neither her dad nor Noah's and is someone else entirely. As she thinks about it, excitement rushes through her as her plan is possibly not foiled just yet. There is still a slight chance that she can find 'O' and the name of Winnie's book, thus ultimately saving Winnie from leaving West 4th Street.

It may be a naïve and foolish plan, but this gives me a chance to work this all out.

"Ready for the main course?" asks Noah with a smile on his face, interrupting the thoughts and ideas running through her head.

Intuiting that Noah may be attempting to move the conversation and date along, Emma nods. The smell of the mushroom risotto and the feeling of her stomach grumbling make her even more eager to dig into the meal. Noah takes out two containers of risotto from his bag, handing her one and a set of plastic cutlery. The pair start to eat their meal in a comfortable silence, allowing Emma to simply take in and enjoy the moment on this whole wonderful night.

The sound of Noah chuckling breaks the silence. Emma watches as he nervously scratches the back of his neck. "So, I feel like I shared enough about my family and trauma. In fact, you probably know a bit too much about me. Tell me about you, what do you do for work? What do you like to do when you're not learning French with my mom?"

Moving around the risotto in the container with a plastic fork, Emma curses to herself. She knows how boring her life is and saying it to someone she likes feels so humiliating. On dates, you're supposed to present yourself in the best light you can, make yourself seem more interesting and exciting than you really are, but she doesn't know how to hype up her boring life. So, she decides to be honest.

"My life is pretty boring, honestly," she admits. "I lived here in the city all my life, even went to college here. Once I graduated, I started working at SpikeSearch as a data analyst and have been working there since. When I'm not at work, you can either find me in a bookstore or at home reading a book." She shrugs her shoulders, "I'm pretty simple when it comes to things. Maybe too simple." Emma glances at him and is surprised not to see the reaction she expected. He wears an expression of curiosity, as if intrigued to know more.

"How so?" he asks.

Do I share with him what has been captivating my mind for the last few weeks? Or would I be sharing too much? I guess the latter doesn't matter too much when it comes to us.

She waits, pondering how to best phrase what she's been feeling. "Ever since that night when George died, I constantly look back at my life and think about how I've been living it."

"I can imagine how witnessing something like that could lead you to re-evaluate everything," Noah responds.

Emma leans back against the bench, resting her head on the brick wall behind them and looking up at the hazy sky above. "In a way, it was like my life flashed before my eyes when I saw his body. It made me realize that life isn't guaranteed. We all think we have ninety years to live our lives, have time to do the things we always wanted to do. But the truth is, we don't know how much we have, and we decide to play it safe. Take a job that pays well but we don't enjoy rather than something we are passionate about. Stay in situations out of convenience and comfort, instead of taking risks. If I were George, I would have left a life so unfulfilled, it's like I was never on Earth to begin with. I don't want to be like that."

"I should have brought a bottle of wine," jokes Noah.

Emma turns and gives him an apologetic look, "Sorry, I didn't mean to get too deep and morbid."

Noah laughs. "I'm used to it. You'd be surprised by the questions fourth graders throw at you." He turns toward her. "With them, I know it's simply childlike curiosity. But with you, the question remains: what in your life makes you feel that way? You wouldn't necessarily have that kind of reaction if you weren't already feeling that way before that night."

First Winnie, now him. What is with the Reynards sensing my unhappiness so quickly?

"Well, before that incident, I was told of a new position opening at work and how my boss was thinking of giving it to me. But when I heard about it, I wasn't excited about the prospect of climbing up the corporate ladder. No, I was freaking out over working extra hours and selling my soul to a company that can lay me off at any moment. Then on that same day, I saw a dead body, and it highlighted even more how unhappy I am. But the past few weeks," she pauses, "I got to do the things I always wanted to do but never made the time for. Learning a new language. Getting out of my comfort zone. Even trying to write poetry. I don't know what it is that fulfills me, but maybe I'm finally getting closer. Do you feel fulfilled?"

Noah nods. "Took me some time, but I do love what I do. Helping kids and encouraging their curious minds. It's crucial for them to have that kind of environment to thrive in, which is why I feel like my role is so much more than teaching them math or grammar. To tell you the truth, I never really wanted to become a teacher."

"Really?"

He nods. "I wanted to become a researcher of dead languages, spending my days in a library analyzing and learning the history of old dialects. But when I didn't get into any of the graduate schools I applied to, I stayed here in the city and was offered a teaching job at Westview. First, I did it just to have a job, but then in a blink of an eye I've been there for three years and haven't thought about leaving. Little did I know when I started that I would fall in love with teaching and the school." Noah grabs her hand, looking earnestly into her eyes. "Sometimes we think we know what we want in life, and then the universe directs us down a different path that will lead us to what makes us happy. Don't think back on your life with disappointment or regret, think of it as you finding your path. Often enough, it will present itself to you on its own time. Whether that is in SpikeSearch or with something else."

Her cheeks redden from their hands touching as well as his insightful words. She smiles down at their conjoined hands. "I wish I was patient enough to do that. Knowing that what I'm doing now isn't working makes my brain run in circles trying to figure out what will make it feel right."

Noah squeezes her hand. "I promise in time you will figure it out."

And for now, she believes in his words, thinking that if someone else's life hasn't gone necessarily as planned and they're still happy, then maybe she can be happy too. The rest of the date is more cheerful and lively as they switch to more lighthearted topics. Several times Emma cries laughing from the stories that Noah tells her about his days of being a teacher and she even forgets the worries and anxiety that have been constantly popping into her mind for days. For the first time in a while, she can enjoy the moment and feel as if she is on top of the world, or in this case, on top of the city.

Like a bat, Emma's ears perk up at the first few musical chords of Frank Sinatra's "Come Fly with Me" playing from the speaker. "Oh, I love this song!" she exclaims while covering her mouth that has a chocolate-covered strawberry inside.

Instantly, Noah gets up on his feet and offers her his hand, "Come dance with me."

Embarrassed, Emma feels more blood flow to her already red cheeks. "Oh, I can't dance. You saw how I was on the charity night, and that was with the liquid encouragement of tequila."

He shakes his head with that dimpled smile showing. "You can step on my toes all you want."

She looks into his eyes. Suddenly, she envisions being so close to him, she can rest her head on his chest, and now the idea of dancing doesn't seem too bad after all. She takes his hand and lets him lead her to the middle of the rooftop. He raises the volume from his phone, and they start to dance clumsily to Sinatra. Emma laughs, feeling like how they were back on the rooftop on that night, drunk and euphoric. But this time, there is no ounce of alcohol in their systems. Noah twirls her, and they both giggle like two young, giddy kids. Before she knows it, she lets go of her reservations and gets fully swept away by the dance.

They dance like this for many more songs afterward, no longer feeling the cold snap of the air on their now warm bodies. It isn't until the slow melody of the Arctic Monkeys' cover of "Baby I'm Yours" plays that they fall into a sway. Her head rests on his shoulder, while his rests on the side of her head. Emma can feel the heartbeat coming from someone's chest; whether it is hers or his, she does not know. The idea that it is the sound of both of theirs beating at the same time sends a rush of giddiness down to her toes.

Thick water droplets soon fall onto their faces, catching onto their eyelashes and forcing them to lift their heads and look up at the sky.

"It's snowing," whispers Emma.

Their gazes look back down and lock on each other, their faces mere inches away. Before she knows it, Noah is leaning forward, and their lips meet in a slow and sweet kiss. Feeling like she's having her first kiss all over again. Emma's kissing dry spell makes her overthink every movement, question every choice of where to put her hands, who should lead the kiss. But eventually instinct kicks in and she allows herself to stop overthinking it and let the kiss take her away. The kiss starts off slow, as their unfamiliarity with one another hinders the intensity. When Noah cradles her face with his hands, it turns more passionate and heated. Emma wraps her arms around his neck, and Noah places his hands on her waist, pulling her closer to him.

They both take a breath of air after what feels like several minutes, their foreheads touching. Emma bites her bottom lip as they look at each other, then breaks out into a grin, finally understanding what the love stories she reads describe about getting swept away. She will never tell him that this was the best kiss of her life, but something deep inside tells her that he may be feeling the same thing too.

A smile creeps on Noah's face as he brushes away a loose strand of hair from her face, pushing it back behind her ear, then playfully pulling on her beanie. "Are you still off work next week?" he asks, smiling like he just won the lottery.

Emma nods. "I go back the week after New Year's. Why?"

"I got the school to approve the trip to the planetarium for next week and wanted to make sure you can still come along."

She can't help the grin from forming on her face and daringly plants a quick peck on his lips. "Oh, I wouldn't miss it for the world."

Once they are tired from dancing and their extremities have reached an uncomfortable freezing temperature, they pack up their outdoor picnic and seek warm shelter. As Emma helps Noah clean up, she secretly steals glances at him. Trying to memorize the way his curls surround his face, how his glasses sit on the bridge of his nose, she wants to take in everything about him. Suddenly the quote from *The Port to Sea* means something entirely new to Emma. "'They say love takes your body, mind, and soul. But in truth, I've never truly felt mine until I laid eyes on you…'" she recites quietly to herself.

"Sorry, did you say something?" asks Noah, lifting his head as he places the blanket back into his backpack.

Like a child trying to convince their parent it wasn't them, Emma shakes her head vigorously with a smile. "Nope!"

Looking at his face, into those warm brown eyes, she can see pieces of Winnie in him. She tries to envision what his father looked like or looks like. Thinking back to what Noah shared with her about his suspicions of his parentage and the affectionate note written on the manuscript page, she wonders if it's truly possible that he may be right. She does not dare tell Noah yet about 'O'. Mainly because she needs to explain how she found out about it, and there is no way she could do that and not break her promise to Winnie. Besides, what if she's wrong? Why plant the idea that his mom had an affair without concrete evidence? No, if she is to bring this up to him, she needs to have concrete evidence, strong evidence that will confirm that his gut feeling is right. To do that, Emma will need to find out who 'O' is and how they are connected to Winnie.

Her search to find 'O' is now back in full swing, and this time it's still just as dire as it's now personal. She envisions the Venn diagram in her head, how the two circles overlap in the middle to show the potential connection 'O' has to Winnie and Noah. As much as she wants to help Winnie find a solution to her troubles and to keep her on West 4th Street, she equally wants to find the answers to the questions that have been gnawing at Noah for years. But she knows she needs to tread carefully. If his suspicions are right, she'll need to be careful about what she reveals and how.

Now that she's back to square one for this search, Emma will need to go back to the source of all of this and double-check if there are any clues that she may have missed. To do so, Emma will have to visit Winnie much sooner than she planned.

Pacing back and forth in her bedroom the next morning, Emma wonders how she is going to make an unannounced visit to Winnie's so it feels like it was purely coincidental and not a thoroughly planned scheme she concocted. Defeated by her lack of ideas, Emma plops onto her bed, the motion making Sadie perk her head up, giving Emma a side eye of slight annoyance. Without noticing

Sadie's irritated look, Emma subconsciously reaches out to pet her, and the feeling of her short and soft curly fur sends calm and ease throughout Emma's body. It is from this new vantage point that Emma spots a small, shiny gift bag nestled underneath her desk by the far corner.

Winnie's Christmas/thank you gift! I forgot all about it!

She reaches for the bag, peering inside to see the metal tea infuser along with the four small mason jars of the locally produced herbs Emma noticed that Winnie likes to use the most: jasmine, lavender, peppermint, and ginger. Emma knows it isn't much, but she at least wanted to give Winnie a gift that she will enjoy and use. She bought the gift items a few days before the charity event and meant to give it to Winnie when she dropped off her dress. But being the absent-minded and easily forgetful person she can be, when something is out of her sight, it's also out of her mind.

Staring at the gift in her hands, it suddenly dawns on Emma that she now has a solid reason to go over to Winnie's. Now all she needs to do is fix her bed hair and get out of her pajamas.

Around ten minutes later, she stands outside Winnie's door, anxiety and adrenaline running through her veins as she rings the doorbell.

Please... please be home...

Never has she ever felt such relief when she hears the door handle turn and feels the whoosh of warmth coming from inside the house. Upon explaining her surprise visit and presenting the Christmas/thank you gift, Winnie invites Emma inside for tea—something Emma was banking on Winnie to do for this to work out.

While Winnie goes to the kitchen to make her a cup of tea with the gifted herbs, Emma realizes that this is the small window of opportunity she is looking for. Quietly, she makes her way to the study, double-checks that the coast is clear by peeking once more into the entry hall, and makes her way quickly to the bottom shelf of the bookcase by the fireplace.

Carefully, she slides the folder out of its slot and opens it out on the couch. Knowing that she can't physically take the folder with her, she removes her phone from her butt pocket and opens the camera app, taking pictures of all the pages so she can examine them all later. She carefully checks for any other details that she might have missed the first time, and indeed, she did miss something. On the back of one of the manuscript pages, Emma finds a pencil sketch of what looks to be a lily. She doesn't know why, but somehow the flower feels familiar.

Remembering she doesn't have that much time to analyze it, Emma takes a picture of it, saving it for later. Once she's checked all areas and taken all the pictures needed, she places the pages carefully back into the folder's sleeves and slides it back into its secure slot on the bookshelf. As if it was never touched.

Now begins the hard part.

June 18, 1989

My Dearest Mémé,

It's been a few weeks since I mailed the letter to Fossettes, and zero days since I last cried.

His reply came in the mail yesterday. In the moment, I wasn't ready yet to read it. I had to hide it in my dresser until I was alone to read it. As much as I didn't want him to reply to my letter, selfishly I was hoping he would. I needed to hear his last goodbye to me.

I made the mistake of reading it today. Instead of closure, it brought on an influx of new tears to run down my cheeks. I thought my heart broke the day I wrote that letter, but it didn't truly until I read his.

He told me that despite the cruel things I said and the reasons I gave, he knows—as well as I—that deep down what we have is undeniably true love. While he is indeed heartbroken by my decision to stay with Russel, he respects my choice and will abide by it. Despite all I said, he still wished me all the happiness and encouraged me to never stop writing. He said that I even inspired him to go after his dream of opening his own store. As much pain his letter gives me, I cannot get rid of it; it is the last set of words he will ever say to me. I can still smell his scent of cedarwood and peppermint on the page.

Russel can never know of this letter's existence. I know I'm at a lot at risk just keeping it. But I need to at least have this. So, I tried hiding it in the closet with the cleaning supplies. Much to my shock, I found a folder underneath a pile of bed linens that contained a few pages of my manuscript. It has my and Fossettes' annotations all over the pages; you can barely read the original typed text. Oh Mémé! I thought I had lost those words for good. It brings me so much bittersweet joy to have some of my story back. Despite the majority of it being illegible, I know what was on those pages. So, I don't make the same mistake twice. I hid the pages and the letter in separate hiding spots.

I know you said that I could always re-write my story from scratch. But deep down, I know I could never do it. That story is my heart and soul, and after everything that happened, re-writing our love story would bring me only sorrow and pain. His missing presence is already a deep hole in my heart, and re-writing this without him would be the ultimate betrayal. To prevent myself from further heartache, I think giving up on writing is the best thing for me.

Russel knows that I'm keeping my end of the deal since he's been showering me in a sea of lavish gifts, trips to the salon and spa, and I've been given time off from the wives' club due to 'my devoted time and service to the company and club.' This is his way of buying my happiness, bribing me to stay silent about what happened with the book and the affair. But I know I will have to go back to the club and act the part of the happy and devoted wife, as I know he could always hurt Fossettes to get back at me.

I do have to say that since we have come to an arrangement, we have been fighting less and Russel has been less argumentative. We have had a few moments that we were able to laugh and reminisce about our years together in high school. We even had a nice evening out to dinner. Who knows, maybe Russel could change, and we can turn things around? I know it will never go back to how we were before we got married, but if we can even go beyond just toleration and to friendliness, I will take that. But I'm not that naïve to hope too much for that.

Being on solid ground with Russel is all the more appealing because soon there will be another member of the family. Mémé, you are going to be a great-grandma! I'm not that far along, only you know of this for now. Once I get it confirmed with my doctor, I will tell ma mére, mon pére, and Russel. You know I've always wanted a big family and a bunch of kids. I'm not out of time yet; maybe I can still have that. Who knows, a baby or two may help Russel and me to have some sort of semblance of a family.

This does mean I will have to postpone my trip to see you. But that doesn't mean we can't find some way to get you here. Once I know my due date, we can coordinate.

With all my love.

Ton petit soleil,

Winnie

P.S. I'm stocking up on peppermint and green tea, as I know I'll need all the energy and nausea suppressants I can get my hands on.

Chapter Fifteen

The sound of children laughing awakens Emma from her trance of mindlessly staring up at the planetarium's glass dome ceiling, watching the white puffy clouds pass by.

"Sorry, what did you say?" Emma asks after Nia spoke beside her. Looking around, Emma makes sure the rest of the kids in her group are all accounted for, counting all eight heads.

"We want to go to see the telescopes, Miss Emma," Nia repeats as she drags Emma to a corridor leading to a museum display of telescopes throughout history.

Emma nods. "Of course, let's gather the rest of our group." She looks around the room and calls out her group's name. "Avengers, assemble!" Inspired by one of the kids' t-shirts, Emma's group decided to call themselves the Avengers, trying to one-up the other two groups by making theirs look more fun.

Instantly, a dozen footsteps rush towards her, with all eight faces staring back at her. A rapturous noise echoes throughout the domed lobby, as her group of small, brave superheroes gather upon hearing their leader's calls. "Now let me see…we have the Hulk." One of the boys laughs as she calls out his nickname. "And I see Thor, Black Panther, Iron Man, Black Widow, Spider-Man, Scarlet Witch." She looks down and tugs onto Nia's hand that is now holding on to hers. "And last, but not least, we have Cap." A wide, wild grin splashes on Nia's face, feeling proud for being given the nickname of Captain America.

"Now, I hear that Earth's mightiest heroes want to go see the telescopes? Who wants to go see them?" asks Emma. All at once, eight hands shoot straight up into the air with 'Me's echoing through the corridor.

Emma puts on her serious face. "Then it is your mission, Avengers, to investigate the telescopes and find me the oldest one on display. Do you accept this mission?"

"Yes, Miss!" responds all eight kids in unison.

Emma can feel a pair of eyes on her, and she knows who it is. Looking up, she sees him, laughing while being circled by nine of his students. Noah flashes a smile at her and winks, sending her a secret message only she understands. She looks away quickly before her cheeks blossom to a red, and the kids catch on to her giddiness from Noah's attention. They already know she is Mr. Reynard's special friend; the last thing she needs is for her infatuation to be caught by a dozen nine-year-olds and get teased by them.

She still can't believe that it has only been a week and a half since Noah kissed her on that rooftop. In some ways, it feels longer, and yet, it still feels like it happened yesterday, still freshly planted in her memory.

They've gone on several dates to the bookstores and movies. They've taken several walks through Central Park that ended up being time for Emma to talk endlessly about what to do about work and for Noah to run ideas on what he and the rest of the Westview teachers could do with the remaining prize money. They also have spent several long nights together. Despite all the time she's been with Noah, she has only seen Winnie once since her spontaneous drop-in. The busy start to her tutoring semester only gave Emma time to come over during a mid-day break.

Now that she goes back to work next week, Emma knows that her fear of their friendship fading may be realized, and it amplifies the failure she's experienced with her search for 'O'. She tried Googling sentences from the manuscript pages with no luck. She tried searching on social media to see if an 'O' is in Winnie's social sphere. But Winnie's list of thirty-five Facebook friends did not indicate that any one of them could be 'O'. But who would be Facebook friends with an ex-lover from their past? After each failed attempt in her search, Emma gets closer and closer to giving up and putting this dumb plan to rest, accepting that there is absolutely nothing she can do to help Winnie.

When she's not thinking about this, work and her impending career decision fill the void. The closer she gets to her return date, the more knots and cramps form in her stomach. Emma doesn't know what she should do and fears she will end up making the wrong choice.

Taking one quick look at Noah, an ache throbs in her chest from seeing him in his element with his kids. He seems so happy and fulfilled with his job and life. Everyone in her generation hopes they can make a living off their dream, to find the job that not only gives them purpose in life but can financially support them too. Knowing that being a teacher wasn't his dream or goal in life reminds Emma that not everything in life has to be figured out before you turn twenty-one and graduate from college. It seems like everyone will go through this phase at some point in their life. At least Emma can feel lucky that she is going through this now rather than fifteen years down the road after sticking to a choice she made back when she was twenty-one.

She wishes that the universe would guide her to her right path, just as it did for Noah by giving him the job at Westview. But she knows that it would be too passive for her to hope the universe would hand her opportunities on a silver platter, instead of actively seeking them out on her own. But where can she look when she doesn't even know where to start?

Hearing the laughter and cries of excitement coming out of the kids forces her to push aside her running thoughts. A smile forms on Emma's face knowing that she and Noah helped to get the funding for this trip. It makes her early mid-life crisis seem so silly and even selfish. Here are twenty-two kids who live a different life than her. They will always get the shorter end of the stick. They will have to work ten times harder than she did just to get where she is at twenty-four. They will face injustice and bias solely on their skin color, economic background, even the name they are born with. As soon as her heart soars from happiness, it shatters with realization. Right here and now at nine years old, these kids feel like they have the world in the palm of their hands, but that may not be the future they will face. Some may have already gotten a taste of that reality.

Emma feels the need to make sure these kids have the best day ever, to feel special for even a few hours of their day.

"Look, Miss Emma!" says Carlo, with his small pointer finger on the display glass, pointing to an ancient telescope. Emma walks over and stands by him, along with the seven other kids who are curious to know what Carlo just found.

"Built in 1608, one of the first telescopes ever made. It's from the Netherlands," Emma reads aloud the display sign right next to the telescope. She looks down at Carlo. "That has to be the oldest one here. Great job finding it, Thor!"

"What's a Netherland?" asks Rina, or Scarlet Witch.

"It's not a thing, but a place. A country actually," replies Emma.

"Where is it?" asks Nia.

"It's in Europe," says Emma. She reaches into her bag and takes out her phone, quickly scrolling through the Maps app to find the country. She kneels down to eye-level with the kids, all eight of them surrounding her in a semi-circle, looking over her shoulder at her phone. "See, it's right here," she points to the country bordering Germany and Belgium.

One of the kids laughs over her left shoulder. "What's so funny, Iron Man?" asks Emma, peering over her shoulder to look at him.

The boy points to her phone screen and giggles. "Antwerp." The rest of the kids laugh along with him, some howling at the funny-sounding city name. Emma laughs along with them, their young, exuberant laughs being nothing but contagious.

"Kids, the show is about to start," interrupts Noah, who is standing in the threshold of the museum. Cheers erupt from the kids as they make their way toward the third group and the theater. He doesn't follow the kids just yet, but he lingers by the entrance, waiting for Emma.

"How are they doing?" he whispers to her as they make their way into the big domed theater, their hands merely inches away from touching.

Emma looks at him and smiles. "They are the best. Nia is going to grow up to be a leader. I can feel it."

Noah nods and smiles to himself. "She is a rarity. So determined and strong. I hope she doesn't lose that part of herself as she grows up."

With that in mind, Emma thinks back to her nine-year-old self. The young girl who was going to become just like the strong literary role models of her youth, like Nancy Drew and Ella of Frell. The girl who never shied away from trying new things and believing she could become anything she set her mind to.

Young girls hear the stories of Amelia Earhart, Cleopatra, and Frida Kahlo and become obsessed with the idea that they can achieve anything they set their minds to. Societal rules be damned. But that drive and those dreams fade away as they get older. Like how kids are with Santa Claus, they see through the façade and stop believing in the magic. That's what it is like to grow up as a girl. When their boobs start to grow and hormones start kicking in, then insecurity and unwanted attention start to creep in. Then soon they'll hear the stories of what women face every day, the challenges and scrutiny they endure just to be equal to a man. The dream and drive they had at nine years old looks more like naivety and wishful thinking than actuality. Emma hopes that the world doesn't diminish Nia's shine, that she can persevere through it, unlike Emma.

"The only thing we can do is make sure she has the foundation to keep that part of her," says Emma.

"That's the one thing I can't stand about being a teacher," explains Noah. "There is only so much I can do in the one school year I have with these kids. After that, I can't control whose hands they're in. Sometimes I worry that some of them could fall into the cracks and how I won't be there to catch them."

Emma places a hand on his shoulder, stopping them in the theater hallway. "That's a big burden you are putting on yourself."

He looks at her with sorrowful eyes, "It's the secret burden we teachers put onto ourselves." He shrugs nonchalantly. "Comes with the job."

She reaches for his hand and gives him a squeeze. "That's what makes you a great teacher. You care about them and their futures. All it takes is one teacher to show them that compassion and love to make a world of a difference to them. And you," she moves his chin for their eyes to meet, "are that one teacher to them."

He smiles down at her. "Look at who's the one giving life advice now."

"You're not the only wise one here, Mr. Reynard," she teases.

"We should go make sure the kids are seated and behaving. Will you sit next to me?"

"Of course." Emma nods and follows him into the massive theater.

Back at home, wide awake in the late hours of the night, Emma is nestled with several pillows on her bed. The sweet, melancholic voice of Kacey Musgraves lowly pulses in her room. Sadie lays down next to her, peacefully snoozing when her owner is anything but calm.

She has six days until she goes back to work. But before then, she needs to resolve the mess she has found herself in. She feels a duty to Noah to help confirm the identity of his father and has the sense that if she doesn't pursue it, he'll never know. But she also feels a loyalty to help Winnie as she continues to show Emma extreme generosity. Questions swarm in her mind, muddying her thoughts by both reiterating her intentions and doubting the good it can do.

What cost am I willing to pay to find the identity of the mysterious 'O'?

Could I lose Noah? Winnie? Both?

What happens when I get the answers and they do more harm than good?

Clutching her head between her hands, Emma's head hurts with confusion, doubt, and its endless spiraling. How did she not see this would be an issue from the beginning? She knows she can't abandon this altogether. How could she when she knows she can help both with their troubles? But she doesn't see how she could help one without hurting the other. Telling Noah would betray Winnie by telling him a secret she most likely has good reasons for keeping. But knowing the truth and not telling Noah would also hurt him and their relationship.

Who do I protect from getting hurt?

Seeing her red notebook resting on her desk, Emma knows how she can at least try to process what she is feeling. As she runs her fingers through Sadie's curly fur, Emma stares at the blank page of the notebook now open on her lap, trying to find the right words to articulate the feelings rushing inside her.

Before she knows it, the pen is in her hand, writing feverishly away.

I wait for shooting stars,
to make a wish come true.
But then that day happens,
my wish gave me you.
Here I am now,
with a heart bleeding blue.
In my hand is a sword,
double-edged for you.
If I can make,
one last wish,
I would undo,
what mine did to you.

She reads the words over again, and a small fire of pride is lit in her. She's surprised yet satisfied that she was able to eloquently write what she is feeling in just a few lines on the page. With a small smile of delight on her face, she shuts her notebook and securely locks it. The notebook's cover catches her eye; the floral design suddenly feels familiar. She lightly traces her pointer finger over the deep engraved marking of lily flowers.

Why does this look so familiar?

Then suddenly, it clicks in her head.

She frantically leans over to her nightstand and grabs her phone. Sadie growls at her for moving, waking her from a deep slumber. With jittery fingers, Emma scrolls and taps away to find the picture. She grabs her notebook and puts it next to her phone, looking at the lily flower on the notebook, then at the lily flower sketch on the back of one of the manuscript pages.

They are exactly the same.

In utter shock, she drops her phone and notebook onto the bench. Her pulse quickens. Her breathing deepens. Her gaze fixes on her window, and her eyes widen like she is having an out-of-body experience. Two thoughts form in her brain at the same time, like two trains speeding toward each other on the same track, about to hit one another. She can feel the impending collision in her cranium.

If the lilies on my notebook are the same as the sketch on Winnie's page...

And if that bookshop owner personally made that notebook...

Then he must be O.

Chapter Sixteen

The bookstore is across the street. Emma lingers on the sidewalk, staring at it like a predator scoping out their next prey. She's standing far enough away that she isn't noticeable, but close enough that she can strike. Her legs are immobilized. Her hands are buried deep in her coat's pockets. Her mind is telling her to move, to go inside, but her body tells her not to.

The traffic is congested for a weekday afternoon. But it is New York City; there is never a time where there is no heavy traffic. Cars and trucks pass by slowly. Pedestrians walk in front and behind her on the sidewalk, not one of them giving her a thought. The commotion around her doesn't help to reduce the self-inflicted anxiety buzzing in her body. Her internal struggle of what to do is causing havoc in her mind.

Another shopper leaves the bookstore, leaving only two people left inside. Since Emma arrived, she has been keeping track of who enters and who leaves, as it would be ideal for her to do this with no one else inside. She knows that what she is about to address with the owner is personal, and the last thing she wants to do is to start things off on the wrong foot. Being considerate to him is the least she can do.

A young couple holding hands strolls in front of her, leading Emma to think of Noah.

An ache forms in her heart, already missing him. It's been only two days since the field trip to the planetarium, but it feels like it's been weeks.

His birthday is next week, and Emma has no idea what is expected from her. Does she take him out for a celebration? Does she get him a gift? Since they haven't gone official just yet, she is stuck in a grey area of uncertainty.

Noah did invite her to a small dinner party that his closest friends are throwing for him. A dinner party feels so adult, but she'd rather have a quiet, simple dinner party over than a long night out clubbing until the early morning with his friends. Nothing screams immaturity more than turning twenty-eight and wanting to re-live your college years. Emma knows what this invitation means. She knows that this shows his true intentions. No guy would have the girl he is seeing meet his close friends if he wasn't serious. She knows she should be happy, elated even, that he took this step. This is everything she has ever wanted, but it all feels too good to be true. She knows what it means if it feels that way: that it usually is.

A taxi honks loudly in front of her as a cyclist cuts in front of him on the street. The driver then gives the rider the middle finger out the window. This typical New York interaction brings Emma back to her senses.

As much as she doesn't want to go in, as confrontation is Emma's least favorite thing in the world, she knows the bookshop owner is her only chance of getting answers. She needs to find out the name of Winnie's book and what her relationship with 'O' was. In order to do so, that means she needs to go inside and read him the legible lines from the manuscript pages in the hope he will provide her with the one answer she has been seeking.

The sheer coincidence makes Emma believe that maybe this is all fate. That the universe guided her to that store, to buy that notebook, all for a reason. She feels called on to find out who 'O' is and be able to give Winnie reassurance that she can stay where she is meant to be.

If fate is behind this, she must go inside. She can't leave now when answers may just be behind that faded red wooden door, waiting for her to uncover them.

Taking a deep breath, she jaywalks across the street and makes her way into the bookshop. The smell of paper and ink brings Emma into a calm state. Being in the presence of the one thing that brings her peace in the world can make even the most daunting and uncomfortable tasks seem slightly more bearable.

No longer caring who else may be inside, Emma looks around the shop to find the curly silver-haired man with the wire-rimmed glasses she met a few short weeks ago. The red leather notebook is resting inside her small backpack; she can feel its weight even more now that she is in the shop, the enormity of the situation hitting her.

She hears him before she can see him. "Ah, welcome back!" says his voice, as he emerges from the dark of the back bookshelves on the first floor. "Is there anything I can help you with?" he asks as he makes his way to meet her at the checkout counter.

"I was wondering if you can help me find the name of a book?" she asks. "I'm afraid I don't know the author, but I have a few lines from the book."

The man nods and smiles. "Being an avid reader myself, I like to think I can identify a book based on a few lines. Do you have something that I can look at?"

Emma walks over to the counter, taking out her phone. "I have pictures."

"That works just fine. I just need to be able to read the words."

Emma smiles and nods. "Thank you so much." She unlocks her phone and goes to her photos, trying to control her shaking hands. Eventually, she finds the handful of pictures she took of the manuscript pages in Winnie's bookshelf and places her phone on top of the counter. "I came across these pages the other day…," she starts, looking at the shop owner as he peers at the picture through the glasses resting on the tip of his nose, hoping to see a reaction. When she gets nothing, she continues. Swiping to the last picture of the manuscript page with fewer scribbles, the note of encouragement 'O' left for Winnie is shown clear as day. "Based on this personal note, the pages could have been written around June 1989." The shop owner hasn't looked up nor has he said anything. Emma proceeds, taking his silence as a go-ahead rather than a stop.

"But lastly, I found this." She swipes her phone screen once more, showing the picture of the small lily sketch on the back of one of the pages. She then reaches into her bag and takes out her notebook, placing it right next to her phone. "The lily designs are the same." Her eyes never leave his face, gauging what kind of reaction he will have. Will he deflect and deny having any part of Winnie's book? Or will he confess and tell her what she already knows; that he is 'O.'

The shop owner takes off his glasses and runs his hand over his face. His face gives nothing away, but his eyes are a whole other story. Emma sees the pain, sadness, and heartache spurred by seeing the notebook and pages side by side. She hadn't noticed them before, but there are tired lines resting on the corners of his eyes, the only physical sign of his age. The rest of him looks like he could be in his forties, a bookish version of George Clooney. If he is indeed 'O', Emma can easily see why Winnie could have fallen for the younger version of him.

After what feels like forever, he finally speaks. "Where did you find these?" he asks, pointing at her phone—not accusatorily, but hopeful. As if Emma is presenting to him a treasure he has been seeking for years.

"A friend of mine has it. She doesn't know that I found it or that I took those pictures," Emma says out of breath.

"You know her?" he asks, not having to mention who 'her' is. "How has she been?" he asks in one giant breath.

And this is exactly why she was scared to come inside. Emma sees a swirl of emotions inside his eyes. Sadness? Anger? Regret? She can't quite tell what it is.

She looks down at the glass counter, uncertain how to proceed. But now that she started this, she can't go back, not when she is this close to finally getting some answers. "You knew her then? Winnie?" she asks, not answering his question about her since she herself doesn't even know how Winnie is.

The mention of her name jolts the owner. It's apparent he hasn't heard it in years, possibly thinking he would never hear that name again. He nods slowly, looking downcast. "I met her almost thirty years ago, in Tompkins Square Park." The shop owner looks up and takes in the whole place, as if he can see a young Winnie strolling through the shop.

Emma points to her phone screen. "You are 'O' then?"

He nods, a small smile of recollection creeps on his face. "Guilty. I helped her here and there when she was writing her book. Hence all the cross marks and annotations. You should have seen the rest of the pages; it was a sea of red and black."

"Did you know that it wasn't her who ended up publishing it?" asks Emma.

The owner looks off to the side, thinking. "I had a hunch it wasn't her," he says after a moment. "Some of the scenes in the published version were very different from how I know she envisioned them. The fact that it was published with a different name was also a giveaway. But since I haven't spoken to her in ages, I never was able to find out for certain. May I ask why you're interested in knowing about her book?" he asks.

The words are on her tongue, ready to be spoken. But hesitation lingers, forcing her to keep her mouth shut. Deciding whether she should tell the owner the truth, or at least half of it, about why she is here. Maybe that way he can see that she is trying to help Winnie, so he may be more willing to help her. "She doesn't know that I'm here, but she did tell me about her book, how it was published without her permission, without her name on it. But she didn't tell me its title." Emma pauses, taking a solid breath. "She also told me that she is in financial trouble and that she may need to sell her house soon. She's done so much for me, and I just want to do something in return for her. I was hoping you could tell me the title of her book, so I can help her return ownership to her. That way she doesn't have to worry about her financial situation, and she can stay in the house where she belongs."

"That's a very kind and selfless thing you are doing for her," says the owner. "But I'm sorry to say that I can't tell you the name."

Disappointment crushes her. She didn't realize that she expected the owner to tell her the name without any real effort until he just denied her that information. After being handed the unexpected, Emma grapples with where she goes from here. "Why not?" she asks, flustered.

The owner gives her a soft look of empathy, a look that says he wants to help her but for some reason cannot. "It's not my place to share," he says. "She never went public with it, so I have to respect that she wants to keep the ownership and her connection to the book a secret for a reason."

"Maybe she couldn't speak up about it. But that didn't mean she didn't want to," says Emma.

The owner takes this in, considering that there could be another reason why Winnie never came forward about her book. "You could be very right about that. The only thing I can tell you, and with certainty, is that if you can get the rights of her book back to her, she would never have to worry again about money for the rest of her life."

It takes Emma a moment to understand what he means, but then it clicks. "It's a bestseller," she says. The owner nods, confirming.

"It's been so long since it was first published, she could have given up trying to fight for it. Lost hope after all these years," says the owner. "She just needs someone to believe her and show her that all hope isn't lost just yet."

"May I ask what happened between you two?" asks Emma, hoping to get insight on the other unknown item, what exactly his relationship with Winnie was.

The man gives her a small, gentle smile. "Winnie and I were together, in love even. So, in love, we had a plan, a plan for us to be together, officially. First, she needed to file for divorce. She didn't have a lawyer, so she was reaching out to attorneys who would represent her. And when everything was settled and finalized, which we knew would take a long time as her husband wasn't an easygoing guy, we could officially be together, even get married one day. But then one morning, that plan went out the window," The man turns his head away, stares out the front window, looking at the constantly moving city.

"What happened?" asks Emma, feeling like she's on the edge of her seat, if she were to be sitting in one.

After a moment, he looks back at Emma and releases a heavy sigh. "I got a letter," he continues, "from Winnie. In just one sheet of paper, my life turned upside down. Instead of saying it to my face, she wrote that she was breaking things off with us. That she realized that she didn't want to leave Russel and felt that our relationship was just a phase and that she never really loved me.

"At first, I didn't want to believe it. I couldn't wrap my head around the words she wrote, how we were so happy and in love one moment, planning our future. Then a switch flipped and everything went away. I wanted so desperately to think that there was another reason, that what she said to me wasn't true. But after a few years when I didn't hear from her, I had to come to terms with the fact that she was never coming back. If she did love me, *if* that was enough, she would have come back to me."

"I'm so sorry," she says. "To go through that kind of love and pain, I can't fathom it, nor wish that on anyone." She looks down at the countertop, unintentionally staring at the notebook.

"I even made that for her too," says the man. "When I found out that she was a writer, I just knew I had to make her a notebook, one worthy of being filled with her poetic words." He runs his hand lightly over the cover. "I finished it a few days before I got her letter. Before I got the chance to give it to her. Since then, it had been sitting in this case, waiting for the next rightful owner." He looks back up at Emma, and this time a small smile creeps up on his face, a hint of a dimple just slightly showing. Emma tries to contain her excitement once she sees that dimple and registers again the color of the owner's eyes—warm brown.

Just like Noah's.

But she dismisses it once she remembers that brown is the most common eye color in the world. And the fact that the owner has the same eye color as Noah is no way conclusive evidence about his parentage.

"You never heard from her since that letter?" asks Emma.

The man shakes his head. "And as much as I wanted to reach out, especially with the technology of today, I never went against her wishes. I stayed away as she asked me to."

The owner pauses. After a quiet moment, he asks, "Is she happy?"

Emma nods. "I think so."

A woman's voice comes from behind them, a customer asking him a question about a book. The owner looks back at Emma briefly with a grateful look, as if he is relieved to finally be able to speak about the secret he had held on to for too long. "Good, I'm glad to hear that," says the owner before he heads over to speak with the customer.

Since she returned home from the bookshop, Emma has been thinking about her conversation with the shop owner, trying to figure out what her next course of action is. But the more she thinks, the more her brain feels muddled with which Reynard is her primary focus. As much as she wants to find the name of Winnie's book, she equally wants to know if there is enough evidence to support Noah's concern about his parentage. It could be entirely coincidental that Winnie had a brief affair before Noah was born, but it's not enough to make Emma fully believe the man said to be his father is not actually his father. But the more she thinks about the messiness of that situation, the more she knows it's not in her place to get involved. That is a family mess she does not want to get entangled with, nor a mess she should be stirring up.

She needs to stick to and focus on the one task that has a clear deadline: getting Winnie onboard with Emma's plan to get her book rights back.

But now as she sits in contemplation while eating dinner, Emma wonders how exactly she should tackle this. She wanted to at least know that Winnie has a solid case before presenting it to her, but now that she can't find the title of her book, there is no way for her to do that. After all that work, in the end, she has to ask Winnie the name herself.

But how do I bring up a topic that Winnie is not comfortable talking about?

"What has you so lost in thought?" asks her mom while taking a sip of wine, washing down the taste of marinara sauce. It is just the two of them for dinner tonight, as Oliver is preparing his opening statement for a case tomorrow. The two Callahan women decided to eat their Italian takeout on the kitchen island, rather than sitting formally at the kitchen table. "I know when something is going on in that head." Abigail turns to face Emma, leaning back on the stool and crossing her legs on the seat. She motions for her to speak. "Tell me. Maybe I can help."

Emma places her fork on her plate, then takes a sip of Chardonnay. "Oh, where to begin?" she starts. It takes her some time, but eventually she tells her mom everything. How it all started when Winnie told Emma about her book and financial bind, and how she also made Emma promise not to share this with Noah. She explains her plan to help Winnie with her dad's assistance to get back the rights to her book that will not only solve her financial conundrum but rightfully fix what was wrongfully taken from her. "I was hoping that when I found the only other person who knows the name of the book she wrote," continues Emma, "they would be able to tell me the name so that Dad can look into the history of the book's publication. That way I can tell Winnie with utter confidence that she has a solid case. But now that the person didn't feel it was their place to share it with me, I don't know what to do."

"What are you not sure about?" asks Abigail.

"Whether or not to tell Winnie about my idea," says Emma. "To get the name of the book, I'd have to go to her directly."

"And I'm guessing there is a reason why you didn't do that from the beginning?"

Emma nods. "When Winnie apologized to me about sharing those details, it seemed like she was ashamed or embarrassed. Ashamed that she is in this situation or ashamed that she doesn't know how to fix it. I was afraid to tell her about my plan. I didn't want to embarrass her or make her feel insulted in any way."

"Well, you're only assuming that's what she's feeling," says Abigail. "There really isn't any way to truly know unless you ask her about it directly. If anything, I think she would be mostly flattered that you care so much to help her rather than feeling insulted. But if I had to guess about what could be going on, it seems like Winnie falls under the category of someone who had to rely solely on herself for her whole life. For those people, it's extremely difficult for them to ask others for help. Whether it's from a lack of trust or trauma from someone they trusted. These people won't ever ask for help unless someone offers it to them. Maybe that's what you need to do for her."

Emma takes a moment to consider her mom's suggestion. As uncomfortable as she feels, she knows that her mom is right. She has to suck it up, be an adult, and talk to Winnie. Her alternative is to do nothing, and that is something Emma knows she cannot do. She cannot go on knowing she could have done something to help Winnie if she has to move away from West 4th Street. Emma simply wouldn't be able to live with that guilt. She has to do what's best for Winnie, not what's best—or easiest—for her.

"You're right," she says. "I can't overthink and assume what she's feeling. I simply need to tell her about my idea, even though that will make me a nervous wreck." She leans over to give her mom a hug, "Thank you for listening and making me see reason."

Abigail pulls Emma closer into her, reciprocating the embrace. "Of course, Ems. That's what I'm here for."

January 14, 1990

My Dearest Mémé,

He is here!

Noah Christopher Peterson. Born on January 12th, 1990, weighing seven pounds and six ounces. I can't wait for you to meet him. He looks so much like you, Mémé. I wonder if he will have our famous dirty blonde hair.

So far, Noah is not a fussy baby. Hopefully, he will stay this way!

Russel has taken fatherhood in short steps. He has been hands-on as much as he can—or wants to—but given that he is leading the biggest project at the company, I know he won't be around to help as much as I'd like. I have a feeling that a baby may not be enough to bring us together. I caught Russel coming home late after a long night of drinking and gambling, as if being a father is making him go back to his old ways rather than changing him in the way I hoped it would. It's so exhausting taking care of one small human being on my own—how can I have more kids? You know I want a large family, but I don't want to raise a family on my own.

For now, I hope Russel's expectations of me will adjust now that Noah is here. I worked with the club until the very day my water broke. I just hope he doesn't expect me to be able to be as hands-on as I was before.

He did make a comment earlier about me joining him at a gala at the Met in a few weeks. This event is 'the biggest of them all' since the company is trying to get the mayor to approve a restoration project at a historical site and needs all hands on deck, including the wives. I'm worried he expects me to look the part. Why is it that women are expected to bounce back post-pregnancy as if they didn't just push a human out of their vagina? Men. If they had to suffer one-third of what we women go through, they would be on their knees begging to take it away.

If only gender roles were reversed...

The only thing keeping me sane is knowing that you and my parents are visiting in just a couple of weeks. I will need all the help I can get with this little bundle of joy and doing what Russel expects me to do. I just wish you were able to stay much, much longer. If it were to be a perfect world, I wouldn't let you go back at all.

I'm afraid I can't write much more; Noah has started to cry again.

I cannot wait for you to be here and meet your great-grandson!

Ton petit soleil,

Winnie

P.S. Could you bring over some of your herbs? I can already feel how sleep-deprived I am going to be with this little one and dying for a large cup of femme forté. You'd be shocked to see the state my inventory is in now.

Chapter Seventeen

Emma stands by the front door, not quite ready to announce her arrival.

Lingering outside, she double-then triple-checks that this is what she wants to do. Because once she steps inside, there is no turning back. Before psyching herself out, Emma rings the doorbell.

It feels like it's been forever since she last stepped in this house. It's only been ten days since she last saw Winnie. But with each passing day, her sense of familiarity with the house slowly weakens, feeling more and more like a stranger as the days pile on.

As the minutes pass, Emma wonders if she should ring the bell once more or just step inside, as she did when she stopped by every day. Either option makes her skin crawl, not wanting to annoy Winnie by ringing again or offending her by barging right in. Eventually, she settles for the latter, hoping old habits can be used as her excuse.

She has never been inside when it was sundown, and seeing the home in the warm late afternoon glow makes Emma doubt for a second if she stepped inside the right house. It's the smell of lavender and freshly ground coffee beans that reassures her she is in the right place.

After walking around the first floor and seeing no sight of Winnie, Emma decides to take the obnoxious approach to find her. "Winnie? You here?" she yells out from the foyer. When she is met with silence, she starts to question whether she got the wrong day. She is about to reach for her phone to double-check their text history, making sure she came by at the correct time for late afternoon tea. But before she can unlock her phone, the back door opens, sending a gust of cold air into the cozy home. Emma's heart leaps out of her chest, as the last place she thought she would see Winnie emerge from is her backyard.

"Sorry!" apologizes Winnie as she stumbles inside, wrapped in winter attire like she is about to go on an expedition in the Arctic while carrying a snow shovel in her hand. "I decided to clear out the back when the snow softened up a bit. They predict we will get some more snow next week." Winnie shakes her head as she walks towards the foyer. "And that's exactly what we don't need, more snow." She starts to remove her layers of clothes in the foyer, placing them in the hall closet. Once she is in her normal outfit of a sweater and a pair of Lululemon leggings, she gives Emma a hug and motions her to get comfy.

Emma takes off her jacket and boots, also placing them inside the hall closet. She remembers to take her notebook from her bag, knowing she will need it to show Winnie the poem she wanted her to look at. Once she is fully out of her winter gear, she follows Winnie into the library where she already has two cups of tea on the coffee table.

The pair sit comfortably on the couch. Emma, making herself at home, takes the merino wool blanket and wraps her bottom half in a cocoon, grabbing her mug from the coffee table as the cherry on top of her comfort cocoon. "How is the start of your semester?" she asks Winnie.

Winnie rolls her eyes. "I thought last semester's students were tough. I have a new student in my roster, and I have never met such a difficult thirteen-year-old in my years of tutoring. Teenagers these days," she says, shaking her head as she takes a sip of tea. "I understand that most of them are forced to take my class because their parents want them to know multiple languages and be these great exemplars of humanity so they can get into an Ivy League school, but what their parents forgot to instill in them is manners and good decency. Enough about me though, how have you been? You said in your text you had a poem you want to show me."

Emma nods and reaches for her notebook. "I wrote this not too long ago, and I actually feel proud of it?" She ends as a question, but more of a question to herself. "I want you to read it, only if you want to." Emma places the pen in the lock and opens it to the first page in the notebook. She takes a deep breath, reading over her poem once more, double-checking her decision to have another's eyes read her words. Having Winnie's eyes read her work.

Here goes nothing...

After another moment of reluctance, Emma hands the notebook over to Winnie.

Winnie examines the leather and engraving detail on the cover, then marvels at the backside. Both wonder and curiosity spread across her face as she runs her eyes over the notebook. Perplexity lingers on her face, as Emma wonders if the lily flowers look familiar to her. Winnie runs her hand once more over the smooth red leather. "This is beautiful."

It was made for you. "Thank you," she says instead, then shakes her head. "I don't know why I said that. I didn't make it," she laughs once realizing how dumb it sounds for her to take credit for something she had no part in crafting.

"You have good taste in notebooks then," says Winnie as she laughs at Emma's slightly awkward response.

Emma stares out the front window as Winnie reads her poem, too self-conscious to watch her reaction. This is the poem she wrote after the planetarium trip, and Emma just hopes Winnie doesn't get too weird if she realizes that the poem was inspired by her son.

Time ticks by slowly. Too slow for Emma. It feels like it's been too long since she gave Winnie her notebook. She dares to peek at her and is caught by surprise. Tears are falling down Winnie's cheeks as she reads and then re-reads the poem. Her fingers are resting over her lips, trying to contain her emotions. It feels like there is a knife wedged into Emma's heart; the last thing she wanted to do was upset Winnie, and clearly that is what she has done. She only wanted to show the one person who motivated her to write poems to feel a bit proud of her progression. But now she has done the exact opposite of making her feel proud.

Emma reaches out to her, then hesitates, not sure if she should comfort her or let her cry in peace. Knowing what she would want someone to do for her in a moment like this, Emma places a sympathetic hand on Winnie's shoulder. "Are you alright?"

Winnie nods, a bit too much, as if she is trying to convince herself as well. She wipes away the tears on her cheeks, then gives Emma a weak reassuring smile. "It's good," she finally says. "A poem should resonate with everyone, even though its meaning may be different from person to person. Just as it should invoke the reader to feel understood," Winnie places her pointer finger on the notebook page and taps it. "You did exactly that, my dear. You should be very proud of it."

The compliment warms Emma's cheeks, and a slight giddy sensation runs through her from Winnie's praise. "Thank you."

New tears start to run down Winnie's cheeks. "I can't seem to stop," she says while laughing them away.

Emma doesn't know when she reached out to hold Winnie's hand. Deep down she hopes she is sending Winnie a signal, letting her know it's okay for her to speak her mind, to unburden herself from all the emotions she's feeling. As much as Emma wants to initiate the conversation, she also knows that she can't. That Winnie must be the one to do it.

A fatigued sigh escapes out of Winnie's mouth, one that tells of her exhaustion and pain in one sound. "I know I never talked to you about my book and what happened to it," she finally says once her tears have stopped. "It's connected to my relationship with my husband. I know Noah must have shared with you what happened to his dad."

Emma nods. "He told me about the accident."

"What else did he tell you about his dad?"

Emma takes a moment to respond, trying to think of what Noah told her versus what O told her or what she found out herself. "He said you were high school sweethearts, and were a happy, loving family when he was a kid. He doesn't remember much else about his dad since he passed when he was so young."

Winnie nods. "I always made sure he would see it that way." A weak smile rises on her face. "I'm happy to know that he still thinks that way."

"What do you mean?" asks Emma, trying to understand what she is vaguely telling her.

"Noah… he… he never knew what his father was truly like." Looking at Emma, Winnie can still see the confusion on her face. "We were high school sweethearts," explains Winnie, her demeanor now shifting to story mode. "Or that is what it seemed to be at first. Swept up in the idea of love, I followed him to New York as he pursued his dream in architecture and I went to NYU, hoping to become a writer. For a while, we were happy and in love."

Emma can see a shift in Winnie. Her voice becomes lower, her body language becomes more rigid as her memories of her younger years flash back into her mind. "Things started to change when Russel started working for Graham & Boch as an architecture apprentice," continues Winnie. "As his new, devoted wife, I supported him in his decision. He was going to work for one of the country's best architectural companies. I couldn't have been prouder. But as he became successful and climbed up the ladder, he started to change. The stress and the workload put such a heavy amount of pressure on him that he started drinking heavily to cope. When I first noticed it, I tried to confront him about it, tried to help him, but he wouldn't have it. He just couldn't see how his drinking was consuming him, how he needed it to function on a day-to-day basis.

"Then one morning, I woke up and no longer could see the man that I married and fell in love with. The smart and sweet boy who charmed me back in high school was gone. He completely changed into someone who slipped easily into alcoholic rages and gambled uncontrollably, someone who lashed out at the people who loved him the most. It was over the dumbest things, but it was just enough to fire him up." Winnie stops and clears her throat, preventing herself from letting her emotions get the best of her.

"After a year of him being with the company," she continues, "our relationship became very fragile and strained. The love we had was long gone. I felt more like a prop to him than a partner. I was in such a dark place at that time of my life. Never had I felt so alone and scared, trapped in a marriage with someone who was becoming more and more like a stranger. I felt so trapped that even being alone in our house would make me panic, feeling like the walls were suffocating me.

"I couldn't breathe in that place, let alone cope with what my life had become. So, I did the only thing I could do: I'd escape the house for hours, venturing around the East and West Village while Russel was away at work. Giving myself some time to breathe and feel at ease. And it was in those blissful, freeing hours that I met him."

"Who?" asks Emma, even though she has a hunch who she means.

"Owen," says Winnie, with a sad smile of remembrance, "the love of my life."

Even though she knew it was coming, Emma's mouth still opens slightly from shock that Winnie said his name out loud, finally acknowledging who he is to her. "How long were you two together?" asks Emma, keeping up with the pretense that she doesn't already know this. Even wondering herself if she should tell Winnie that she met him and knows where he is. But for now, she allows Winnie to finish her story.

"Only for a few months."

"What happened?" she asks, eager to finally hear her side of their love story.

"Russel found out about us. Before he did, I was all set and ready to leave him. Being with Owen made me realize what love is supposed to be, and that gave me the courage to file for divorce."

The mention of Winnie and lawyers makes a lightbulb suddenly turn on in Emma's head. Maybe this time she will get the final, truthful answer regarding why Winnie was so uncomfortable around her dad. "I know you went to my dad's old firm about a potential case. Was it actually about seeking a divorce from your husband?" Winnie nods, confirming the true reason.

"But what I still don't understand is why they never took on your case. I mean it seems like you had grounds for the divorce, with the way he has been treating you. Was it the affair? Would that have expelled the case, making it go into your husband's favor if that was brought up in court?" asks Emma.

Winnie shakes her head. "My contact with your dad and the other lawyers was very limited. They didn't know the specifics of my case. Once they heard who my husband was, they wouldn't go anywhere near it." Seeing the confusion on Emma's face, Winnie elaborates. "I didn't know then when my husband first joined his company, and I don't think he did either, that they had a partnership with some illegal groups in the city."

"You mean like the mafia?"

"Not necessarily them, but some organized crime groups, yes. I had suspicions that my husband's company laundered money for them and in return the groups would persuade companies to let them have any building project or available land they wanted, some sort of quid pro quo. I think your dad's previous family law firm knew that as well and didn't want to get involved with the wife of someone who had that kind of connection. Before I could even find another lawyer who would help me, despite my name, Russel found out about Owen. Then I had no choice but to stay with him."

The wheels turn slowly in Emma's head, trying to understand why Winnie would be forced to stay with him. "Did he threaten you?"

Winnie shakes her head. "Worse. He would have gone after Owen and-" She was going to say something else, but something stopped her from speaking aloud.

"And who?" asks Emma, feeling like she has been sitting on the edge of the couch during this whole conversation.

She looks over at Emma with so much pain in her eyes, even Emma could cry. "Noah."

Emma scrunches her eyebrows inward, confused as to how Noah could be involved in this, and then her eyes bulge in shock once she connects the dots.

She was already pregnant with him at that time…

"Noah wasn't his," says Emma, not realizing she said it out loud. She can feel her pulse beating rapidly now that she finally got the proof to confirm Noah's real parentage.

Winnie nods. "I was terrified of Russel also finding out I was pregnant when he found out about Owen. So, I had to cover it up and make him believe it was his without a doubt. You know…" she trails off, not feeling fully comfortable with revealing exactly how. But it didn't take too long for Emma to connect that she is referring to their physical relationship. "If he found out that the baby wasn't his, I know he would have resorted to…" she looks down at her hands resting now on her lap and barely murmurs, "ways to terminate it. I told him as late as possible not to make him question the timing of things exactly." Winnie shakes her head at herself. "I also naively thought that maybe a baby would help our relationship, possibly glue our family together."

"And did it? Help, I mean," says Emma.

"I wish I could say it did, but Russel kept up with his ways. I knew then that if he wouldn't change for a child, he would never change."

"Did any of your family know about what was happening?" asks Emma.

"Only my mémé did. After Noah was born and Russel was still being Russel, she came to visit. After seeing in person what I'd been writing to her for months, she decided that I needed her. That Noah and I needed her. She moved in with us and stayed with us until she passed."

Not wanting to think for another second what Winnie's husband would have done to her if he had ever found out the truth, Emma instead asks what she is dying to know now. "Does Owen know? About Noah?"

Winnie shakes her head. "I found out about the pregnancy around the same time Russel found out about us. I would have told Owen, but by then I was trapped. To protect him and Noah, I had to keep him in the dark and leave him, no matter how much it pained me to do so."

Emma looks back at Winnie and notices how different she seems; her usual cheeriness has been replaced by grief and pain as she unravels her story.

"You sacrificed your happiness to protect the ones you love," Emma proclaims, letting the weight of Winnie's history settle into her. She feels the soul-crushing weight of all of it. "When your husband died, did you think to find him? Owen?"

"Of course," Winnie responds instantly. "Once I got the call informing me about the accident, the first thing I thought of was finding him."

"And did you?"

Winnie shakes her head. "No."

"Why? You were free to go to him."

"I had Noah to think about," says Winnie. "I couldn't confuse and hurt him more if I told him the truth. He was only eight at the time. Besides, eight years had gone by since I last saw Owen. For all I knew, he could have left the city, found someone else, and gotten married, started his own family..." Winnie stops to collect herself from choking up. "The thought of him moving on—I feared that if he did, it would mean that our love wasn't what I thought it was, and that terrified me. I decided that I'd rather be left in the dark than to face that reality. Even if there was a chance he would have taken me back, it would have broken my heart to see him again after all that time and be hit with the truth that I had clung on to a love that wasn't real."

Emma is utterly speechless, having never heard such a heartbreaking story. For her, the love stories she reads almost always have a happy ending, despite the rocky road that leads them there. Now she realizes that the narrative that true love will always prevail is just a naïve dream for the protagonist to cling on to, believing that their suffering will eventually lead them to their true love in the end. Those stories are just that—stories, made up to instill that false hope into hopeless romantics. Winnie's story is a rude awakening for those romantics like Emma.

But after hearing both Owen's and Winnie's sides of their love story, Emma knows that they still love each other. Even after almost thirty years since they went their separate ways, their love is still very much alive. A part of Emma hopes that maybe one day these lovers will find each other again and finally get their happy ending. It breaks her heart to know that there is a very realistic chance that they will remain as they are now, brokenhearted and insistent on believing that the other stopped loving them long ago.

"He really did take everything from me. My heart, my happiness," says Winnie, breaking the silence. Emma knows that she is not referring to Owen, but Russel. "Even…" she starts saying, her eyes darting to the corner of the bottom bookshelf.

Emma follows her eyes, staring at the faded green folder. She gets up from the couch and walks to the bookshelf, bending down to pick up the folder from its tight corner spot. Emma stares at it in her hands, a raw, naked feeling creeping over her, acknowledging that the reveal of Winnie's book is just about to be revealed. She lifts it with the cover facing Winnie. "Even this?" she says.

Winnie's cheeks become ashen as she sees Emma hold onto her other secret. Winnie slowly nods her head, panic swimming in her eyes. "Even that."

September 1, 1998

It feels silly to write this. But I've heard that this may help with my grief. Help me process and accept that I've lost you. The one person I couldn't live without. So here I am, writing a letter to you that I know you will never read. It will be stashed away along with all your letters and mine that Pépé mailed to me a few weeks ago.

It's been two months since you died, and yet it feels like it was yesterday that I last heard your voice, last felt your touch. I don't know if there will ever be a day that I don't miss you. Most days, the pain is just too much.

And my poor Noah. He lost two important people in his life so soon and so quickly. He thinks I've been sad about the loss of Russel, but all my pain comes from losing you. For his sake, I keep up that charade, as he not only lost his great-grandma, but he lost his dad too. I don't think I can ever tell him about the true nature of his father. I know it would be best for him to keep thinking only good things about him, about our family.

It's been eight years, and I still think about him. My Owen. My Fossettes. I even see him in Noah, maybe too much. It's a curse for my son to look so much like the man I love, the man I couldn't be with. But we both know that I cannot complain about something that I purposefully did.

I have thought about finding him every day since Russel died. But every time I muster the courage to do so, I just can't do it. I keep thinking of Noah and how the truth would be too much for a young boy to handle. He just lost his father; he doesn't need to be hurt even more. Besides, I know after everything I did to him, Owen may never want to see me again. I don't know how you can show up in someone's life eight years later after doing the most heartbreaking thing to them.

All I know is this: I will always love him. My Beck.

I just hope that he knows that his Madeleine never once stopped loving him.

Just as I hope you know how much I love you.

Goodbye my mémé. Until we see each other again.

Ton petit soleil,

Winnie

Chapter Eighteen

Emma watches Winnie flip through the manuscript pages as if she is reading her own words for the first time. She sits next to her on the couch, waiting with anticipation for her to speak. Ever since Winnie told her that she wrote a book, along with its unfortunate publication and her financial worries, she's been anxious to know the name not only to proceed with her idea, but to finally find out the bestseller Winnie wrote—and didn't get the credit for.

Emma waits patiently for Winnie to finish. But her patience soon runs out. "Can you tell me the name of your book?" she asks, unable to wait for even another minute to get her answer.

"You've probably been dying to know since I told you about it," says Winnie, smiling.

"Oh, you have no idea," laughs Emma.

"I've already spilled my secrets. What's another going to do?" says Winnie, as if she's trying to convince herself that it is okay to say it. She takes a deep breath, then looks at Emma. "It's been more than fifteen years since it was published. I was actually surprised they used the title I gave it. The book I wrote, poured my heart and soul into, is *The Port to Sea*," says Winnie.

At first, Emma thought she had misheard her. She thought she had heard her say the title of her favorite novel. Which is why she had to double-check. "Did you say *The Port to Sea*?" she asks. "One of the best love stories to have ever existed?"

"I wouldn't call it that," says Winnie, "but yes. You heard me correctly."

This moment feels too surreal for Emma. Even though she knows Winnie, looking at her now, she sees her in a completely new light, absolutely starstruck. Sitting right next to her is the writer who brought Madeleine and Beck to life, inspiring thousands of hopeless romantics with their love story. One that had ultimately proved that despite life's challenges, true love will always find its way.

"You know," says Emma before she loses the courage to ever say this out loud, "I've read your book probably more than anyone else on the planet. Your prose and the way you portrayed Madeleine and Beck's relationship were so real and raw. It feels like more than one of those sappy romance books—it feels like a love story that could really happen. You showed women an accurate portrayal of unconditional love that's still a healthy relationship, proving to us that we can have that kind of love. That we do deserve that kind of love. I want to thank you for bringing that story into my life and to the lives of all the other women and young girls like me."

A painful smile rests on Winnie's face upon hearing Emma's words, feeling a mixture of happiness and sadness at the same time. "I've always wanted to hear those words. To know that..." she takes a moment, collecting herself, "my story touched the hearts of others makes all the pain and loss I suffered from writing it, worth it." Winnie reaches out to grasp onto Emma's hand. "Thank you."

"Wait a minute," says Emma as she connects the dots of the story Winnie is telling and the story she wrote. "Is *The Port to Sea* based on a true story? Are Madeleine and Beck, you, and Owen?"

Winnie nods with a proud, yet sad smile on her face. "Yes."

"Holy s-," starts Emma, her mind blown knowing that her favorite love story is based on a true one. Madeleine and Beck are *real*, not just some made-up characters in a book. And she knows one and met the other! Then she realizes there is still one part of the story Winnie hasn't told her yet. "How did the book end up getting published under C.K. Rothschild?"

"Russel found out about my affair because of my story," admits Winnie. "I stupidly left my pages all over our dining room table while he was away on a work trip. Of course, he had to come home a few days earlier than expected. While I stepped out to see Owen, he found them read through all of it."

"When I got back, he acted like his usual self, didn't even give me one hint that he had uncovered it. But those pages, our annotations, were enough evidence to convince him I was in love with someone else. He then hired a private investigator to follow me. They tracked me to Owen's, proving my infidelity to him. He then burned every page of my manuscript. Even all my copies.

"But if your husband burned all the copies, how did it get published?" asks Emma.

"Well, little did I know that when he said he destroyed it, he didn't burn every copy. He kept one for himself and sold it off to a publisher. Knowing my husband, he probably thought he would get a good price for it, and it would help pay off his gambling debts. But somehow, the universe was still looking out for me."

"What do you mean?"

"The publisher only gave him half the money they agreed to upfront. The rest they would pay once the book was published. He gave them the manuscript in June 1989, but the book wasn't published until 2004."

Still not following, Emma's eyebrows pull inwards, not comprehending the significance of the time gap.

"My husband died in June 1998," says Winnie, practically spelling it out for her.

"Oh," says Emma once it clicks in her head. "Your husband wasn't alive to see it get published and get the other half of the money."

"I never knew that he did this, until one day in March 2004, a letter addressed to my husband arrived. It was from the publisher, explaining how due to an office move, the manuscript had been lost. One day in 2002, my story was rediscovered and was set to be published. So along with this explanation, they also provided a check with the remaining fifty percent that they owed him. Imagine my surprise when I saw this letter, telling me that my story was getting published but under a different author. I was reminded again not just of what I lost, but I also got to see who my husband truly was: a self-centered, cold, manipulative man."

"So, there was never a C.K. Rothschild?"

"No. I could imagine my husband made up that name, his way of further hurting me by ensuring my name would never be tied to the book I created. That, and he only saw the dollar signs that came along with it. When my story ended up becoming this bestselling phenomenon, it felt like my whole world crumpled underneath my feet again. The world would never know that it was my masterpiece."

"And if Russel didn't steal your book, you could have published your book and you wouldn't be having to worry about money now," says Emma, understanding what Winnie meant back when she told her this information weeks ago.

Winnie scoffs. "I would have been set for life with the number of copies sold over the years."

Emma, taking this as her opportunity, places her hand over Winnie's. "But what if we can fix that?"

Confused yet intrigued, Winnie raises an eyebrow. "How could we fix that?"

"Well," starts Emma, "after we do some digging about the actual contract with the publishing house, my dad is willing to help you fight to get your rights back. To get your book back."

Emma can see a hint of hope forming in Winnie's eyes. "You would do that for me?"

"Of course, in a heartbeat. So how does that sound? Would you like him to take a look, see if there's something we can work with?"

Winnie takes a moment, thinking over this means not only for her, but also for Noah. "Let me think about it for a few days. I'm unsure if I want my past to be dug up and put on full display."

Emma squeezes her hand. "Only if you want to. Take your time and think about it."

Hopefully not too much time so our efforts won't be too late.

"Did you ever try to write another book?" asks Emma. This question has been lingering in her mind for the past several minutes, as she knows that someone with Winnie's talent should be doing nothing but writing books.

Winnie sighs deeply before answering. "My mémé kept trying to convince me to. She knew how much writing meant to me and how much that story meant to me." A chuckle escapes from her. "That was the one downfall of having her live with me. She pestered me day and night about it. I thought about trying to write another story, but then Russel died, and shortly after that, my mémé passed too. After I lost her, I was just so heartbroken and lost, and I had to raise an eight-year-old boy all on my own. I got so overwhelmed trying to stay afloat with my grief and my duties of motherhood that I could not fathom writing anything. Doing the one thing that brought me so much joy and happiness into my life just didn't feel the same anymore. Especially when the last person who believed in my writing was gone."

"How come you never told Noah about your book?" asks Emma.

A tired sigh comes from deep within Winnie. "How could I? To tell him about it, I also would have to explain what I did, what his father did." She shakes her head. "I never was able to tell him the truth of who his dad truly was, what our relationship truly was, or what he did to me for years." Winnie places a hand on top of the opened folder. "I hid for years. At first from Russel, and then from Noah. When he moved out, I finally felt like I didn't have to hide it anymore." Winnie looks at Emma with relief and contentment. "You have no idea how good it feels for someone to finally know the truth."

"I'm happy you feel that you could share that with me. But…" says Emma, thinking about what her knowing the whole truth really means. "It also kind of puts me in a weird predicament with Noah. With us dating and all," says Emma, panic and anxiety already consuming her.

Winnie squeezes Emma's hand. "I know. It wouldn't be fair for me to ask you to keep my secrets from him. I know I will have to tell him now." Winnie looks out the window into the street where it is now pitch dark. "I'm just terrified he will never forgive me if I do."

And now I'm terrified he won't forgive me for knowing before him…

Emma clenches onto their conjoined hands, hoping to give Winnie the strength and courage she will need to tell her son the truth.

Chapter Nineteen

It's been two days since Winnie told Emma everything, yet it feels like it's been much longer.

For those two days, Emma has been desperately wanting to tell Noah, but she knows better than to tell him what should only come from Winnie. When he texted her earlier that he was going over to his mom's house for brunch, Emma knew right away that it wasn't going to be a normal meal with his mom. In a matter of hours, she knows his life will be turned completely upside down.

And there is nothing Emma can do to help. He needs to hear this from Winnie, a conversation all on their own, as mother and son.

The only thing she can do is be there for him when he is ready to talk about it. Although there are so many ways this could go wrong, she keeps hoping that the whole revelation goes well and that he understands why she didn't tell him before.

Emma tries to keep herself occupied by reading *The Little Prince* in her room, getting lost inside the world within its pages. She gets so entranced by the story that she nearly misses Noah's call.

"Noah?" she answers, her heart beating out of her chest.

"Hey. Are you home?" he asks, his voice sounding so faint that Emma could barely hear him.

She sits upright, placing the book on her nightstand. "Yeah, I'm just reading. Is everything okay?"

"She told me everything," he says.

Emma's heart breaks into a million pieces once she hears the pain in his voice. "Where are you?" she asks, wanting to be there with him, to hold on to him while he processes it all.

"Outside."

Rushing out of her bedroom, she puts on a coat and a pair of shoes, not noticing whose they are. As soon as she shuts the front door, she takes him into her arms. Emma can feel that he is upset, and rightfully so. Once they break apart, they sit on the front stoop, watching the afternoon traffic of pedestrians and cars go by. Emma sits close to Noah, but not so close that their bodies touch. She wants to give him some space to process everything, but not too much space that it feels weird or uncomfortable.

"What's going on inside that head of yours?" she asks after they sit in silence for some time.

Noah runs a hand across his face, showing how disheveled and confused he is. "Where do I start? The fact that my dad isn't my biological dad? Or that he tormented my mom for years? Stole my mom's book and sold it off to spite her? Or the fact that it took this long for my mom to tell me the truth, telling my girlfriend all of this first before telling me, her son?"

Emma's heart skips a beat when he says "girlfriend", something she's never been called before. It takes her out of the moment for a second. She can't help the small, giddy smile that creeps up on the corners of her lips.

The sound of a police siren in the distance brings her back to the moment, remembering that as Noah's girlfriend, she needs to be supportive and attentive as his world is being pulled from under his feet. There will be a time and place later for Emma to digest Noah casually dropping the 'g' word.

"I'm still trying to process all of it," says Noah, rubbing his left temple. Emma can hear the emotional strain in his voice.

"How are you feeling, about all of it?" asks Emma.

"Confused, hurt, feeling like my life and family were all a lie," he says as he plays with his shoelaces, looking more like a kid than a grown man. Emma knows that feeling too well, needing to do something physical while trying to think, to process everything, even to try to hide behind the pain. "Everything I know about my family wasn't true. This whole time I thought my parents were happy and loved each other," he starts to massage both his temples now, releasing any tension building up in his head.

Then his head perks up, a realization suddenly hitting him. "Now I know why we never talked about him after he died. It wasn't because she was heartbroken from losing him. She was relieved. She was no longer trapped by the person who was causing her so much pain. By not talking about him, that allowed her to move on from him. Here I was, thinking it was because she was fragile and too emotionally broken by it." Noah shakes his head at himself, feeling foolish for not seeing the truth earlier. "How did I miss that? What he was doing to her for all those years."

Emma places a hand on his shoulder. "Would you have wanted to see that? You were so young when it happened. Your mom protected you from seeing that for a reason, Noah."

He nods. "I know, but I still feel that I could have done something, at least comforted her when she needed it."

"Just imagine being in her shoes: what would you have done for your child in that situation?"

"You're right," he says after pondering it for a moment. "I would have done the same thing." Suddenly he stands up, pacing back and forth on the sidewalk in front of her, as if walking will help him gather his thoughts. "I want to be angry at her for lying to me for my whole life," he says passionately, "but now that I know what she did, for me, even for Owen, my heart hurts more from knowing what she did to protect me than from her lying to me." Emma can see tears form in the corners of his eyes as he stops pacing in front of her. She can see he is thinking; she can almost feel the wheels turning in his head. Then a deep, tired sigh escapes his mouth. "Good god, she has done so much for me, and I haven't known. After all these years..." He wipes away the tears with his hand just as they are about to fall down his cheeks. "And now she tells me that she may have to sell the house too." Noah shakes his head in disbelief. "She can be so stubborn and strong-willed. I just wish she would have told me these things. I can help her. She doesn't have to figure it out all on her own. She doesn't have to protect me anymore."

"Maybe she doesn't know how not to," suggests Emma.

"Thank you for seeing that she needed help and still offering it even though she never asked," says Noah. "She has always felt that she has to do things on her own, and now I know why. It's from her wanting to be in control of things, never wanting to feel so helpless and trapped ever again." He runs a hand through his hair, coming to a realization. "Which is what she must be feeling now with the house and everything."

Noah sits back down as silence emerges again. Emma wants to give him as much time as he needs to process and talk. The last thing she wants to do is bombard him with questions all at once. But the one thing she feels she needs to ask is how he feels about the man who is his biological father. "How do you feel about Russel not being your father?"

"I barely remember the man. I have zero emotional attachment or connection to him. When my mom told me he wasn't my father, I should have had some strong reaction to it. But instead, I was non-chalant, neutral. What's really throwing me off is the fact that I have a living, breathing father, when for so long I thought he was gone."

Everything Noah is currently experiencing is unimaginable to Emma, having been raised by two parents who not only love and adore her, but love and support each other. While Emma tries to comprehend Noah's conundrum, she wonders if both he and Owen would be open not only to meeting, but also to having some sort of relationship. But she knows now it isn't the right time to open that can of worms, when everything is still fresh and raw. "And her affair? I can imagine that must have come as a shock to you."

"Surprised, yes. But I don't feel like it's my place to judge her for that, you know? She was unhappy and trapped in a marriage to someone she didn't love. I don't fault her for falling in love with someone else. I mean, I wouldn't be here today with you if she didn't." He looks at Emma with tenderness and compassion in his face, as if he can understand why his mom fell for someone else. "You know, when she first told me about Owen, I thought it was just a fling, someone to distract her from her misery. But when she showed me her manuscript pages, with all of their notes, you can't read that and not think that they truly did love each other."

"It's sad when you think about it," says Emma, "two people who clearly loved each other and were forced to be apart."

"What saddens me the most," says Noah with a sigh, "is that my mom confided in you before me."

Silence emerges between them once more. Emma feels nothing but guilt building inside. Here he is, knowing that his mom confided in Emma before him. She can easily imagine he believes that her friendship with his mom is closer than what they have, and what that means for them. The guilt eating inside her prompts her to feel the need to come clean about *every* detail. Picking at the hair tie around her wrist, her left foot jittering up and down, Emma anxiously tries to build up the courage to speak up, but every time she opens her mouth, nothing comes out. Her stomach starts to turn; the longer time stretches, the worse she starts to feel. Confrontation is not something she handles well, but this time she knows she must do this.

"I have to tell you something," she suddenly blurts out, surprised by hearing her own voice in her ears.

Noah picks up his head that had been hunched over, resting in between his hands. "Sure, what's up?" he says. Seeing the exhaustion in his eyes makes Emma stop and question whether now is a good time. His mom just turned his life upside down; the last thing he needs is someone else adding to it.

But now that she opened her mouth, she knows she can't back out.

Here goes nothing. Let's try not to screw this up terribly, Emma. Okay?

"Your mom told you about the pages of her manuscript I found?"

"Yeah."

"Well, I noticed on one of the pages there was a handwritten note for her. I didn't know who it was since they only signed it with the first letter of their name, but the message they wrote made it pretty clear that the person truly loved her, and that she may have loved him back."

Noah's eyebrows crease inwards, curious to know where this is going. He motions for her to continue.

"I didn't think about it too much since I wasn't familiar with your family story and what happened to your dad, so I brushed it aside. But when you told me during our first date about how you always had this gut feeling that your parentage may not be what you've been told, it got me thinking back to those pages and that note. I wanted to make sure, *really* make sure, that I had actual proof before telling you. I didn't want to say something then end up being wrong and having you accuse your mom of something that isn't true.

"I thought if I could find the man who wrote that note on the page, he may know about your mom's book and provide clarity on your parentage."

"And did you?" asks Noah, "Find him?" His voice conveys not one ounce of emotion, neither upset nor angry. The dry ambiguity in his voice leaves Emma unable to gauge what he is feeling, making her fear her worst-case scenario has come true.

"I did," says Emma, "but by luck actually." She explains to him about the bookstore and the notebook, and how she connected the owner to his mom's pages and its note. "When I went to go see Owen at the store," she continues, "I didn't know for sure that he was your father, but I did find out that he and your mom were together. I didn't get the whole picture of all of it, I swear. But I realized after that it wasn't my place to dig into something like that. So, I left it. But when I went to go see her a few days ago, my goal solely being helping her, it was like she was ready for the wall that she built up and kept for all these years to finally fall down. It felt like she wanted to tell someone about what happened to her all those years ago, just waiting for the right moment." Not knowing what else there is left to say, Emma stops talking, waiting for Noah to say something. Anything that indicates how he is feeling about this.

Noah runs a hand across his face, and a heavy sigh escapes him. Heavy silence lingers for a few moments, but it feels like forever to Emma. Her heart beats loudly in her chest; she can feel it pulsing from her head to toes. The anticipation is slowly killing her, making her second-guess the way she phrased and worded things. She runs over the entire conversation in her head to see if she said anything incorrectly or missed any signals from his body language.

"You knew for weeks that there was another man in my mom's life?" Noah eventually asks.

"I didn't know that exactly," says Emma, hoping to make it clear that she wasn't sure about that all this time. "I only knew that there was a slight possibility."

"Possibility or not, you didn't think to tell me about it sooner?" he asks. Emma could hear the pain and hurt in his voice.

"I thought that telling you this without knowing for certain would make a mess of things. I didn't want you and your mom to get into it when it could turn out to be nothing at all, that I was completely wrong about everything."

"I just..." starts Noah. Emma sees in his face how he is trying to balance his rationality with his emotions. "It upsets me to know that you had information about my real father and knew where he was, and you didn't share it with me."

"I know, and I'm sorry I didn't tell you sooner. I just didn't know how to tell you without making things worse."

After a few more minutes of silence, Emma watches Noah think, he finally gets up and stands in front of her on the sidewalk. "Listen, I appreciate you telling me this," he stops and looks down the street to his right, closes his eyes briefly, then turns to look back at her. "But with everything going on, finding out my mom had been lying to me for years, I feel like I can't trust anyone. I'm not saying that I don't trust you, but after my mom dropping a bombshell like that, I can't think straight." He raises his hand to rub his left temple, "I just need some time to think and process everything."

"Of course, take all the time you need," says Emma, knowing that is the right thing to say and meaning it, while also trying to understand what he means by needing time.

A sigh escapes his mouth, running his hand across his face. "I think I need to be on my own for a while."

"As in we're breaking up?" asks Emma, hoping to be wrong.

Noah nods his head. "I think that would be best for the both of us."

"Okay," she says meekly, her heart plummeting into her stomach. She nods slowly to process what just happened.

After they say their goodbyes, Emma watches Noah walk down West 4th Street until he is a tiny blip in her vision and then disappears around a corner, wondering if that's the last she'll ever see of him.

She knows that it's not only the freezing air that is making her feel numb. She heads back inside the rowhouse robotically, feeling wholly detached from her body. She walks mindlessly to the family room and plops onto the couch, staring blankly at the wall while Sadie places her head on her thigh, giving her comfort.

Chapter Twenty

It's February, and Emma is back at her desk at SpikeSearch. Valentine's Day is just around the corner, with March soon closing in. Her two-and-a-half-week adventure with Winnie and Noah feels like a lifetime ago, just a footnote in Emma's short story of her life.

For the past five weeks, Emma has kept her contact with Noah very brief, knowing he needs time alone. The last time she heard from him was when she texted him about their latest class trip a week and a half ago. The conversation didn't go beyond more than two text messages each. Emma can't lie to herself; she is aware of how every day she hopes to get a text or call from him, ready to patch things up and maybe even get back together. But as the days turn into weeks, Emma knows that she has to come to terms with the fact that he may never come back at all.

She hasn't visited Winnie either, as she feels doing so will only muddy the waters more than clear things up. Thankfully, after explaining what happened between the two of them, Winnie understood and holds nothing personal against her for not coming over. For now, they have settled on the occasional text exchange to catch up; Winnie always asks whether Emma has heard anything from Noah as she too hopes that he will come around. But the text messages don't fill the void where their friendship used to be.

Besides, Emma can only imagine how busy Winnie is going to be now that she is working with her dad. It's been only a few weeks since Oliver started looking into her case, and Winnie and he have already had several meetings and phone calls about it. It's taking him much longer than expected to get the contract from the publishing house. His associates are even reaching out to find the exact editor that made the original deal with Russel, trying to get as much detail as they can about what exactly went down with this book deal. The slow-moving progress is killing not only Winnie, but Emma as well. When a day goes by with no updates, that is another day getting closer to when Winnie needs to decide about her house.

And as happy as Emma feels that there is a chance Winnie can keep her house and get her book back, Emma can't help but look at her life and feel nothing but emptiness and sadness.

Every day that goes by, Emma slowly slips deeper and deeper into self-hatred and regret. Regret over saying anything to Noah at all. Regret for getting involved in something that was none of her business. Regret for leaving her comfort zone to begin with. If she had stayed in her bubble, she never would have gotten into this situation. Yes, she never would have met Winnie or Noah, but she would much rather have that than deal with the pain of losing them. Emma knows that this is what happens when she foolishly thought she could make her life look different.

If I hadn't *left work early that day, none of this would have ever happened…*

"Emma?" says a voice off to her left, taking her away from her thoughts.

Looking away from her monitor, she sees Astrid and Ben standing next to her, waiting for a response to a question only she can answer. And with that question, Emma is instantly reminded of the apprehension she felt as she stepped back into the fluorescent-lighted glass box that is her cubicle. How the sweat accumulated on her clammy hands as she met with Wyatt. How her soul crushed after he offered her the job. How she felt panic once she said 'Yes'. She doesn't regret accepting the job; she knows that this is what she is supposed to do. What any zillennial in corporate America is supposed to do: seek promotions and raises, climb the ladder of rankings within the best Fortune 500 companies. If she is to go back into her bubble—and prevent her from creating further destruction down the road—staying with SpikeSearch and taking the promotion is a no-brainer.

"I'm sorry guys, I was reading an email. What were you asking?"

"We tried running the fourth-quarter metric analysis for Mika," says Astrid, "but Ben and I keep getting different numbers."

Astrid tilts her monitor over so Emma can see the issue they are facing. Emma takes a deep breath and tries to focus intently as Astrid tells her what's going on. This is her first debacle to handle as a manager. Deep down, she's terrified this may be something she can't fix and prove to everyone that maybe she isn't fit for this after all. It doesn't take Emma too long to realize what the issue is: Ben is using outdated data in his code, and she has him run it again with the most current dataset. Now his metrics match Astrid's.

"Sorry, Emma. I should have double-checked the timestamp of the data. Bit of an oversight on my part," says Ben, feeling embarrassed for doing something only a rookie is known to pull.

"Don't worry about it, Ben," says Emma with a reassuring smile. "It happens to the best of us."

Feeling relieved at handling her first managerial crisis, Emma goes back to preparing for the presentation. She goes through the mundane tasks of reading reports and taking notes, while dipping into her artistic skills to create a presentation that doesn't scream 'I just copied an Excel template'. Wanting to prove she can do this role, she gives her all to prepare for her first meeting with the directors and vice presidents of the company. She works hours straight to get it as perfect as can be.

She has been so heads-down that once she glances up at the time, she is shocked to see that it is already 6:30 and that everyone else has left for the day. Rubbing her screen-tired eyes, Emma glances at her phone and sees that she received a text an hour ago.

From Noah.

Her heart instantly falls to the floor, and panic starts to rise up in her, as she cannot fathom why he is contacting her. With shaky hands, she unlocks her phone. Reading too quickly the first go-round, Emma re-reads the paragraph, making sure she read and understood it all correctly.

`Noah: Hi, if you're free after work, can you meet me at the High Line? I need your help with something.`

Checking the time once more, she sends a reply and rushes to pack up her things, hoping she didn't respond too late.

Emma: Of course! I'm heading out of the office now.

Emma practically runs to the High Line, feeling like the protagonist at the end of the rom-com where they run to the airport to profess their feelings. But she is very much aware that this will not be the case for her.

She ends up being the first to show up, giving her more time for her mind to race and her nerves to heighten.

The normally vivid green foliage is gone, leaving just the cold silver metal bridge with mounds of snow underneath the railings. Needing something to do, Emma leans up against the railing and kicks the snow off the High Line and onto the street below with her Docs. She checks the time on her phone for the seventh time in the past five minutes, hoping he will show up soon, so she doesn't die soon from an anxiety attack.

Then she hears him calling her name.

When she bolts straight up to face him, the sight of his dimple and curly hair—which she thought she'd never see again—makes her want to melt right into his arms and never let go. But instead, she stands still, waiting for him to reach her, wondering what he needs her help for. As he gets closer, she can see that he isn't his usual cheery self, but he isn't cold either.

"Hi," she manages to say once he stands nearly a foot away from her.

"Hi," Noah responds with a hint of softness in his voice, a smile breaking in the corner of his mouth.

I miss you is what she wants to say but manages to not do so and embarrass herself. "How are you?" is what she settles for instead.

"I'm good. The kids are doing their job of keeping me on my toes," he replies with a slight laugh. "How have you been?" he asks, and Emma can tell he genuinely means this, not for conversation's sake.

"Good as well. I took that promotion at work, so I've been busy getting up to speed." Internally, Emma cringes. Her skin starts to crawl behind her neck, wanting to shiver away the feeling. This feels like an awkward half-forced conversation you have when you run into people from high school, not a conversation with someone she has completely opened up to.

"I've heard," says Noah. "From my mom," he clarifies once he saw the surprised confusion on her face. "Which is why I asked you here."

"About work or your mom?"

"My mom, but also…" Noah takes a moment, collecting his thoughts. Whatever it is he wants to say to her, he has clearly thought about the numerous ways he could phrase it, just as she would. "First, I want to say that I understand why you didn't tell me about Owen and that it should have come from my mom. If the roles were reversed, I wouldn't know what to do either. And now I see that waiting to understand the full picture was the right thing to do. Eventually, I came to realize that I was so upset at my mom for hiding this from me all my life that I felt hurt by everyone. You didn't have to tell me about what you knew, but you still did because that's just who you are. You are open, honest, and will always do the right thing, no matter what the cost is to you."

Emma waits, slightly breathless. Taking in everything he told her. Dread creeps in slowly, as she has a hunch she knows where he is going with this. Her worst fear of their fate is possibly coming true. "And?" she asks, waiting.

"I don't know how much time I still need. I clearly still have a lot to work through. Bringing you into this, when I'm still not in the right headspace, wouldn't be fair to you."

Slowly, Emma nods her head, understanding while trying to refrain from showing her disappointment and heartache. Naturally, her instinct would try to reassure him that they can make it work. But deep down, even she knows that to continue now would set them up for failure later. "Okay," says Emma, "I understand." Although externally she seems level-headed, internally is another story. Deep down, she thinks that maybe love was never meant for her and that she never should have believed she could find it with Noah.

"You said before that you needed my help with something?" she asks, wanting to end this conversation now and move to a different topic.

"I do," says Noah. "I think we should tell my mom that we know where Owen is."

Shocked that this is coming from Noah, Emma tries to rationalize his idea. "Do you think that's a good idea?"

"It may not be, but there is a man out there who doesn't know why his lover left him and that they have a son together. He deserves to know the truth too, Emma. Not just me."

"And you want me to be there? To help you tell her?"

"Yes, of course. You two have this special bond. If she were able to open up to you and tell you all her secrets, then I have a better chance of her listening to us and agreeing to meet with Owen in person."

Emma glances away from him and stares at the street below them, watching the cars pass by, thinking of what to do. "What do you think?" he asks. Looking back at him, Emma can see his eyes almost pleading with her not to make him do this alone.

"One of her reasons for not finding him was the fear he may be with someone else. There is a chance her heart may get broken if she does go to see him." Emma stops, giving herself one last moment to feel confident in her final decision. "But we can't hide this from her, Noah. I agree with you that she should tell Owen the truth. He deserves to know just as much as you did." Emma glances back up at him. Having to spearhead another confrontation makes her skin crawl, and she wants to hide somewhere far away so she doesn't have to face it. But if this is what she needs to do to make up for the mess she caused, she knows she has no choice but to do it. "So, yes," she finally says, "I'll help you."

Noah gives her a gracious smile, showing off that dimple, "Thank you."

Chapter Twenty-One

"Stop checking your phone," says Emma. She places her hand lightly on Noah's arm, gently moving it to let his phone rest on the table. Glancing down, she can see his leg is bouncing rapidly, anxious. She is just as nervous as he is. They have no idea how this conversation with Winnie will go.

"I'm sorry," says Noah as he places his phone screen down on his kitchen table. The lingering smell of grilled cheese hangs in the air. Emma offered to make them to provide comfort to both Noah and her. In times of heightened anticipation, Emma uses comfort food to help cope with it. She hopes that this too will help him. But looking down at Noah's plate, he barely ate half his sandwich.

"Would you like a cup of tea?" offers Emma, thinking if food won't help, maybe a cup of calming tea will.

Noah doesn't answer. Instead, he cranes his neck to glance once more out the window behind him, looking with intense anticipation for Winnie to show up on the sidewalk, heading to his apartment building. When he doesn't see her silver hair, he looks back over at Emma, realizing he did it again. "Sorry."

"You said that already. Ah-" she raises her hand in the air, holding up her pointer finger, interrupting him before he speaks. "If you say sorry one more time…"

Noah gives her a forgiving smile. "*Desolé*," he says with a hint of the French accent that Winnie carries whenever she speaks French.

A light chuckle comes out of her, and she shakes her head. "*Je sais.*"

"I meant to ask you about the promotion," says Noah, trying to occupy his mind by talking about something else. "I'm actually surprised you ended up accepting it. What made you change your mind?"

"You want the honest answer?" she asks.

"Of course," says Noah, shifting to face her. One of the things she loves about him is his ability to give her his undivided attention, knowing he listens to everything she says and even gives solid advice when asked.

Suddenly feeling self-conscious, Emma looks down at her clasped hands. "I know I messed everything up, Noah. This is what I get for getting out of my comfort zone for once and meddling in something that's not any of my business. So, I'm going back to what I know best and what I'm good at, staying where I know I won't fuck anything else up."

"But I thought that was exactly what you didn't want to do?" he asks.

Emma shrugs and shakes her head. "Things change."

"Well, I mean if you are happy then I guess that's all that matters." Emma can tell he feels a little guilty, knowing that the way things ended with not just them, but with everything, has had some influence on her decision.

Before Emma says anything else, Noah suddenly bolts right up as something catches his attention outside. Peering out the window, Emma can easily spot where his focus is now. Winnie is making her way down the block and to his building.

Once Winnie walks into the apartment, Emma can see her clearly. She's caught off guard by the lightness and happiness now on her face. Winnie's practically glowing, bursting at the seams. A very stark contrast to the slight swirl of sadness that she had always carried with her. The only thing Emma knows that could have caused such a transformation in her is the unburdening of her lifelong secrets. Now that she no longer has to hide everything from her son, she can finally feel like herself. Emma's heart swells lightly with joy from seeing Winnie so elated, knowing that in some way she helped Winnie get to such a state.

Emma reminds herself of today's game plan, and her heart plummets to the pit of her stomach. What they tell Winnie will not only dim her lightness but possibly form a dark cloud over her head and heart. For Winnie and Noah's sake, Emma smiles cheerfully, hoping her face doesn't sabotage her this time by conveying her inner turmoil.

"Should I be excited to see the two of you together?" asks Winnie as she takes a seat in front of them at the kitchen table.

Confused, Emma looks at Noah, hoping he provides some clarity. Seeing the guilty look on his face, she realizes that Noah didn't tell Winnie that they're on speaking terms again, but not back together.

"We…" starts Noah, not quite sure what to say without hurting Emma's and Winnie's feelings. He clears his throat. "I admitted to Emma that I was blindsided a few weeks ago, and I can see that there was no right thing for her to do in that situation. We're still figuring out where we go from here, but that's not why we're here. As two people who love and care for you, we wanted to meet with you in person to discuss something."

Winnie lifts her left eyebrow. "And what is it that you want to discuss?"

Noah clears his throat and pulls off the band-aid. "Well, it's about Owen."

Emma feels like Winnie's heart just stopped beating. She doesn't need to see the frozen, expressionless look that is now on her face to know it.

"What about him?" barely murmurs Winnie.

"Well," starts Noah. He nervously glances at Emma, looking for reassurance. She nods to encourage him to go on. "We wanted to let you know that we know where he is and felt that you should know."

The color in Winnie's cheeks suddenly turns an ashy white, and the whites in her eyes are showing like a deer in the headlights. The words coming out of her mouth are barely audible. "How do you find this out?"

Emma raises her hand a smidge, as if she were a young kid back in grade school, too shy to answer a question. "That would be me. I unknowingly went into his bookshop a few weeks ago. I didn't know that he was your Owen until I saw the lily flower engraved on the back of one of your manuscript pages. You see, the same flower design on the page was also edged onto the cover of a notebook I bought from his store."

"He's...still here? In the city?" she says incredulously.

"Doesn't seem like he ever left, Mom," says Noah.

Winnie sits silently for several minutes, processing everything they told her. Emma starts to worry that they broke her with this information until she finally does speak up. "Why are you telling me this?"

"Now that you've told me everything, we thought that you may want to find him," mutters Noah.

Winnie reaches forward to hold onto Noah's other free hand. "I didn't tell you about him so I can go find him. What we had..." She stops to take a moment to collect herself, "our romance. Was so long ago. Even if you did find him, that doesn't mean he wants *me* to go find him. He could be married with kids, be happy with his own life, however that may look. What good would come if I barged back in after all this time?"

"Doesn't he deserve to know the truth now?" interjects Noah. "To know the real reason why you left him? To know that he has a son?"

Winnie shakes her head after his every sentence. "It's complicated, Noah."

"No," he says, not so loud that he comes off as angry, but with clear frustration. "What's complicated is that you're still keeping secrets. Owen... he deserves to know, just as much I do. Maybe even more." Noah takes a moment to collect his thoughts, then speaks in a lower voice. "Just imagine being in his shoes. Never knowing the real reason why the woman he loved decided to leave him. Never knowing for twenty-eight years that he has a child." He reaches with his free hand to grasp onto Winnie's other hand, both clutching onto each other. "I can imagine how much you and Owen need closure. But think of how much I need it too. I mean, I have a father who is alive. I could possibly even have a relationship with him too."

Tears start to fall down Winnie's face after finally hearing what she has always known what she must do. Emma imagines how much it means for it to be coming from Noah. "You're right," she says as she wipes away her tears.

Noah cocks his head. "So will you do it?"

Winnie wipes away her remaining tears and sniffles as she nods. "Yes, I promise I will speak with him. But I will only do it under one condition."

"Yes?" asks Noah.

"I don't think I'll be able to do it on my own," says Winnie through a ragged breath. She looks over at Emma with pleading eyes. "And since you have already met him, will you come with me?"

Emma looks over at Noah, checking to see if he is okay with this idea. After he gives her an approving nod, she looks back once more at Winnie. Being the one who caused all of this in the first place, she knows she must do the right thing to atone for her meddling, as she knows that Winnie would do the same thing, with no questions asked.

She places her hand on top of Winnie's. She hopes not only to reassure her but tell her in that one gesture that she will always be there for her, without a doubt. "Of course, I'll come with you."

Chapter Twenty-Two

Emma waits outside Winnie's front door, feeling nervous and on edge while bracing herself against the chilly February air. Like she too is about to see her long-lost lover for the first time in almost thirty years. But for Winnie's sake, she knows she can't come across this way, as Winnie must be feeling the same, probably even more so. It took Winnie a few days to set a date for when they would do this, wanting to delay the inevitable, a tactic Emma knows too well.

But as nervous as she is, Emma is there for support, and that means telling her everything will go alright, even if there is a very good chance that this encounter will not go as desired. Emma knows that there is only one thing she can do to give Winnie the encouragement she needs to do this, and it's not solely by her coming along. It's the one thing that can remind her what she always meant to Owen: the notebook.

When Winnie opens the front door, ready to head to the East Village, Emma sees that she is on the verge of a panic attack. Her breathing comes in short, rapid breaths, her hands tremble here and there. Emma places her hand on Winnie's upper arm. "Are you alright?"

Winnie nods. "I think so." She turns around to close and lock her front door, then looks out onto West 4th Street. Emma imagines that she's taking it all in, knowing that the next time she comes home, her life will be forever changed.

"Before we go," says Emma as they step onto the sidewalk, making Winnie turn back around to face her. "There's something I want to give you." Winnie watches as Emma unzips her backpack and takes out her red leather notebook—sans the few poems Emma already wrote in it— and its matching pen from inside.

"I want you to have this," she says as she hands them over to Winnie.

Mesmerized by the design, Winnie takes the notebook, a sense of recognition sweeping over her. "You know when I first saw this, I knew that the design was familiar, but I just couldn't quite place it." She looks back up at Emma, "Owen made this, right?"

Emma nods, "He made it for you, actually."

"When?"

"He said he finished making it just before you left him." Emma motions to the notebook, asking if she could take it for a second. Once it's in her hands, she opens the notebook, showing Winnie how the lock works and then flipping through its pages. "It's been sitting at his shop for all these years, waiting for its rightful owner to claim it. Waiting for you to come back." Emma runs her hand over the intricate lily cover design, marveling at the smooth details. "Now that I think about it, it seems a bit like fate that it ended up in my hands. As if the universe was trying to connect us all together."

She hands the notebook and pen back to Winnie. "I think it says something that Owen waited this long to give the notebook away. Maybe he was secretly hoping you would come back?"

"But he let you have it, it's yours now," says Winnie.

Emma shakes her head. "I can't get in the way of fate. This was meant to be yours, always has been." She reaches out to hold onto Winnie's hand, "Maybe now you can reclaim the part of yourself that someone wrongfully took from you."

Winnie runs her hand across the leather, feeling the love and craftsmanship Owen poured into it. She looks back up at Emma, with a look of re-ignited determination and gratitude. Emma knows that sometimes we need others to remind us of what our calling is, and a storyteller is what Winnie is destined to be. "My dear, thank you," says Winnie as she embraces Emma.

Seeing the joy and lightness that now encompasses Winnie, Emma knows that her idea worked. Now she just hopes that this feeling will stay until they arrive at the bookstore.

"How do you like the new job?" asks Winnie as they start to walk along West 4th Street.

Deep down, Emma knows Winnie genuinely wants to know, but she also understands that Winnie wants to talk about just anything to keep her mind off any spiraling thoughts she may be having.

"It's been an adjustment," Emma replies. "But I know once I get the hang of things, it will be a lot better."

Winnie is silent for a minute, either trying to figure out if Emma is embellishing or if she isn't. She has always been able to see the truth, despite what Emma has said. Now knowing how her mind works, Emma takes her silence for disbelief. "My team is great," she continues, hoping to dissuade her from thinking that she isn't happy. "I had my first meeting with the higher-ups the other day, and it went well. That's another thing I will have to get used to, speaking in front of a room full of people. But we all have to overcome our fears at some point, right?"

Emma knows she is rambling and probably sounds like she is covering up the truth. But this time, she truly does mean it. The job has been good so far. Challenging? Yes. Does she have to do things that put her on the verge of having a panic attack? Yes, but isn't that what will help us grow and develop? By doing the things that we are most afraid of.

Winnie gives her a smile. Emma is not able to decipher if it's genuine or meant to placate her. "That's great, dear. I'm glad to hear it's turning out to be different than you initially expected."

As the two continue to walk towards the East Village, Emma considers this time as ample opportunity for her to ask Winnie questions she has had since the day she met her. Now that Winnie shared very personal details about her life with Emma, she feels that she can ask these questions without feeling intrusive. There is only one thing that Winnie hasn't explained to Emma. "Can I ask you a question?" she asks.

"Of course. I'm now an open book," laughs Winnie, "So ask away."

"How come you never went back to visit Martigues?"

"Oh, that was from a lot of things," says Winnie. "I always had plans to go back home when I was younger. But Russel always made excuses for reasons why I couldn't go. Looking back, I think he just didn't want me that far out of his sight. When my mémé came to live with us after Noah was born, I never really had a reason to go back. But when she passed, I couldn't ever bear to go back home. She was my home, and with her gone, I could never step back on that soil without her. I know it wouldn't feel the same." A sad smile creeps up on her lips as she recalls something. "In fact, Owen and I planned to move to Martigues once my divorce was finalized. Well, that was all before Russel found out about us. When you really think about it, going back there would not only remind me of my mémé, but the love that I lost as well."

"Even now? You still wouldn't go back?"

"I honestly don't know. I haven't thought about going back to Martigues in ages."

When they are a few feet away from the bookstore, Emma notices that Winnie has gone silent. Instinctually, Emma reaches out to hold onto her hand, not planning on letting go unless Winnie says otherwise.

Winnie hesitates at the faded red door, causing Emma to stop short from opening it. "I just need a minute," says Winnie, bracing herself for what is about to happen. "Do I look okay?" she asks while adjusting her hair and jacket.

Emma nods. "You look as beautiful as ever." She means it.

Winnie takes one last deep breath. "Okay, let's go."

Walking into the bookstore, Emma leads the way, almost using her body as a shield, guarding Winnie from any onslaught. The bell on the door chimes as they close it, signaling their arrival to Owen.

"I'll be right out," says Owen somewhere deep within the store. Emma looks all around the store—the checkout counter, the upstairs area—and is not able to see him. Then suddenly the door next to the checkout counter opens and out comes Owen from the back office.

"Oh! Hello again," says Owen as he lays his eyes first on Emma, the more recognizable of the two.

It isn't until Emma motions her head in Winnie's direction that he finally looks at her and realizes who she is. His eyes widen in shock, almost in disbelief, as if he's seeing a ghost.

Suddenly it's as if everything is in slow motion. Looking at Winnie, Emma can see she looks just the same as him. Both are in pure shock. It feels like they will never break from this catatonic state, until Owen finally walks away from the checkout counter and towards them. His face flips from confusion to shock, then back once more.

"Hi," says Winnie, breaking the silence first.

"Is it really you?" asks Owen in disbelief.

Winnie nods and takes a step closer, "Yes."

Emma tries to prevent a grin from coming onto her face, her inner fangirl wanting to break free. Before her is the couple of the love story she has adored for ages, and she is the first, and maybe the only, person to know who they are and get to see them together in person.

I can't believe it. It's really Madeleine and Beck!

Stop, Emma. Get a grip! We are here to support Winnie, and some serious shit is about to go down here.

Emma doesn't know if it's her imagination showing her what she is to see, but she can see their chemistry, pulling them closer to each other like magnets. It isn't until now that Emma starts to hope that maybe her favorite love story can have a real happy ending in real life. That a second chance of finding true love is not out of the realm of possibility quite yet for these long-lost lovers.

"Emma here told me how she found you. I thought I would stop by and see how you are," says Winnie, sensing that Owen is still a bit too shocked to speak just yet. She looks around the bookstore with a mixture of sadness, longing, and happiness on her face. "I'm glad to see that you opened the bookstore you always wanted, and it's still here after all these years. How are you? Hopefully, life's been treating you well?"

The shock slowly wearing off, Owen finally seems to return to his normal self. "If you count getting married and then divorced as part of 'doing well', then I've been thriving," he jests. Emma doesn't realize she has been holding her breath, waiting for Owen to speak. She releases a deep breath once she hears the slightly humorous, not spiteful, tone in his voice.

"Any kids? Divorces can be painful once kids are in the picture," says Winnie.

Owen shakes his head. "Thankfully, our marriage failed before kids came around." In a subtle, quick movement, he looks down at Winnie's left hand and sees that she is not wearing a wedding ring. It is quick enough that Emma just barely missed seeing it. "And you?" he asks.

A knowing smile comes onto Winnie's face, as if no time at all has passed. "I know that what you really want to know is why I'm here, after all this time. You've always been sensitive to people's feelings, always asking the polite things first instead of what you truly want to say. But I didn't come here not to talk about what happened with us and act like our history never happened."

Emma sees relief spread across Owen's face, as if he had been worried that this was going to be that kind of talk. "Why did you come here then?" he asks.

"To tell you the truth," says Winnie. She looks over at Emma for reassurance, then looks back over at Owen. "The whole truth. That is, if you would like to hear it. I'd completely understand and respect if you don't want to go down memory lane and bring back up any unwanted feelings."

Skeptical, Owen looks at Emma, looking for an outsider's take on what he should do. Emma nods silently to him to tell him that he should hear her out. He glances at his wristwatch, then heads over to the front door.

Oh no, is he really going to kick us out? Could he still be that upset with her for what happened that he is too stubborn to see otherwise?

But thankfully, he only went to the door to flip the sign to 'closed' and lock it. He then motions for Winnie to head into his back office. "We can talk in there."

Winnie looks at Emma like a deer in the headlights since she did not plan to do this part without her. Emma gives her hand a reassuring squeeze, telling her that she doesn't need her to do this. "I'll be right out here," she says, hoping that just knowing she is nearby will be enough.

Winnie looks back at the office door, and for a split second, Emma thinks she is about to forgo this whole thing and leave. Then Winnie proves her otherwise by standing taller and curtly nodding to herself in determination. Emma watches her follow Owen into the office and shut the door, hoping that everything will go alright.

They end up talking for much longer than Emma expected. Once a half-hour passes, she grabs a book and starts reading, unsure of how long she will be waiting. She's relieved not to hear any raised voices so far.

By the time they emerge from the office two hours later, the sun has already set and Emma has reached chapter ten of the random thriller novel she picked up. But still on high alert, Emma stands up from the couch she had been lounging on, anxious to see their faces. She feels like a kid who's waiting to see how bad of a fight their mom and dad just had.

Thankfully, Owen doesn't look angry; rather, he looks astonished. Winnie looks relieved, happy to finally have this weight off her shoulders and possibly content with how their conversation went.

Before Emma can silently ask Winnie how it went, Owen starts to speak, making her turn away from Emma. "Can I meet him?" asks Owen. Emma knows 'he' can only mean one person.

"Of course, you can. But he will also have to be ready for that."

"Right, of course," says Owen, shaking his head for not thinking about how Noah may feel about all of this.

Winnie hands over a small piece of paper with her phone number on it. "I'll reach out to you about what he says. Thank you again for hearing me out." Owen takes and places the paper into his pants pocket.

"Sure," is all Owen says as he unlocks the front door and holds it open for them.

"So, how did it go?" asks Emma once the bookstore is several feet behind them.

"As well as I hoped it would. He was rightly shocked and upset with me for not telling him about Noah, but he did understand why I couldn't." Suddenly Winnie stops short on the sidewalk, causing

Emma to stop short with her. "Do you think it's wishful thinking for me to think that we could all be a family?"

Emma shrugs. "Anything is possible."

"But nothing is guaranteed," finishes Winnie with a sigh.

They start heading back to the West Village in comfortable silence.

Emma is utterly speechless and in full admiration of what Winnie just mustered the courage to do. Even though she can't fathom ever having to do such a thing herself, she can feel that witnessing such an event is already changing her. Encouraging her to face head-on the things she's been too in denial to admit for weeks.

Ready to admit what she's been truly feeling over the last five weeks, Emma stops short. "I think I made a mistake," she blurts out.

"With what, dear?" asks Winnie, turning around to face her.

"Taking on the new job. I think I let my emotions get the better of me and made a clouded decision. I did what I thought was the right thing, instead of what I wanted to do."

Winnie looks at her with both relief and pride. "I knew you would eventually come to this conclusion. Do you know what it is you want to do?"

Emma pauses, trying to articulate the thoughts she's had since the night of the charity event. She felt it in Noah's classroom and at the planetarium. "For weeks, I haven't been able to shake the feeling that I could be doing something less self-serving. That with the connections and access I have, I have an opportunity to help those who really need it. But I haven't been able to figure out exactly how to do that."

Winnie waits patiently as Emma thinks, the look on her face showing she's on the cusp of figuring something out. She thinks about how easy and fun do nation got people to help organizations in need and the number of client connections SpikeSearch has. Finally, an idea starts forming in her head. Excited by the idea, Emma grabs her phone and feverishly starts typing out notes she does not want to forget. Exhilaration starts rushing through her. For the first time ever, Emma knows what her purpose is. A wild grin spreads across her face, like a mad scientist finally solving an enigma. She looks back up at Winnie in disbelief and shock. "I think I may finally know how."

Chapter Twenty-Three

Frantically typing away at her desk, Emma tries to finish and polish the latest edits of her proposal to the CEO, making the changes Wyatt and Mika gave her in their meeting earlier today.

All thanks to her epiphany two weeks ago, she found a way to incorporate the idea of the do-nation charity game into a new form of marketing that SpikeSearch could spearhead. If approved, their clients will be able to utilize an app containing games and challenges for their consumers to play and compete for. Whoever wins the challenge gets a prize for that company's service. In return, the visibility and extra traffic coming from the challenges will mean more money raised for the organization SpikeSearch selects to receive the donations for that month. The more viewers and participants in the app, the more consumers for their client, which means more money to be given to organizations in need. The more traction the app gets for its marketing tactics, the more new clients will come to SpikeSearch's door to have the rights to use it. A 'win-win-win' situation.

Emma learned from the do-nation event that everyone will try to win something for a grand prize or recognition. And what better way to use that inclination than to have it benefit non-profit organizations?

After thoroughly researching and investigating her idea, she felt confident enough to bring her idea to her director and VP to see if the company would even consider it, and much to her surprise, they did not need much convincing. After reading the numbers, the business plan, and the legality of her plan—all thanks to her dad—they immediately bought into her idea and agreed to help her present it to the CEO later this month. If approved, Emma will become the director of a new branch under the research and development business unit, guiding this application to fruition. Until then, Emma needs to make sure the proposal is as perfect as it can be as she cannot and will not let this idea flop.

Before she knows it, it's almost seven and she's one of a few still in the office. If she doesn't leave now, she will be late for dinner at Winnie's.

She rushes to pack up her things and put on her jacket, beanie, and mittens. She doesn't know what to expect at tonight's dinner. At first, it was supposed to be just Emma and the Reynards, celebrating the fact that Winnie's case didn't even need to go to court since Oliver was able to come to an agreement with the publishing house directly. Not only will the publishing house make a mass announcement to explain its wrongdoing by publishing *The Port to Sea*'s with the wrong author, but they will also publish a revised edition of the book with Winnie's name starting in January of next year. Thanks to that agreement, Winnie will start to get royalties of any copies sold along with a nice sum of money to amend the relationship between the author and house, leaving the door open in case Winnie decides to write another book. A huge win for her.

It wasn't until earlier this week that Noah came up with the idea for Winnie to invite Owen to the dinner as well. Since he helped Winnie immensely back when she wrote it, Noah felt he should be included in the celebrations too. That, and to provide him with an opportunity to meet his biological father.

Now that this dinner is half celebration and half father-son meeting for the first time, Emma knows that there are a lot of expectations from everyone attending. She just hopes that it will go as seamlessly as possible.

The weather forecast predicted that the city would get only a few inches of snow over the course of the next five hours, which is nothing compared to the snowstorms the city has endured over the many years. As Emma rushes out of her office building in Astor Place, she's surprised to see at least four inches of snow on the ground.

She shivers as the cold, wet snow seeps into her shoes and soaks the bottom of her jeans. It wasn't supposed to snow like this.

She looks up to see a hazy sky with snow falling at a rapid rate, feeling like she is in a snow globe that is being shaken. Worry starts to creep up her spine. Whenever the weather ends up being much worse than what is predicted on TV, Emma knows that a natural calamity is always around the corner. Preparing for the worst, she nestles her face into her scarf and jacket and makes her way over to Winnie's.

The walk ends up being much worse than she expected. Snow clings to her hair and hat. Trudging through what is now five inches of unshoveled snow has tired her calves. The cold air burns her lungs, making it slightly harder to breathe. Other than that, she finds it quite peaceful to be walking along the city streets with not a soul in sight.

In what should take only twenty minutes to get to Winnie's, it takes Emma nearly double that to finally reach her front door. She rings the doorbell with shaking fingers. A rush of warm air hits her cracked cheeks as Winnie opens the door, making her realize how frozen the rest of her body actually is.

"Oh, thank goodness you are here," says Winnie, with eyes pleading silently for help, making Emma wonder exactly how the dinner is going. "My god, it looks like a snowstorm out here," exclaims Winnie, suddenly realizing the snowy catastrophe awaiting them outside. "You walked all the way here in *this*?"

"I didn't think it was going to be this bad, honestly," says Emma with quivering lips.

Winnie ushers her inside. "Come in, you must be freezing."

Emma's body starts to thaw slowly as she warms up by the library's fireplace and then eventually follows Winnie to the living room. She can hear Noah and Owen's voices echo in the entry hall, and it sounds like neither of them knows how to talk to one another, especially when Winnie isn't with them. Emma feels the mood shift instantly once Winnie returns, with her following.

"Look who's here," says Winnie as they enter the living room. A smile of relief washes onto Noah's face once he sees that Emma is here.

Seeing them together, Emma realizes just how much Noah looks like Owen. Both have the same curly hair, soft brown eyes, glasses, and tall height. They even have the same dimple. Emma imagines that if she were to see a picture of a younger Owen, he would have the same chestnut-colored hair as Noah. But there is still some of Winnie in Noah—her perfectly straight nose and defined bone structure. He is the perfect mix between his parents.

Winnie motions for Emma to take a seat next to Noah on the couch, then heads to the bar cart. "It's getting pretty bad out there, looks to be more than just some light snow," says Winnie as she pours Emma a glass of wine.

Once Emma settles into the couch and has a few sips of wine, she finally registers how awkward this situation is. The only thing she can relate to this very moment is when she sees her gynecologist and the awkward tension of knowing that a stranger will be seeing the very intimate parts of herself. Thankfully, she and no one else will be getting *that* personal tonight, but emotionally, they will be just as vulnerable.

The first hour goes by with some minor bumps in the road. At first, the conversations are superficial, talking only about their jobs and life in the city. Emma sits on the side, feeling for each one of them. There is no guidebook on how to introduce your son to your ex-lover who happens to be his real father. But she can see that they all are trying their best, learning together as they go.

"Emma, Noah, can you help me check on the food in the kitchen?" asks Winnie once the conversation about Noah's school has become an uncomfortable silence.

Eager to leave the tense room, Emma and Noah follow her into the kitchen without hesitation. The kitchen table is set. Napkins are neatly folded on the table with the most beautiful floral arrangement resting in the center. She knows that it must have taken Winnie hours to prepare for tonight.

The three of them huddle together in one corner of the kitchen island, like a set of close friends about to gossip with one another.

"I'm not the only one feeling that this is going awkwardly, right?" whispers Winnie.

Relief not only washes through Emma, but she can see that Noah is relieved that Winnie was the first one to acknowledge this. Winnie, reading both of their faces, puts her face in her hands, shaking her head in disbelief.

A feeling creeps up the back of Emma's neck, a feeling that something isn't quite right. It takes her a second to realize that it's the lights. They've been gradually getting dimmer for the past minute. Emma was about to say something until the lights decided to flicker more obviously this time. The three of them look up at the ceiling lights in unison.

"Uh-oh," echoes Owen's voice from the living room after the lights flickered for the fourth time. Then suddenly the power goes out, leaving them in the dark.

Emma rushes over to the kitchen window and investigates the conditions of the snowstorm. The snowflakes have gotten bigger and are coming down faster. Visibility has drastically gone down since she was outside an hour ago. The clanking of ice pellets can be heard on the roof and windows. The cracks in the windows start to moan as the wind gusts speed up. "It looks like a blizzard out there," says Emma.

A bright glare shines from over her right shoulder. Turning around, Emma sees Winnie on her phone, trying to figure out what is going on, just as Owen walks in from the living room. "It's been declared as a blizzard. The city is to stay put until it dies down and the trucks can clear out the streets," says Winnie.

"And the power?" asks Noah.

"Something about a transformer failing. Only lower Manhattan is having an outage. They don't know how long it will be out for."

Silence emerges, only the sound of the roaring wind and sleet hitting the windowpanes is heard. All four of them thinking the same thing: that they may be stuck here for a long time.

"What do we do now?" asks Emma, as Winnie takes the marsala chicken out of the oven, shutting off the gas. She places the chicken dish on top of the stove, then throws the oven mitts onto the island with defeat. It could be her mind playing games with her, knowing that the heat is no longer running, but Emma suddenly feels a lot colder.

"We can still have our dinner," says Noah, attempting to salvage the night. "We can light candles on the table, drink some more wine, and wait for the power to come back on." He looks at everyone, waiting for a response. Emma hears the optimism in his voice.

"Would be a shame to let the meal go to waste," says Owen, siding with Noah.

Winnie takes a minute to consider Noah's idea. "I mean, the dinner is cooked," says Winnie, as if she's trying to convince everyone what they already know is a good idea.

"I can go upstairs and grab the candles," says Noah.

"I can help you light them," offers Emma.

"I'll go check to make sure we have enough firewood for a while," says Owen. "Considering the power company didn't prepare for a blizzard, it may be quite some time until they can even get to the transformers."

"Okay," says Winnie, looking a bit cheerier knowing that everyone isn't ready to give up on tonight just yet.

Thirty minutes later, after everyone has completed their tasks and Emma has let her parents know that she is safe, they sit around the candlelit kitchen table. A fire is going steadily in the library. Winnie even brought out blankets from the linen closet to keep everyone warm while eating. They start to eat the three-course meal as Owen pours everyone a fresh glass of wine.

The tension that was felt in the beginning of the evening has slowly dissipated, as if it left with the power. Emma doesn't know if it's the amount of wine consumed or the intimate setting of their new environment that creates a sense of calm and ease around them. But whatever it is, she's just thankful it has helped them to get to this moment.

Looking at Noah, Emma can see how much he has changed over the course of the night. She can see by his body language how much more at ease he is with Owen, how he can joke with him, making her hope that they can form a genuine connection after tonight.

"So, you're telling me that you two met because someone died?" asks Owen after Winnie fills him in on how Emma met the Reynards.

They both respond at the same time.

"Yup," says Emma.

"In simple terms, yes," replies Winnie.

"And if you hadn't gone to my store and bought that notebook, you never would have known who I was." Owen takes a deep sip of wine, shaking his head at the absurdity of it all. "It's strange how we all got here. If Emma hadn't walked home on that night, she never would have met Winnie. If she hadn't walked into my store, she never would have run into me." They all take a moment, letting that idea sink in. How easy it could have been for this moment never to have happened at all, just because someone made two seemingly mundane decisions.

Owen tilts his head to his left, facing Winnie. "Just like if you didn't stop at Tompkins Square Park on that day, we wouldn't be here today."

A deep blush creeps onto Winnie's face, suddenly feeling shy about her infidelity. Talking about it privately is one thing; openly mentioning it is something she will have to get used to now that everyone knows about it.

"You know," says Owen, changing the subject quickly as intoxicated minds tend to do, "you look so much like someone. I just can't place who." He looks at Emma in deep thought, his pointer finger tapping his left cheek. Suddenly he snaps his fingers, and excitement runs across his face. "That's it! 'Please don't take my man!'"

An exasperated laugh comes out of Emma as she rolls her eyes. "Not again."

"See!" exclaims Noah, poking Emma's side. "I told her the same thing. She looks exactly as Jolene would if she were a real person."

"You were so obsessed with that song when you were a kid," says Winnie. Then it dawns on her. She looks at Owen. "You used to play that song all the time in your apartment."

"Like father, like son," mutters Emma.

Unintentionally, Emma's comment opens the gates of a detailed retelling of Noah's childhood. The good, the bad. The funny, and the sad. It doesn't matter; Owen wants to know about every little part of Noah's life. Winnie brings all of them down memory lane, embarrassing Noah every possible moment she can.

During her stories, Emma only half-listens to her. Most of the time, she is getting distracted by watching Owen as he listens intently to Winnie. Just as it's clear as day that Winnie still loves Owen, Emma can see that he still loves her just as fiercely. Since she started speaking, Owen hasn't taken his eyes off her, with a glint of affection in his eyes. Even a stranger off the street could see the sparks between them, feel the chemistry they have. Emma doesn't know what's more infuriating: the obvious, visible love they still have for each other or the fact that both of them are afraid to speak up about it.

"Excuse me for a second; I'm going to check on the fire to see if it needs more logs," says Owen as he gets up from his chair.

Emma glances quickly at Noah, wondering if he saw the same things she did and will take the initiative to discuss it with his mom. Having Noah's attention, Emma quickly looks at Winnie and then where Owen is, hoping he can understand what she's silently communicating. A smile forms on his lips as he takes a sip of water and gives her a nod. A nod that, yes, he sees it too.

Noah takes Winnie's hand. Her gaze lifts from her plate to his eyes. Emma can see that so much is already being communicated between them. From the look of understanding in Noah's eyes to the look of hope and longing on Winnie's. "You still love him, don't you?" he asks Winnie.

"I don't think I ever stopped," she mutters, "even after all this time."

"Then go after him, Mom. You did so much for me, sacrificed so much for me. I want you to be happy. You deserve to be happy and be with the person you truly love."

"Noah, I..." starts Winnie, but then she loses her words, becoming speechless.

"In no way do you ever need my permission," says Noah, "but if you do need my blessing, you most certainly have it."

Tears of happiness start to pool in her eyes, then she swiftly wipes them away when Owen comes back to the kitchen.

"Looks like the snow stopped," says Owen. The others get up from their seats to peer out the kitchen window and still see an overcast sky but no snowflakes falling.

"How much do you think we got?" asks Noah, looking at Winnie's small backyard.

"At least a foot for sure," says Winnie. She reaches for her phone. "City still says to stay put. They're at the transformer, but it's going to take a few hours to get it back up. Snow trucks are out plowing, which is good." Winnie checks the time, "It's already past midnight." She looks up at her son, Owen, and Emma. "Who knows when the roads will be good enough to head back out. I insist you all stay over until it's better in the morning." Knowing there is no alternative, and no disagreeing with Winnie on this, the others agree with her.

"Emma should get the guest room," says Noah. He looks over at Owen. "We can take the couches in the living room and study."

Winnie starts to get up from her chair. "I'll go set up the sleeping areas for everyone."

"Let me take care of Emma and me, and you can help Owen out in the study," insists Noah. While Emma and Noah make their way upstairs to the guest room, she wonders if his suggestion has more to do with giving Winnie and Owen some time to talk alone.

"Did…" she starts to speak, about to ask him about it, but when she looks at him, a gut feeling tells her that there is something else on his mind.

"Can we talk?" he asks once the candles he brought up have been lit.

Emma's heart plummets to the floor upon hearing the three words you absolutely never want to hear. "Sure," she says as they sit on the edge of the bed, dreading every second.

"Just a heads up, I'm probably going to ramble and say things that don't make any sense, but I feel that it is important for you to know." Intrigued yet cautious, Emma shifts her body to face him, then motions for him to proceed.

"I don't think I really understood what my mom lost," says Noah. "Not until tonight, after seeing them together, and finally reading her book. She did all of that just to protect me. I know she wishes that things could have gone differently for them, and I do too. But seeing the regrets she carries—the would've, could've, should've—has made me realize that I could be doing the same thing myself."

"How so?" asks Emma.

Noah looks into her eyes, the soft brown hues melting her heart by the look he is giving her. "With us," he says.

Emma's heart rate increases, hope pulsing throughout her body. *Could he be suggesting we get back together?*

"Thirty years from now," continues Noah, "I don't want to look back at my life and have those same regrets. I don't want to look back and wonder if I threw away something that could have been great, just because I'm afraid of something." Noah sees the confusion on her face, trying to figure out where he could be going with this. He reaches out for her hand. "What I'm trying to say is, I don't want to lose you. I don't want to throw away what we could have.

Did I already miss my chance?" he asks, optimism and hope slowly draining from his face as he waits for Emma to react. She doesn't mean to take this long; she is still shocked by what he said and is struggling to comprehend that it's real.

When Emma realizes that this isn't a dream, she reaches out to tousle one of his curls and leans a bit closer to him, then cups her hand on the right side of his face. "No," she says with a smile, "you didn't miss your chance."

He leans forward to rest his forehead with hers, a smile curling up on his face. "No?" asks Noah with hope flowing back onto his face.

"No," whispers Emma.

Then in one swift movement, Noah lightly tilts his chin to hers and kisses her longingly. From this kiss alone, the rising temperature from their body heat warms them up enough from the freezing cold air in the room.

After what feels like several long minutes to Emma, they eventually break apart, both grinning like little kids on Christmas morning, giggling from euphoria. They both lie down on the bed facing each other, bundled in layers upon layers of blankets, creating their own intimate blanket fort. They end up talking for hours about the things they missed during their time apart, telling jokes about the dumb things they've done. And as they catch up, Emma hopes that maybe by now Winnie and Owen have rekindled as well.

Talking for what feels like days, Emma's mouth is now as dry as sand on a hot desert day. Her throat feels tight and desperate for water. She glances at the time on her phone and sees that it is almost dawn, shocked that she and Noah have talked all through the night. Emma unravels herself from their safe haven and makes her way out of the guest bedroom to the hallway bath.

Out in the hall, she hears hushed voices, trying to contain their infectious laughter. Not being able to resist, Emma tiptoes to the stairs and slowly makes her way down. She stops halfway, just at the right spot to peek into the study.

She isn't surprised to see that Winnie and Owen are still up, talking excitedly.

She's surprised to see how they are sitting. Their bodies are now nestled right next to each other on the couch, with Winnie's head lying comfortably on Owen's shoulder and his arm wrapped around her, his hand running up and down her arm. Emma's favorite wool blanket covers them, the glow of the still-burning fire wrapping them in warmth. Emma's heart tugs a little at the sight of their proximity, knowing that it probably didn't take them too long to get to this point.

Emma doesn't need to eavesdrop on their conversation. She knows from their body language alone that the pair finally declared what they had been dying to say from the moment Winnie stepped into the bookstore.

Tears of happiness run down Emma's cheeks as she quietly heads back upstairs, no longer feeling parched. She doesn't need to wonder anymore. She knows that the real Madeleine and Beck finally got their storybook happy ending.

Epilogue
Fifteen Years Later

The warm sea breeze blows through Emma's hair, her long hair flowing freely in the car. Her arm rests relaxed and lazily outside the car door, moving her fingers along with the rush of air. The strong sun rays send small kisses to her skin, reminding her how the sun here changes her pale skin to a light tan, her freckles becoming more pronounced by summer's end. The smell and feel of sea salt are all around. On her hair, skin, everywhere you go there is the scent of the ocean's aftershave.

Martigues is just the same as it was.

Boats line up along the canals. Cobblestone streets. Bright colors painted on the buildings' walls. The sandy beaches and azure waters of the Côte Bleue. The constant sound of seagulls chirping. It has become Emma's second home after visiting every summer for the last fifteen years. But this time, it feels much more somber knowing that there will be a key presence missing from their visit.

As Noah parks their rental car into the short driveway, all the Reynards remain unmoved in their seats as he turns the engine off. Neither one of them is ready to head inside the quaint cottage that will be missing its core presence. A presence that gives a magical and endearing feeling. The feeling of home, even when it's thousands of miles away from their own. Emma takes Noah's hand, reassuring him that he is not the only one still grieving.

"Why aren't we leaving?" asks the small voice behind them, still clueless to how the death of a loved one will carry on long after they are gone. How even a simple object, or scent, can bring back memories of that one person they will never be able to see or hold onto again.

Emma turns around in her seat, giving a small smile. "We are just giving Daddy some time before heading inside. Why don't you help me take out our bags from the trunk and bring them inside?"

"Okay!" says the eight-year-old girl as she jumps out of the car, eager to finally stand up and stretch her tired legs after their long trip.

"We'll be inside," Emma says to Noah and places her hand on his shoulder. "Take all the time you need." Noah nods, then leans down to plant a kiss on her hand.

Once they lug their suitcases to the front door, Emma pauses before knocking on the wooden turquoise-blue door, bracing herself for what she will feel on the other side. But that moment is cut short as her daughter bangs excitedly on the door, eager to get inside and see the person they have travelled all this way for.

"Mad Bug," exclaims Owen once he opens the door, hugging his granddaughter tightly. "Oh, you've gotten so big!" says Owen as he twirls her in the foyer, the girl's infectious giggles bringing some joy to the melancholic environment around them. "You aren't my little Mad Bug anymore," he says as he places her back down on her feet.

"I'll always be your Bug, Pop Pop," ensures Maddie.

"I know you will," he says as he leans down to give her a kiss on the top of her head. "Now why don't you go ahead inside? A plate of your favorite madeleines is waiting for you on the kitchen table." Emma and Owen linger by the front door as they watch the sea of untamed auburn curls make a mad dash for the kitchen.

The pair don't have to speak or utter a word, just by a look alone, they know that they both still feel the pain and sadness that first struck them seven months ago. In one swift move, they both cling onto each other in a tight embrace. After a few moments, Emma hears Noah's footsteps behind her, getting closer to them.

"Noah," says Owen as they break apart from their embrace, while Emma discreetly wipes away tears.

"Hi, Dad," says Noah with a weak smile. Owen rushes over to

hug his son tightly, something he has been wanting to do since he saw him nine months ago.

It took the family time to grasp Winnie's sudden stage four cancer diagnosis at the start of their last trip. After the pain and anger became a sorrowful ache, they soon realized that the timing of it all was a blessing. It allowed Winnie to spend her last few months with the people she loved most, and to have all of them here with her when it was eventually her time to go. Nine months isn't enough time for their grief to pass, but by following Winnie's instructions of having the family back together for this summer at the cottage, they know that they can at least grieve together.

"I'm so happy all of you are here," says Owen with a cracked voice as they break apart.

Emma places a comforting hand on Owen's shoulder while giving Noah a look of forlorn heartbreak.

"Oh please, come inside and get comfy. You all must be exhausted from the trip," says Owen once he regains his composure and gestures them to head inside.

The cottage doesn't feel the same, as if it too knows that it has been missing something. Looking around, Emma sees that Winnie's items are still in the same place as they were last summer, knowing that Owen would always keep her spirit alive in the cottage they have called home for the last fifteen years.

As she heads to the kitchen, she takes a quick glance inside the living room. She spots the familiar green color of *The Port to Sea* resting, with its pages opened, on the armrest of the lounge chair, waiting for its reader to resume its story. Emma wonders what part Owen stopped at during his hundredth time reading his love story. A small smile rises on her lips as she glances up to see Winnie's second novel, *Amour, Amour et Douleur*, still in its special place front and center in their massive wall-to-wall built-in bookcase.

As Emma walks into the kitchen, she feels Winnie's presence suddenly hit her. As if she can expect her to walk into the kitchen at any minute and give Emma a hug. But when she looks over at her daughter sitting on Owen's lap, Emma can see why she feels that way. Looking into her daughter's eyes, she sees Winnie's eyes staring back at her. Listening to Maddie's giggles, she hears Winnie's infectious laugh underneath. Emma never realized until this moment just how much of Winnie is in Maddie, right down to having the same courageous and creative mind. With these remnants of Winnie in her daughter, Emma can put her mind at ease knowing that her presence will never truly leave them.

"Everything all good at Westview?" asks Owen once the family settled into the kitchen with refreshments and madeleines.

"Westview is just as good as ever. Maddie will be starting fourth grade there this September," says Noah with a smile of pride.

"How does it feel to have your dad now be the principal at your school?" Owen asks Maddie.

She shrugs her shoulders as she happily eats another madeleine. "I know some kids would be embarrassed to have their dad be the principal, but I don't." She looks over at her dad with a grin on her face. "I like having Daddy be in charge."

Emma and the others laugh at her animated daughter. Needing a moment like this to break the heaviness from settling into their bones.

Humor. She definitely has Winnie's sense of humor.

"And all is well at work?" Owen asks Emma.

"Do-nation has successfully launched across the US and Canada," Emma says proudly. "There is ongoing talk of it going global, but I want to focus on the areas we're in now before thinking that big."

"You know what Winnie would say," says Owen.

"Go big or go home," finishes Maddie.

"Exactly, Mad Bug," says Owen as he tickles Maddie on the side of her neck and gives her dozens of kisses on the cheek, her giggles filling the cottage.

"I miss Mémé, Pop Pop," says Maddie once the tickling subsides. Looking into her grandfather's face, Emma sees the grief-stricken look in her daughter's profile. With that look alone, Emma feels the tears build up in her eyes, ready to fall down her cheek again.

Owen plants a kiss on Maddie's head and gives her a comforting embrace. "I know my bug, I do too. We all do."

"But," continues Owen, trying to sound cheerful. He takes Maddie off his lap to grab a small blue box wrapped with a gold bow from behind him. "There is a way to fix that."

"How?" asks Maddie.

Knowing what resides inside the box, Emma and Noah await the emotional waterfall that is about to pour onto them.

"Mémé asked me to give this to you," says Owen as he gives Maddie the gift. "She wanted to make sure you still had a part of her with you."

With fervor, Maddie opens the box to find Winnie's copy of *The Little Prince* along with her first edition copy of *Winnie the Pooh.* A squeal comes out of Maddie upon seeing her two favorite stories. Despite the time difference, Winnie always made sure they had their virtual story time.

As Maddie flips through one of the book's pages, a single sheet of paper falls out onto the kitchen table.

"What is that, Mads?" asks Noah, as Maddie opens the folded sheet of paper.

"It's a letter," says Maddie. "It's from Mémé!" she exclaims once she sees her grandma's nickname signed on the bottom.

Not able to read Winnie's immaculate cursive, Maddie hands the paper to Emma. "Mommy, can you read it to me?"

"Of course," says Emma, as Maddie moves to sit on her lap, scooching back to lean against her mother.

"My dearest Madeleine," starts Emma, "*Mon rayon de soleil.*" Emma stops to prevent the tears from coming. "Oh, how I wish I could be there with you," she continues with ragged breaths. "Catching fireflies in the field, reading to our heart's content on the beach, hearing your spirited laughter. I know it doesn't feel like it, but I'm with you right now. In the sea breeze. In every freshly blossomed lily flower. Even in the stories you read. I'm there, right beside you.

One day when you are old enough, your mom and dad will gift you one last book. A book that tells the story of how our family came to be. But until then, *mon rayon de soleil*, these books will give you the knowledge you need; despite every obstacle, every challenge, we Reynards will always find our way to right where we need to be."

www.ingramcontent.com/pod-product-compliance
Lightning Source LLC
Chambersburg PA
CBHW021252280626
47169CB00021B/2962

* 9 7 8 1 6 4 5 3 8 5 8 6 8 *